D0108749

INCENDIARY
DESIGNS

INCENDIARY DESIGNS

Michael Allen Dymmoch

THOMAS
DUNNE
BOOKS

St. Martin's Press ✹ New York

This is a work of fiction. With the exception of Deen Kogan and her dog, Miata, the characters depicted herein are products of the author's imagination. Any resemblance to real persons or events should be construed as coincidental.

INCENDIARY DESIGNS. Copyright © 1998 by Michael Allen Dymmoch. All rights reserved. Printed in the United States of America. No part of this book may be used or reproduced in any manner whatsoever without written permission except in the case of brief quotations embodied in critical articles or reviews. For information, address St. Martin's Press, 175 Fifth Avenue, New York, N.Y. 10010.

The excerpt on p. 138 is from "Against the Picts," from *Poems* by John Fowles. Copyright © 1973 by John Fowles. Reprinted by permission of The Ecco Press.

Production Editor: David Stanford Burr

Library of Congress Cataloging-in-Publication Data
Dymmoch, Michael Allen.
　　　Incendiary designs / Michael Allen Dymmoch.—1st ed
　　　　　　　p.　　cm.
　　　ISBN 0-312-19245-2
　　　I. Title.
　　PS3554.Y6I5　　1998
　　813'.54—dc21　　　　　　　　　　　　　98-19413
　　　　　　　　　　　　　　　　　　　　　　　　CIP

First edition: October 1998

10　9　8　7　6　5　4　3　2　1

For
CRAIG LUTTIG
MIRIAM MORGAN SCHNEIDER
and
PHIL SPARBER

ACKNOWLEDGMENTS

The author wishes to thank the following for answers to various technical questions or for general information on topics of which the author was ignorant: Commanders Hugh Holton and William Guswiler; Neighborhood Relations Officers Angelo Falbo, Sheila O'Keefe, and Sergeant Looney; Bomb and Arson Sergeant Irene Jones; Detective Jack Stewart, and "Pat" (News Affairs) of the Chicago Police Department; Tom Novara, Shadows and Light Photography, Milwaukee, Wisconsin; Carol Fitzsimmons, M.S.W., A.C.S.W.; pharmacist Luci Zahray; Joseph Grandt; Craig Luttig; and James G. Schaefer. I have taken liberties with the information given me. Any errors are my own.

Thanks also to my editor Ruth Cavin and her staff, and to cover artists Alexander Barsky and Alan Dingman of St. Martin's Press; my agent, Ray Powers; independent editor, Yohma Gray; the reference librarians at the Northbrook Public Library, Northbrook, Illinois; Judy Duhl and her staff at Scotland Yard Books, Winnetka, Illinois; Janis Irvine and her staff at The Book Bin, Northbrook, Illinois; Nancy, Teresita, and Soon Ja at the U.S. Post Office, Northbrook, Illinois; and the Red Herrings of Scotland Yard Books. All of you helped me bring Thinnes and Caleb to life.

—mad

ONE

At dawn the street lights still glowed orange over Lincoln Park. The air was warm for March—midforties—but ghostly mist hung in the art-deco canopy of fat-budded treetops. And moisture-laden air, too ill defined for fog, condensed in the foreground. In the distance, fog obscured Cannon Drive as it made its way between leafless crabapples and witchy, skeletal sycamores. The fog hid Diversey Harbor and the lake to the east, and Clark Street, west of the park. Caleb felt he had the planet to himself and he decided to run as far as Diversey before heading back.

Just north of Fullerton, screened from the view of nearby high-rises by the mist and a brick Park District building, half a dozen people were gathered in the parking lot west of Cannon. They were dressed in white robes, like graduation gowns, but their collective body language suggested a clan rally rather than a chorus. They were chanting something unintelligible. White witches or satanic cult? The group was suddenly too interesting to ignore.

Caleb slowed. As he got nearer, individuals in the group shifted position so as to keep facing him, paying him far more attention than a lone runner warranted. They didn't speak, but their stares gave the same message gang members broadcast on their home turf—stop at your peril. As he came even with them, he smelled gasoline. Then through an inadvertent crack in the human wall he glimpsed the silhouette, then the familiar blue and white of a police car. And with a jolt like an electric shock, he realized that a man in the back of the group was emptying a gas can on the car's roof. Where were the cops?

One of the group suddenly slammed the top of the squad car with a head-size rock. Two other men and a woman jumped on the bumpers, rocking the car. A fourth man sloshed more gas over the roof. With a rush of adrenaline, Caleb realized there was someone in the car. He rushed forward and crashed between the people, blocking the hands that reached for him. The word No! filled his mind as he grabbed the gas can and flung it as far across Cannon as he could.

The man he'd taken it from snarled something. Caleb ignored him until he realized that the man had matches. Others in the group shoved Caleb. The woman screamed, "Blasphemer!" Someone else yelled, "Stop him!" They began to chant again: "Fire! Fire! Fire, next time!"

Focusing on the match-holder, Caleb grabbed for the matches. The man tried to put his body between Caleb and the lights, but Caleb reached around, wrapping him in a great bear hug, and took them. The man twisted away and screamed at his confederates for a light. Caleb dropped the matches. As he kicked them under the car, he noticed gasoline dribbling from the fuel tank, pooling on the pavement. He looked at the man in the car, a police officer. Caleb had an instantaneous impression of his face, eyes focused and widened. He had seen the look before—in Nam—the transformation of resigned despair to forlorn hope, hope he didn't dare believe . . .

Caleb tried the door—locked. The gas fumes were nauseating. The mini-mob pressed forward with its mind-numbing chant. He whirled to face it. "Get back!" The authority in his voice surprised even him and made members of the group hesitate. The chant faltered. He took a step forward. "Back!" His

2

size—six-two—and sudden proximity, more than the command, forced them to retreat slightly, like a wave that would reform and return. He heard a woman cry, "I have a lighter!" The chanting resumed.

"Fire! Fire! Fire next time!"

He needed something to break the window with. There was a rock sitting in a dent in the car hood. As he grasped it, he tried to spot the lighter and saw a woman hand it to the fire-starter. Caleb smashed the rock against the passenger-side front window. Glass crazed, and tiny glass cubes scattered. Gasoline fumes wafted outward. The chanting died. Caleb dropped the rock and lunged at the fire-starter, slapping the lighter from his hand. A growl rumbled from the mob; the fire-starter parted it in search of his lighter.

Caleb turned back to the car and reached through the jagged hole to unlock the door. He jerked it open and thought, Thank God! when the small clunk of the electric lock told him the battery was still alive. A wave of fear washed over him as he remembered that the slightest spark could ignite the gas.

Appearing semiconscious, the police officer lay across the center of the back seat with his arms pinioned behind him. Caleb yanked the rear door open and was aware of odors: fear and gasoline. He snarled another "Get Back!" at the group and reached in to grab the cop's shirt and drag him across the seat. The man's face was white with shock or fear, and Caleb noticed that his uniform was wet, his skin clammy with gasoline. Caleb was electrified by sudden rage, then nauseated. Simultaneously, he noticed the little mob advancing, and the absence of the officer's gun belt. *Where was the gun?*

By the time he got the cop out of the car, the fire-starter had retrieved his lighter, and Caleb had to decide—run or grab for it again? The lunatics moved closer. The rasp of the lighter decided it. Caleb squatted, put a shoulder to the cop's waist and

3

stood back up running, pushing off in the direction of the nearest cover.

The group was scattering now. There was a whoosh as the gas fumes ignited. Caleb felt the flash, the sudden heat on his legs and arms and through his thinning hair. The unconscious cop shielded him from further damage as they were propelled forward by adrenaline and the fireball. Caleb dropped, rolling the injured officer beneath him as a reflex, a flashback from the war. He kept moving, dragging the downed cop, until they reached the building and rounded the corner. The cop's hands were still pinned behind him, handcuffed. Caleb ripped the gasoline-soaked shirt off him and was flinging it away when the squad car's gas tank blew with a roar like a bomb blast. The shirt burst into flame as it arced back toward the car. The crackle of flames was answered by the small patter and clatter of falling debris.

The injured man seemed to regain his focus, to realize his danger; then he passed out. A distant siren cried and was answered by a kindred chorus. Caleb put his face against the officer's chest and wept.

TWO

The vague threat in Thinnes's dream mutated. As he fought his way to wakefulness, the Klaxon softened to a phone ringing. He pushed up on the bed and stretched to reach for it. As he lifted the receiver, the orange cat curled between his feet and his wife's, jumped down and streaked away. He looked at the clock. Six-thirty A.M. was too early even for a weekday. And it was Sunday. Nobody should be calling him today. He put the receiver to his face and said, "Yeah?"

The voice that answered was deep and unruffled. "Thinnes, I need you." Evanger!

"Sunday," Thinnes said, not wanting to move or talk or even think. "My day off."

"There's been an incident down on Cannon Drive, and I need someone I can trust to deal with it."

He meant someone he knew wouldn't talk to the press. "What kind of incident?" Thinnes was coming awake in spite of himself. Damn Evanger!

"Damned if I know. Some nuts tried to set a patrol car on fire—with an officer inside. And his partner's missing."

Shit! "Officer needs assistance" wasn't a call any cop could ignore. "Twenty minutes," Thinnes said.

"Fifteen. A car's on its way."

Thinnes grunted and hung up. Next to him, Rhonda stirred

5

and asked, sleepily, "What is it, John?" She lay curled with her back toward him and didn't open her eyes.

"Overtime," Thinnes told her. He shifted around and kissed the nape of her neck, all that was exposed to the relative chill of the room. "Go back to sleep."

She rolled on her back, still without opening her eyes, and smiled. Her "hmmmm . . ." trailed away as she slipped back into sleep.

Thinnes carefully slid from under the covers and off the edge of the bed. He stood for a moment, looking down at her, fighting his desire to stay. This wasn't how he'd planned to spend his morning. Damn Evanger!

Twenty minutes later he opened the closet door at the foot of the stairs and reached his star and holstered .38 down from the top shelf. Toby, his son's yellow Labrador retriever, sat expectantly on the mat in front of the outside door. "No time this morning, pal," Thinnes told him. "Get Rob to take you out." He put on his jacket and raincoat, and pointed, with his thumb, into the family room at his right. "Go lay down."

The dog obediently retreated and lay with his head on his paws just inside the doorway. He gave Thinnes the soulful look dogs use and thumped the floor with his tail.

"Sorry, bub," Thinnes said. "I've been hustled by better cons than you. Why don't you try that on Rob?" The dog sat up and cocked his head. Thinnes pointed up the stairs. "Go find Rob."

The dog bounded past him. Thinnes went to the door and unlocked it. Toby stopped halfway up, looking expectant. Thinnes shook his head and let himself out.

The car that was waiting at the curb in front of the house was pointing against the traffic, but since it was obviously an unmarked police car, nobody was going to hassle the driver about it. Thinnes locked the dead bolt on his front door and walked

6

out to the car. He opened the driver-side door and told the man at the wheel, "I'll drive."

The driver started to protest, then shrugged and got out. He was young, an inch taller than Thinnes—six-one—Hispanic, not a detective, a tactical officer dressed in street clothes. Thinnes had met him before but he couldn't put a name to the face. Thinnes got behind the wheel. On the seat, there was a McDonald's tray with two large coffees. Getting in, the tac cop picked one up and offered it to Thinnes.

Thinnes said, "What's this?"

"Your boss said not to talk to you 'til you had at least twelve ounces of coffee under your belt."

Thinnes grunted, popped the lid, and took a trial sip. It had the right amount of cream and sugar and was nearly cool enough to drink in spite of the hot warnings on the cup. He slugged down half the contents, put the cup back in the tray, and pulled away from the curb. They got as far as Lincoln Avenue before either of them spoke.

Thinnes heard the tac cop mutter, "Nice," as he outmaneuvered a Lexus driver trying to cut him off. He grunted. After a short pause, during which he negotiated a tight turn and passed an indecisive motorist, he said, "Give me the story on this 'incident' we're going to. They find the missing cop yet?"

"Arlette Banks. No. I didn't get much of the story. My sergeant told me to report to Lieutenant Evanger, and *he* told me to get coffee and pick you up."

Thinnes nodded. Neither of them spoke until he turned the car onto Diversey Parkway.

"How's the dog working out?" the tac officer ventured.

"How? . . ." Then Thinnes remembered where they'd met before: a death investigation, fifteen months ago. Name was Azul, Jaime Azul.

"You still got it?" Azul persisted.

"Yeah."

"Figured you for that kind of sucker when you paid Noir to clean the mutt up."

Noir was Azul's partner. They'd been patrol officers in Twenty when Thinnes met them. It wasn't surprising they'd made tactical by now.

"You still with Noir?"

"Sure," Azul said. "But he's out with a broken ankle, so I'm baching it temporarily."

"How'd he break it?" Thinnes was happy to have the subject off the dog. "Hotdogging?"

"Sort of. Trying to impress a girl on a ski hill."

Thinnes shook his head and they rode in silence 'til they turned on John Cannon Drive.

The first officers on the scene had responded with dispatch. They'd assisted the victims, cordoned off the scene, and taken a preliminary statement from the only individual capable of giving one. "They only took the statement," their sergeant told Thinnes. "They didn't try to make sense of it."

Thinnes looked around. Cannon Drive was ablaze with red, white, and blue flashing lights from fire trucks and squad cars. Yellow police-line tape surrounded the smoking hulk of the incinerated squad car, and harried uniforms battled rubberneckers to keep traffic moving past the scene. "They find Banks yet?"

The sergeant shook his head. "Every cop in town's looking."

"How's her partner?"

"Nolan," the sergeant said. "The medics thought he'll probably make it, but he's in bad shape. He was beat up pretty good and soaked with gas. That's a fact. And, according to our witness, he was almost torched, then bounced around during the rescue attempt. They took him to Illinois Masonic."

The nearest trauma center. Thinnes ground his teeth. St. Joe's was less than a block away, but it wasn't set up for serious emergencies. "You don't sound too confident in this witness," he said. "What's *his* story?"

"Claims he was jogging up Cannon Drive. When he gets near Fullerton, he hears chanting—couldn't understand it, but what the hell, this is the city, so he doesn't worry about it. When he crosses Fullerton, he spots a bunch of kooks dressed in white robes—like choir robes, he said—gathered in the parking lot by the Park District building." The sergeant pointed to the brick building next to the smoking remains.

"Was this a Klan rally of some kind?"

"Guy said no, no hoods, no crosses or flags."

"Go on."

"His story is these nuts stop chanting when they spot him, and he notices they're acting peculiar, so he slows down for a look. Claims he smelled gas, then saw one of these nutcases pouring gas on the patrol car. Then he spots Nolan. Claims he saw red and didn't even think about how stupid it was to butt in. He shoves through the crowd and drags Nolan outta the car, then runs like hell. Makes it to about a yard from the corner of the building when one of the nuts torches the car. He and Nolan fall or get pushed over by the blast and roll the rest of the way behind the building. And a second or two later, the gas tank blows."

"What about the offenders?"

"Claimed they scattered when the arsonist started flicking his Bic."

"Any evidence to corroborate?"

The sergeant shrugged again. "Mobil unit's going over the scene. There's footwear impressions and some trampled grass—what didn't burn up. But this is a public park, so it's anybody's guess."

"Where's the witness?"

"They transported him with Nolan."

9

"What kind of shape's he in?"

Another shrug. "Bruises and contusions, a few shrapnel cuts, few first- and second-degree burns."

"Mentally?"

"He wasn't an obvious psycho. Didn't seem drunk. No clear signs of drug use. Put it this way. Either he torched the car himself in which case he's a major nut case, or he's a genuine hero and the luckiest son of a bitch in the city."

"You got any feeling about which?"

The sergeant shook his head. "You're the detective. I'll leave it up to you. You need anything else?"

"The witness's name."

"Caleb. James A. Caleb."

"No shit!"

"You know 'im?"

"Big guy, early forties, thinning hair?"

"That's him."

"You'd better put out a flash on a bunch of pyromaniacs in white robes."

THREE

Illinois Masonic is a complex of dark red buildings at 836 West Wellington. When Thinnes got there, the two patrol officers who'd escorted the ambulance were pacing the hall outside one of the treatment rooms. They spotted Thinnes as he came in and met him halfway.

"They find Banks yet?" the older one asked.

"No. How's Nolan?"

"Still in surgery." The copper hitched a thumb toward the treatment room he'd been guarding. "Witness is in there."

Caleb sat on the examining table and shivered in spite of the blanket he was wrapped in. The excitement was wearing off and a poisonous cocktail of neurochemicals was replacing the adrenaline. He was beginning to experience depression. He'd suffered from it for so long it seemed comforting at times—the devil you know. He felt the onset of a self-loathing that was familiar, too, a habit he had thought he'd broken. It was partly self-disgust at having lost control, partly a profound feeling of loneliness. In times of distress, friends and family were a palliative or at least distracting. But he was estranged from his family. And he didn't want to burden his best friend, Anita, with the story until he could relate it without emotion. It wouldn't frighten her, but it might induce in her an anxiety he couldn't assuage. And he had no significant other. The self-disgust was also due, in part, to this strange self-pity he was overcome by. Get a grip on yourself, he thought.

"How're you doing?" Thinnes asked.

"I'll live."

"What happened?"

Caleb told him.

Thinnes asked, "What about Nolan's partner?"

"Nolan is the officer I dragged out of the car?"

Thinnes nodded.

"He was the only one I saw. If I'd thought about it, I might have wondered why he was alone, but I didn't have time to think."

"Why'd you get involved? Why not just call for backup?"

Caleb gave him an I-don't-believe-you're-asking look before shrugging. "It would have been too late."

FOUR

When Thinnes got back to the scene, the perimeter had been expanded. The yellow barrier tape stretched from North Pond, west of the smoke-blackened building, across Cannon Drive to North Lagoon east of the scene. Marked units cut off Cannon Drive at both ends of the block detouring traffic onto Clark Street. The crime-scene players were still crisscrossing the area, stopping occasionally to retrieve things they put in small plastic bags or manila envelopes. Oster had arrived. He'd been Thinnes's partner for a couple of years. As usual, lately, he looked worse after he'd had a few days off. Thinnes wasn't sure whether it was because he *was* worse, or because he was just more likely to notice Oster when he hadn't seen him for a while. This morning the older detective looked like shit—tired and rushed. He'd shaved, but he hadn't tied his tie. And his shirt ballooned out from his pants, making him look fatter than usual. He always looked stressed; Thinnes was waiting for him to keel over from a heart attack.

He was talking to a medium-complected Hispanic, five-eight or -nine, maybe a 170 pounds—solid, no fat. Oster introduced him as "Art Fuego, Bomb and Arson." Chicago was a little different than other towns in that arson—and the deaths resulting from it—were investigated by the cops, not the fire department. Arson dicks, and the explosives technicians who made up the bomb squad, were sent away for special training.

Thinnes pointed at the burned-out squad. "I thought the gas tanks on these things were designed to not blow up."

"Well, sure," Fuego said, "under normal circumstances. But opening the filler, punching a hole in the tank, and lighting a fire under it isn't considered normal use."

"So what do you think?"

"The white costumes are a new wrinkle."

"And?"

Fuego shrugged and waved to indicate their surroundings. "They could hardly have picked a better spot to pull this. Except for the remains of the lighter and match book, there's nothing here we can tie to them. I mean, we picked up a lot of stuff, but who knows how long any of it's been here."

"What about the gas can our witness mentioned?"

Fuego shook his head. "Must've taken it with 'em. What *about* our witness?"

"We've got him working on a composite."

"We might as well go see how he's doing, then. I don't see anything more turning up here."

"Okay," Thinnes said, "but have someone check all the trash baskets in the park and the Dumpsters and garbage cans in the area—case any of 'em decided to ditch their costumes. And have patrol put it out that anybody making a stop should keep an eye out for white robes." He looked at Oster; the older man was standing with his hands in his suit-jacket pockets staring across Cannon Drive and over the lagoon, at the lake beyond it. "Carl, d'you bring us a car?" Oster didn't seem to have heard. "Carl!"

Oster started. "Yeah, what?"

"We got a car?"

"Tac guy—Azul—said we should keep the one he brought

14

you. He'll bum a ride back when they're done with the canvass."

"Are you okay?"

"Yeah. I just need some coffee."

Thinnes thought he heard him add, "Irish coffee," under his breath.

FIVE

The police officers who'd driven Caleb to the hospital were pressed into service chauffeuring him to Area Three Detective Headquarters. They'd taken his statement earlier and, beyond asking if he was okay, didn't speak to him. When they got to 2452 West Belmont—Belmont and Western, the site formerly occupied by the Riverview amusement park—they turned him over to Detective Swann, a middle-aged black man with a mild disposition and a strong resemblance to the late Mayor Washington.

Caleb had been to the Area many times since his first visit in 1993. The squad room seemed brighter; it had recently been painted a paler shade of yellow. The red tile floor was unchanged. The open space had been partitioned by dividers between the tables, and computers replaced the typewriters that had been used for filling out reports.

Swann skirted the desks and headed, first, for the table where two large coffeemakers stood. Someone had posted a sign that said: ALL DRINKS INCLUDE SALES TAX.

They looked at mug shots first, computer-generated images that came on the screen like wanted posters from some electronic post office. Swann showed him a series of pictures of men in the age category Caleb had estimated for the fire-setter. There were an amazing number. None of the pictures looked familiar, though; after the first few dozen, the men all began to look related. And they all seemed to have the same vacant expression.

When he and Swann had exhausted the usual suspects, Swann took him to the room off the case management office, where the Identisketch computer was kept. It was a painted concrete-block cubbyhole, ten-by-twelve, with a blind-shaded wall of windows overlooking a parking lot, and two chairs and two desks, one occupied by the computer Swann called the Etch-a-Sketch. There were no bulletin boards with Polaroids or photocopied pictures to mislead witnesses.

Caleb had thought, in the surrealistic moments of the incident, that the fire-setter's image would be burned into his memory. Now he found it wasn't so. The face merged with the faces of other madmen—Rasputin, Charles Manson, Adolf Hitler.

Having studied memory, he understood that the brain didn't function like a biological VCR. Memories weren't stored like movie film that could be played back on command. They were more like coded files stored in various places in the mind, and reconstructed when retrieved, sometimes fabricated from inference and hearsay and bits of other memories (or others' memories) like a puzzle put together from pieces of like shape and color that happened to be near. To really remember something, you had to take careful note of it, study how its parts fit together and how it fit as a figure in its ground, how it differed from similar members of its class. Caleb had not had time to notice much more than *man, white, not young, not old, eccentric, dangerous* before the immediacy of the situation forced him to react.

He could remember individual features—the cursing mouth, the bulbous, broken nose—and how the man had avoided eye contact. It had not been the sad, practiced avoidance of a schizophrenic, or the shy avoidance of an autistic person, or even the guilty avoidance of one who knows what is right or at least what is acceptable yet does the opposite. There was an ecstatic element to the fire-setter's oblivion, as if he were high on chemicals or on the *opiate of the people.* Caleb and the officer had not been so much invisible to the fire-setter as inhuman, irrelevant, inconsequential. Whatever had caused his high, it had become a self-sustaining reaction.

Caleb was at a loss as to how to combine the disparate parts into a coherent picture. Perhaps it was the stasis of the fixed image that made the sum of the parts so much less recognizable than the whole. Why was it so easy to say what it was not?

Detective Swann was very patient, very good at his job. He didn't push, didn't lead. He let Caleb study the relation of each new feature to all the others and decide if it fit. Caleb was grateful and took his time. Better to get it right.

SIX

The car Thinnes had commandeered had flashers on the headlights but no Mars light. He wasn't in the mood for a leisurely drive back to headquarters, though. He put the flashers on and floored it, slowing only enough at intersections to avoid killing anyone. Oster didn't comment. At Western and Belmont, Thinnes slewed the car around a WLS minicam van and cut into the drive ahead of it. He left the car in the fire lane of the dark brick building, facing the wrong way and, with Oster following, pushed through the glass doors into the District Nineteen lobby. He tossed the keys to the uniformed sergeant in the square brick enclosure that served as the district's front desk.

He was halfway to the stairs when the sergeant said, "Hey Thinnes, they want you." He leaned over the polished granite countertop and hooked his thumb in the direction of the district commander's office. Oster kept going toward the stairs. Thinnes nodded and changed direction. The sergeant hadn't specified who "they" were but, given the missing cop, it could be anyone up to a deputy superintendent. Hell, if Banks were "connected" it could be the superintendent himself.

Thinnes went down the hall and knocked on the commander's door. He heard, "Come," and went in, then relaxed. The district commander was a dark-eyed black Irishman who looked Italian; he was forty-eight, five-eleven, 190 pounds. He was sitting at his desk across from Evanger, Thinnes's boss, who was acting head of Detective Area Three while its commander was on vacation. Evanger was a light-skinned black, midfifties, six-one, two hundred pounds. He had receding, close-cropped hair, a narrow, prominent nose, and a wide, stern mouth. He'd shaved his mustache since Thinnes saw him last. Both men had Starbucks coffee cups in front of them and looked as happy to be rousted on a Sunday morning as Thinnes felt.

The DC pointed to an empty chair and stifled a yawn. Thinnes had to fake a cough to hide his own answering yawn as he sat down.

"What're the damages?" Evanger asked.

"One officer missing, one hospitalized—they're working on him. We've got every car in town looking for Banks."

"What's the story?"

Thinnes was sure he'd heard it, but he repeated the highlights, anyway.

"What's with the witness?" the DC asked.

"A solid citizen," Thinnes told him. "A well-to-do shrink. In fact, a department consultant. He was out jogging and literally ran into it."

"If he's not goofy, why'd he get involved?"

"Reflex probably. He was a medic in Nam."

The DC nodded.

"How're we gonna handle this?" Evanger asked.

Thinnes saw that he was being given the reins. If he succeeded, all to the good. If not, he'd be the fall guy. He said, "Patrol is looking for Banks. Our witness is upstairs looking at pictures. If he comes up empty, we'll have him build a composite on the Etch-a-Sketch. And I sent everyone I had out to canvass the buildings overlooking the scene on the off chance some peeper with a telescope saw something. But it's gonna take a while. There's a lot of buildings, with a lot of windows."

"You have anybody at the hospital?" Evanger asked.

"Not yet."

"Ferris is here."

Thinnes shook his head and tried to keep his disgust from showing. "I'd rather send him out to interview peepers."

"You're calling the shots. Where's Oster?"

"Upstairs trying to find out if any cop-hating torches have been released recently. We've gotta look on the bright side."

"There's a bright side?" the DC said.

"Yeah," Caleb said. "It's Sunday. If it was Monday, we'd be up to our assholes in reporters." He stood up and looked at Evanger, "Channel 7's setting up as we speak. Can you run interference?"

Evanger nodded. "I'll try to stall them."

Thinnes went upstairs. Unlike TV squad rooms, there were no desks or chalkboards, no partitions to separate the violent-crimes dicks from their property-crimes counterparts. Everyone worked at tables that were separated by partitions you could look over.

Oster was at one near the operations desk, which was behind a counter along one wall. He looked marginally better. His tie was tied if not snugged, his shirt tucked in. His color was better, too—not as gray. He looked up when Thinnes entered, and he nodded but kept listening to the phone wedged between his ear and his shoulder. The polystyrene cup in front of him was empty. Thinnes picked it up and filled it at the coffeemaker, along with one for himself. While he was standing there, trying to remember what he'd been going to do next, Kate Ryan came by with a coffee mug that said, ONLY ROBINSON CRUSOE HAD EVERYTHING DONE BY FRIDAY. Ryan was a natural redhead with green eyes, and eyebrows and lashes so pale they were almost invisible. She said, "Damn," softly when she tried to fill the mug and got just a few muddy drops. She put it down and told Thinnes, "Move it or lose it."

He took his two cups and went back to the table where Oster was making rapid notes on the margins of a rap sheet.

Putting the cups down, Thinnes watched Ryan stalk out of the room with the coffeemaker. It wasn't her turn to make coffee, and under normal circumstances, she'd have driven to McDonald's to get herself a cup before making it out of turn. But circumstances weren't normal. The pressure they were all feeling had caused most of them to revert to their older, pre–politically correct selves.

Thinnes turned to Oster. "What've we got?"

"Shit. We got shit." Oster shoved a hefty stack of computer printouts and faxes toward Thinnes. "This is all the cop-hating torches we came up with." He tapped the pages with the middle fingers of his right hand. "I crossed out all the ones I know are dead. An' I put *C* by the ones that're in County, *S* by the ones in Joliet, *M* for Menard, *P* for Pontiac—you get the idea."

"Yeah. How up-to-date are they?"

Oster shrugged.

"You want to go over and sit with Nolan, get his statement when he comes to?"

Oster looked around. "Why me?"

"It's you or Ferris. And when Nolan comes out of it, I don't want any fuckups."

The phone rang and Thinnes let Oster answer. His expression soured as he listened to the caller. When he put down the phone, he said, "They just found Banks—what's left of her."

Thinnes waited for the punch line; it came like a kick in the gut. "She was beaten to death."

SEVEN

Arlette Banks turned up in a vacant lot in an industrial area. A half-dozen marked squads and a fire department ladder truck—but no engine or ambulance—were parked along the near-side curb. Yellow police-line tape had been stretched across the open sides of the lot, and grim-faced coppers crowded against it.

Thinnes parked near the squad cars and got out. The small discrepancy of the odd fire truck irritated him enough to make him ask about it. "Flat tire," he was told. "Rest of 'em took off on another call when they couldn't help Banks."

He'd arrived ahead of the ME; the crime-scene guys were still taking pictures. He walked over and ducked under the tape, and a patrol sergeant hurried over to fill him in.

The factories on either side were surrounded by high fences topped with coiled razor wire. The building that had originally stood on the lot had been dismantled, its intact bricks and blocks salvaged. The broken pieces that were left had been put to use. On Banks.

The first officers on the scene, a salt-and-pepper team, were the ones who'd found her. The sergeant pointed them out to Thinnes. "They only found the body because we've been monitoring the lot for illegal dumping."

The white officer was a rookie, probably under twenty-five. He looked ready to puke. His partner, a woman in her thirties, and big, seemed ready to do murder. Thinnes walked over to them and introduced himself.

"Tell me about it," he said.

"We been watching this lot," the woman said. "An' when we went by earlier, it was empty. This time we come by, there's been a dump. So I get out to see if he's—maybe—screwed up an' left something' we can use to nail him. An' I find Banks. We never expected—"

"God!" his partner said, "the flash they put out was real vague—missing—so, you know, it was a shock. But this place is perfect . . ." He waved his arms at the closed and abandoned buildings across the two streets that the lot fronted on, ". . . for something like this."

Thinnes nodded. "Anything here—besides Banks—that wasn't here the last time you were by?"

Both coppers looked.

"Just . . ." The rookie nodded at the remains.

His partner took longer, then pointed to a hubcap against the curb nearest the body. "Don't recall seein' that, but I could be wrong. It wasn't there yesterday for sure. Somebody would'a salvaged it by now."

Thinnes said, "Thanks. Stick around." He went over for a closer look at Banks. The bloody pulp of her head and upper body was half buried under masonry debris. But her shoes and uniformed legs were almost pristine. Why?

He signaled the photographer. "You get this from all angles?"

"S' the cardinal Catholic?"

"See if you can get the firemen to run their ladder up for you and get a couple aerial shots?"

"Why?"

"You got something better to do right now?"

"You're Thinnes, aren't you? They warned me about you."

Thinnes pointed to the hubcap. "Get a couple shots of that,

24

check it for prints, and bag it. And find out what kind of vehicle it came from."

"Yeah, yeah, yeah," the tech said, but he started shooting the hubcap.

Thinnes turned to the sergeant, who'd wandered over to eavesdrop on his conversation with the evidence tech. "Have 'em pick up everything that's breathing within a mile radius of here for questioning. And make sure when they're doing the canvass they ask if anyone noticed somebody changing a tire around here this morning. And have someone check every gas station and repair shop in the area—see if anyone had a flat fixed."

EIGHT

Thinnes stopped back at the hospital before returning to the Area. Nolan was in recovery, Oster informed him, but not conscious yet. Nolan's wife was pacing the hall outside the intensive care unit. She was of Italian ancestry. She had black hair and eyes and was a smoker. Before he approached her, he watched her take cigarettes out of her purse and put them back three times in as many minutes.

When he couldn't stand her nicotine withdrawal any longer, he walked over and said, "Mrs. Nolan, I'm Thinnes, Area Three." A cop's wife would know what that meant.

She nodded. "You catch the bastards?"

"Not yet. Is there anything you can tell me? Your husband get any threats lately? Been in any arguments?"

She shook her head. "Don't think I haven't been racking my brain trying to come up with something."

Things back at the Area were getting nuts. There was a TV reporter with a minicam camped out in front and a radio reporter lounging near the police entrance. "Funny," he heard a black patrolman tell the guy, "but there were three people gunned down on the south side last week, and I didn't hear of any of you beatin' feet down there to cover *that*."

Up in the squadroom, Jaime Azul was typing something at one of the unassigned tables near the coffee pots. He paused to salute Thinnes with his index finger then hooked a thumb toward Evanger's office. "Boss wants to see you."

"Thanks. You lookin' for something to do when you finish that?"

"Could be."

"I need someone to canvass Nolan's neighborhood, someone who speaks Spanish." He took the address from his pocket and held it out.

Azul took it. "Yeah, sure."

"Mrs. Nolan says he didn't have an enemy in the world. See if the neighbors agree."

Rhonda picked up the phone on the second ring. When she said hello, Thinnes said, "Hi."

"I heard," she said.

They'd been planning on a movie at the Old Orchard Theater, and maybe some window-shopping before dinner at Maggiano's. It would have to be postponed. Thinnes said, "Sorry."

"Not your fault."

"I really am." He stifled the urge to ask her what she'd do instead.

"I know."

"Rain check?"

"Sure."

There was a long pause. Neither of them could think of anything to say, yet neither wanted to hang up. Rhonda caved in first. "I guess maybe I'll go to my mother's."

Thinnes thought, both of her parents live there, but the house is "mother's." He said, "Have fun."

"John, is it bad?"

Bad as it gets, he thought. What he said was, "I have to go tell a man his wife's not coming home."

"Why you?" She didn't manage to keep the resentment from her voice.

Thinnes ignored it. He was learning not to take it personally. It wasn't meant personally. "It's my case."

"Oh."

"Page me if . . ." There was no point in finishing. *If you need me* was stupid because he couldn't come until Banks's killers were nailed down. *If you want to talk . . .* They were talking now. There didn't seem to be any point in telling her how he felt—that if his feelings were electricity, they would have long since shorted out the phone wires, that if they were gold, he could've bought Kuwait. Instead he checked to be sure no one around him was listening, then he told her what he thought she wanted to hear. "I love you."

She sighed. "I'll hold that thought."

"Just don't expect to see me any time soon."

NINE

Son of a bitch!" Fuego held up the composite sketch and shook it. "I know this guy." He and Thinnes had been watching detective Swann put the finishing touches on the drawing under Dr. Caleb's direction. "I sent him to the shit house once," Fuego continued. "Name's Brian Fahey, aka Wiley. He must be out on parole." To Caleb he said, "Funny you didn't spot his graduation picture."

Ryan, who'd stuck her head in to see how they were doing, added her two-cents worth. "Let me guess. He sets fires for fun and profit."

"Fun, mostly." Fuego said. "He's not good enough to make much profit. Gasoline fires are a new trick for Wiley. His usual MO is the old standby cigarette in a matchbook. Uses wax paper for a trailer. Pretty unimaginative but effective."

"I'm afraid—" Caleb began.

"Guy lights a cigarette and sticks it sideways in a pack of matches," Fuego said, "then puts the matches in contact with some combustible material—like a couch cushion."

Caleb nodded. "I see. When the cigarette burns close enough, it sets the matches off. Why not just put the cigarette on the couch?"

"Too good a chance it won't generate enough heat for ignition."

"What's a trailer?"

29

"Something that leads the fire to other combustibles. And, unlike an accelerant, wax paper doesn't soak into rugs or floorboards and leave evidence for arson cops."

Ryan said, "This Wiley a rocket scientist?"

Fuego laughed. "Some sarcastic dick gave him that handle. Sommabitch is dumber than a box a hammers. He thought it was a compliment, started telling all his equally bright friends that the cops think he's a genius." He turned to Caleb. "Only problem we got is, in order to prove arson, you gotta eliminate all other possible causes of the fire—including acts of God."

Ferris entered the room just in time to hear this last. He was short and obnoxious, with receding auburn hair and a permanent sneer. He said "Isn't it an act of God that mopes like Wiley are so dumb they think they can get away with murder?"

Fuego looked insulted. "Not *my* God!"

TEN

Thinnes managed to control his anger until he got out of the car at the home of Arlette Banks. He'd followed the district commander's car, carrying the commander and the chaplain, and curbed his squad behind it on the street. The house was small and well maintained, with carefully trimmed bushes and mulched, dormant flower beds.

When the quiet man who'd married Arlette Banks opened the door for them, a sudden surge of rage made Thinnes feel light-headed. He steadied himself against the porch rail. As the chaplain said, "Mr. Banks?" Thinnes fought the urge to hit something. Anger interfered with thought; homicide cops had to keep it under wraps.

Banks needed a full second to understand the chaplain's question. He was a medium complected black man with a trim Afro and mustache. He said, "Arlette?" His expression showed the likelihood that he thought his worst nightmare had come true.

"I'm sorry, Mr. Banks." The chaplain really did seem sorry.

Banks swallowed as tears filled his eyes and spilled over. He backed through the doorway and gestured for them to follow. Inside, he stopped in the center of his neat living room. He crossed one arm over his chest and covered his face with the other, sobbing silently. Thinnes felt overcome by his own anger,

31

and he could see the commander alternate between discomfort and shaking rage. Banks seemed to have forgotten them.

He stopped crying when a child's voice called, "Daddy?" He rubbed his cheeks dry against the shoulders of his shirt and wiped away the last of the tears with his palms. He seemed to have himself pretty much in control by the time a girl of about five came running into the room. She stopped when she spotted the strangers, then crept forward to stand next to her father, reaching up to take his hand.

"Daddy?" She hung on his hand and shifted from foot to foot.

"What, honey?"

She looked up at him and said, "Are you sad, Daddy?" She lay her cheek against the back of his hand.

Banks had to swallow before he could answer. "Yes, honey. I'm sad."

The girl looked up at him again and patted the hand. "When mommy gets home you'll feel happy."

He clapped his free hand over his mouth and sobbed, and the chaplain hurried over to put an arm around him. The girl rested her cheek against Banks and stared at Thinnes and the commander.

When Banks had himself under control again, the chaplain moved away. Banks said, "Lena, would you do me a favor?"

"Sure, Daddy."

"Would you go call Aunt Dolly and ask her if she can come over right away. Tell her it's very important."

"Okay, Daddy." She skipped from the room with nervous, backward glances, giving the impression she was putting up a brave front.

"Dolly's my sister," Banks said when she was gone. "She'll come and watch Lena. I'll have to notify Arlette's parents."

Thinnes didn't envy him that duty.

Lena skipped back into the room with a portable phone

that she held up toward her father. "Aunt Dolly wants to talk to you."

Banks reached for the phone but before his hand contacted it, he waved the girl back and pressed a hand over his mouth, muttering, "I can't."

"I'll talk to her," the commander said. He looked at Lena. "May I?" She handed it to him. He walked toward the front door, saying, "Is this Aunt Dolly?" into the phone. He went outside and pulled the door shut.

Thinnes, meanwhile, introduced himself to Banks. "I'm sorry to have to bother you at a time like this, sir, but there are questions. . . ."

Banks sighed and turned to the chaplain. "Reverend, could you read Lena a story?"

"Surely."

"Lena," Banks told his daughter, "Detective Thinnes and I have to talk business."

"Grown-up talk?"

"That's right. The reverend will read you a story in the kitchen. Do you want to go choose a book and show him where the kitchen is?"

She nodded solemnly and held her hand up for the reverend. He closed his huge hand around it, and she led him away.

The commander came in and put the phone down. "Your sister's coming," he told Banks.

"I always knew this would happen," Banks said. "We talked about it before Arly got pregnant. We decided that life is uncertain at best, so why not? We always agreed that the secret of happiness is to find what you love to do and do it well. Arly loved being a cop. And she was good." He looked from the commander to Thinnes. "How?"

Thinnes won the waiting game. The commander finally said, "She and her partner were attacked by a group of deranged individuals. Arlette was . . ."

"Beaten to death, Mr. Banks," Thinnes finished for him. "I'm sorry."

"And Nolan?"

"He's in surgery. We're hoping he'll be able to give us a description of your wife's killers."

Banks nodded but didn't seem hopeful or particularly interested. Shock, Thinnes decided. He asked the usual questions, discovering nothing. Banks had had no enemies that her husband knew of, no vindictive neighbors.

"What do you do for a living?" Thinnes asked him.

"I teach sixth-grade science."

"Just one more question, sir. Can you think of anyone who'd harm your wife in order to hurt you?"

"No." Banks's expression made Thinnes think he couldn't even imagine anyone doing such a thing.

"We're gonna get these people, Mr. Banks," the commander said. "You can put money on it."

ELEVEN

Save for his cats, Caleb's lakefront condo was deserted. He locked the door and set the alarm. Sigmund Freud was perched on the back of a nearby chair, with his feet gathered under him. He stood and pushed his rump upward as Caleb ran a hand down his back.

"Where's Psyche?" Caleb asked.

Freud followed him as he got a glass of cabernet from the bar at the far side of the room and drifted into the bathroom. The cat watched him undress. He dropped the borrowed scrubs on the bathroom floor and used the full-length mirror behind the door to inspect his bruises. Tomorrow they'd be horror-film spectacular.

When he had finished showering and was ensconced—with a refill of cabernet—on the couch in the living room, Psyche made her harlequin appearance. The small, white, orange, and black cat strolled out of hiding with affected indifference, but when Caleb picked her up, she purred like a vibrator.

For a few minutes, he sat and stroked her and stared at the desert landscape on the wall over the fireplace. The painting had recently replaced his lover's portrait. Chris had died nearly seven years ago, and the migraine of Caleb's loss had faded to a wistful loneliness. He hadn't felt despair, which can be a kind of passion, or passion itself, for ages. Though the memory of his

35

love lingered, it was devoid of the extremes of feeling that gave the word its meaning.

He put the cat down and took up the book he was currently reading. He'd found himself doing this more lately, even turning down invitations in order to stay home and read. During the past year, he'd been going through the motions, dating occasionally, frequenting Buddies' and Gentry and enjoying the atmosphere, but going home alone. Occasionally he allowed himself to be seduced by a gorgeous face or figure, or an original line, but the attraction rarely lasted the evening. He'd begun to examine friends of long standing with an eye toward getting beyond friendship, but there was something irritating or intolerable about each that would have prevented domestic tranquillity. Too often, he found himself wishing he were home, preferring the company of his cats to most of the people he was meeting.

As a psychiatrist, he recognized this ennui and lack of initiative as symptomatic of depression, but, he rationalized, reading was like getting the best conversation from interesting people, with the annoying quirks and personality traits filtered out. He agreed with the anonymous authors of Genesis that it's not good for man to be alone, but he didn't want to settle for sex or friendship. He wanted passion. He wanted romance.

He had a routine life, a condo on the Gold Coast full of exquisite possessions, and season tickets for the Lyric and the Bulls, but no one with whom to share them.

TWELVE

Nolan had suffered a concussion, two broken ribs, moderately severe lacerations of the liver, and minor bruises and burns. The doctors had had to operate to repair the lacerations. Thinnes didn't get to interview him until he was stabilized and moved to intensive care. He was still groggy, Oster reported, but at least they'd taken the tubes out and he could talk. Oster had waited to question Nolan until Thinnes was present.

Nolan's first words were, "How's Banks?" So Thinnes didn't escape breaking the news.

Nolan was outwardly quiet while he took it in, but one of the nurses came rushing into the room to see why his monitors were going crazy. Eventually she went back to her station and Nolan told his story.

He and Banks had been near the end of an uneventful tour. They'd stopped—it was a habit—to get coffee and donuts before heading back to the District to wrap up their paperwork. They were pulling out of the donut place when they'd heard a woman screaming, and a man flagged them down. He'd pointed to a nearby alley, then run down it.

"You didn't call it in?" Oster sounded unbelieving.

"We didn't know what it was yet. We pulled down the alley after the guy, and there was a body lying facedown—no sign of anyone else. Banks got out to see what was wrong; I reached for the radio. Something came up alongside the car—I could just see the movement out of the corner of my eye. Then something hit me.

"The next thing I remember, I was in the back seat of the squad with my hands cuffed behind me and some asshole pouring gas all over the car. I thought I was a goner. Then this big, half-naked guy came charging up. I realized he was probably just a runner, but to me he looked like Jesus Christ and the marines all rolled up in one."

The killing of a cop usually brought out the worst in the Department, even though—since certain court decisions and an epidemic of civil lawsuits—justice was no longer summary or administered ex officio. The minute Arlette Banks was reported missing, every station in the city was suddenly like an ant hill kicked open. Fire ants!

The way things worked—when they worked like they should—was that the cops contacted their snitches and word got around that things would be uncomfortable until the killer was in the bag. You didn't worry about probable cause, either. Probable could always be found. Some cops manufactured it, but Thinnes never had. Never had to. Long ago—maybe three weeks into his Academy training—he'd noticed that citizens in *the land of the free* had more laws telling them how to act than any three other countries. Anybody you observed for more than five minutes was bound to break one of them.

As soon as they got back to the Area, Thinnes sent Oster back to the hospital with mug books, one of which contained a picture of Wiley Fahey. Then he checked to see if Fuego had gotten hold of Wiley's parole officer yet—he hadn't.

The squad room was unusually busy and as serious as a funeral—no casual conversations, no bullshitting. Every detective in the room—and the property crimes dicks were in on it, too—was either on the phone or going over records. There wasn't any of the black humor, either, that usually lightened up the atmosphere.

"Thinnes," Swann called. "Viernes for you. On one."

Thinnes picked up the phone. "Yeah, Joe?" Viernes's name was actually John, like Thinnes's, but everyone at the Area called him Joe. It was an inside joke that only those who knew Viernes or spoke Spanish got.

"Maybe some good news, Thinnes." "We followed up on that hubcap from where they found Banks. Looks like it came from a church van that got a flat. Guy working on his car three blocks east of the scene noticed some idiot driving on a rim. White Ford van—which is consistent with the hubcap. He—the mechanic—noticed the church name, something like Congregation Church, on the side. We found a gas station three blocks farther down, where they sold the driver a used tire. The flat was shredded. Anyway, they wrote down the license because the schmuck paid with a church check. I got the mechanic and the gas station attendant coming in to look at pictures.

"The van is registered to a Conflagration Church." Viernes spelled it out. "On Western. Place is closed up like a tomb right now. My snitches tell me it's run by a Brother John."

"You locate the van yet?"

"Just a matter of time."

"This John, he a priest?"

"Some kind of mail-order minister, I think. I tracked down somebody who's heard of the outfit. Guy collects nutcases for a hobby. He's sending over a video of the head hardcase." There was a short pause, during which Thinnes could hear traffic noises. Then Viernes added, "Too bad we're not allowed to keep files on these turkeys. Be a lot simpler."

"Yeah," Thinnes said.

"Anyway, after you see this video, you got any questions,

contact Detective Flyer, over at Four." Viernes gave Thinnes Flyer's pager number.

"Thanks, Joe."

Thinnes brought his coffee mug when he went into Evanger's office to report. Evanger was drinking coffee himself, out of a large Starbuck's cup.

Thinnes sat down and summarized what he'd done since he last reported in. "I sent Carl over to the hospital with pictures, but its pro forma," Thinnes said. "The sketch from our witness was pretty damn good. What I can't believe is we don't have an address on this guy yet!"

"Sunday," Evanger reminded him. "People fall off the ends of the earth on Sundays."

"Yeah. Well, Felony Review is going over the paperwork as we speak. And as soon as we get an address for this low life, we'll have a warrant."

THIRTEEN

The video arrived before Thinnes had a chance to make even a small dent in the pile of notes he'd acquired. It was labeled Lewis English. He took it into the Identisketch room and ran it in the machine they used for reviewing surveillance videos.

The set was dark except for an overhead spot trained on the lectern and the man behind it. The harsh lighting made the speaker's face look skull-like, made him seem a little crazy. With his wild hair and beard and mesmerizing eyes, he reminded Thinnes of Charles Manson. It was obvious he'd studied acting or public speaking. He maintained eye contact with the audience. And the camera was clearly one of the audience. He sucked the viewer in along with his unseen chorus, who amened at nearly every pause. It made Thinnes think of John Kennedy's "Ask not" speech and Martin Luther King's "I have a dream," which pissed him off because he knew this guy's speech was some sort of sophisticated con.

"God!" English paused, circling the audience with a look. "Sent flood to punish the sons of Adam for their wickedness!" Another pause. "He sent plague to bring great Pharaoh low. Next time! It will be fire! There will be a conflagration the likes of which have not been seen since Hiroshima! Fire to sear the soul of the unbeliever! Fire to cleanse the nation of the contagion of godlessness! Fire to temper our resolve to be among the righteous!

41

"My brothers and sisters, we have a mission!"

By the time Thinnes had run through the tape again, Oster was back, reporting that Nolan had positively ID'd Brian "Wiley" Fahey as the nutcase who'd poured gas on his squad car and tried to set it on fire with Nolan in it.

Thinnes added that to the information he already had in his warrant application. While he waited for Fuego to get back to him with Fahey's address, he called Detective Flyer.

Like every other cop in the city, Flyer was looking to do what he could to get Banks's killer. He was nearby when Thinnes paged him, and he said he'd be right over, happy to help and delighted to talk about his favorite hobby. When he came into the squad room, he walked over to where Thinnes was reading the pile of phone notes the sergeant had just handed him.

"How's it goin'?" Flyer asked. He took the empty chair next to Thinnes.

Oster stood and rested his arm on the desk partition on Thinnes's other side.

"We got a couple leads," Thinnes said. He pointed to the videotape. "What are we looking at here?"

"Lewis English, aka Brother John—among other aliases— founder and chief beneficiary of the Church of the Divine Conflagration. He formed it while he was doing time in County for fraud."

"Divine Conflagration," Thinnes said, "sounds like the name of a rock group."

Oster said, "Sounds like a bad pun to me."

"So where do we find this guy?" Thinnes asked.

"Rosehill Cemetery. He died three weeks ago in County, where he was waiting to bond out on a charge of disorderly conduct. Apparently he was arrested exhorting his flock to burn down a neighborhood adult bookstore. The state's attorney was trying to decide if they could get a jury to buy conspiracy to commit arson, too."

"So this is an anti-porn group?"

"Also anti-abortion, drugs, gay rights, women's lib, immigration, affirmative action, and the ACLU. And they claim battered women's shelters lead to the breakdown of the traditional family. There's some indication church members torched a couple of abandoned buildings since their leader bought it. A few of the crazier ones've been picketing County, claiming the cops beat English to death."

"Any question about that?"

"Nope. ME called it natural causes. Guy had a pipe bust an' he bled to death—officially a burst aneurysm. We called up his bruise sheet—nothin'."

"What's his connection to Brian Fahey?"

"Wiley Fahey is one of his more outspoken disciples. He used to be the reverend's chauffeur and general flunky. Since English died, Fahey seems to have taken over as chief instigator. He's the most outspoken advocate of the police brutality theory."

Thinnes said, "So what's *with* these people?"

"We tried to convince 'em to blame God for the reverend's demise, but since when does a nutcase take a cop's word for anything?"

Oster frowned. "You tellin' us these assholes beat Banks to death and tried to set Nolan on fire because they think cops killed their nutcase leader?"

Flyer shrugged. "I've seen 'em come up with crazier theories."

The search warrant gave them permission to look for "one standard red gasoline can, accelerants and incendiary devices, and documentary evidence supporting a conspiracy to commit arson or murder." Oster looked like he was all in, but he wouldn't be left behind. They brought Fuego to identify any "accelerants and incendiary devices" they might find.

"If that means matches, lighters, and gasoline," Oster said, as they were getting in the car, "we would probably handle it without help from Arson."

"Look on the bright side, Carl," Thinnes said. "If we find anything *he'll* have to carry it out."

"That's fine with me," Fuego said. "As long as you guys haul away any bodies we find."

"Humph. I s'pose that means we gotta call for an explosives tech if we find an M80."

"It's called division of labor. Or job security, if you like."

The landlady let them in after insisting she hadn't seen Fahey for a week—not since the day before the rent was due. In fact, the apartment looked as if no one had ever lived there. It had all the warmth and charm of a thirty-nine-dollar motel room. It was piled with boxes of old office equipment, including a manual typewriter and reams of flyers—propaganda for the Conflagration Church. The three detectives put on gloves and sorted through everything. The first item of interest was a handout demanding FREE BROTHER JOHN and a blurb suggesting that tax deductible contributions to the church could be sent to a post office box in Uptown. Eventually they came across lists of church members and contributors and an unopened envelope that looked like a bank statement.

"I guess we better have someone go over this for finger-prints," Thinnes said.

"No incendiary devices," Oster said. "Not even a match-book. Tough luck, Fuego."

Thinnes had been lifting the equipment out of the boxes to see if anything interesting was stashed underneath. "Hel-lo," he said, as he extracted an adding machine. He put it aside and reached a fat white, leather-bound album from the bottom of the box. "I want to bring *this* to show and tell."

FOURTEEN

Patrol found the white van in an alley off Western, near the late Lewis English's residence. The Major Crime Scene techs had photographed it in place and had it towed to the District garage. They were processing it for fingerprints with cyanoacrylate fumes—Crazy Glue—when Thinnes caught up with them.

The van was a Ford Club Wagon, new enough for Thinnes to wonder where English got the money for it. The rear bumper had minor damage from a collision and bumper stickers that said: GOD IS THE ANSWER and JESUS SAVES. Someone had used a marker to add WHAT'S THE QUESTION? to the first, and AT CITIBANK to the other. The license plate bracket was an add-on advertising a Ford Lincoln Mercury dealership. In the upper corner of the rear window was a faded parking decal, C8, with no company name or clue to where the lot might be. Below it, a strip of yellowed, dried cellophane tape hung from one side of the band of adhesive it had been part of, marking where one end of a License-applied-for placard had been attached vertically to the window. The card itself dangled from a strip of tape below the adhesive line with its number facing into the van. Thinnes walked around to the passenger side, where THE DIVINE CONFLAGRATION CHURCH showed in self-adhesive letters. Someone had "keyed" both doors. The antenna was bent. The windshield was cracked and had three city vehicle stickers on it—none current. The message on the driver-side door had been

45

reduced to CONFLAGRAT ON CHURCH, though shinier patches of paint stood out like ghosts of the missing letters.

"What've we got?" Thinnes asked.

Before the tech answered, he looked behind Thinnes, who turned to see what was happening. An unmarked Caprice had just pulled into the garage. Thinnes felt the hair rise on his back. As the overhead door closed behind the car, the technician's supervisor, got out. Bendix was balding and out of shape. His usual sour expression was in place, and the perpetual cigar was clamped between his jaws. Halfway between the van and his car, he paused to relight the cigar, waving the spent match to cool it and dropping it in a jacket pocket out of reflex. Whatever else his faults, he'd never been accused of contaminating a crime scene. "Figures you'd be in on this, Thinnes," he said.

"Nice to see you, too, Bendix," Thinnes told him.

Bendix turned to the tech and said, "What've we got?"

The tech looked uncomfortable. "No prints on the outside," he said. "Looks like it was wiped clean. Ditto on the spare rim, but we got a partial from the tire iron. Guess he didn't wipe it carefully enough. Oh, and on a hunch, one of the beat coppers checked the storm drains in the vacinity—came up with these." He took a plastic bag out of the box he'd been collecting evidence in; it held a bunch of keys. "Ignition key fits."

"Log 'em and give 'em to the great detective here," Bendix said, hitching a thumb toward Thinnes. "Maybe he can figure out what the rest of 'em fit."

The tech nodded.

"What else?" Bendix demanded.

The tech reached into his box and took out a large brown paper evidence bag with the date, case number, and other pertinent information scrawled on the outside. He held the bag open so Bendix could look inside. Thinnes crowded in to see, too. The bag contained a roll of white fabric that looked like the material graduation gowns were made of. Left in the box were an assortment of paper and plastic envelopes. Thinnes could see a matchbook in one and a paper that could have been a dealer invoice for the van. He pointed. "Think I could get a photocopy of that?"

"Sure thing." The tech took the bagged invoice and started to walk toward the office, then must've realized that that would leave his evidence in the temporary custody of Thinnes, in violation of protocol. On the other hand, giving a detective evidence before it had been processed was also against SOP.

"Gimme that," Bendix growled. He puffed the cigar as he took gloves from his pocket and pulled them over his stubby fingers. Then he grabbed the invoice and stalked off with it.

Thinnes restrained the urge to offer the tech his condolences.

"Hey, Thinnes," the sergeant said when Thinnes walked into the squad room two hours later. "AFIS got a hit on that partial they found on the church van, and—surprise!—it belongs to one Brian Fahey."

"Surprise." Thinnes got his coffee mug and walked over to get coffee.

Ferris was sitting at a table next to the coffee table. He had his feet up and the *Sun-Times* spread out in front of him. "Thinnes, what were O.J.'s last words to Nicole?"

Thinnes didn't want to know.

" 'Your waiter will be right with you.' "

Thinnes shook his head. He wondered if anyone would remember O.J. jokes after Simpson's trial was over. How long would it take before a question like Ferris's would be answered with a puzzled, who? huhn?

"What you got there?" Ferris asked, pointing to the album Thinnes had under his arm. "Wedding pictures?"

"Evidence," Thinnes said.

"Lemme see."

"Go collect your own evidence."

Ferris laughed, and Thinnes realized he'd only asked to see the album to annoy him. "You got your report on the canvass done yet?"

"It's not written up, but I can tell you nobody saw a thing. Too dark. Too foggy. Too early."

"Well, get it written up. I need it ASAP."

"Why? You're not anywhere near ready to close the case."

"I've been on more than twenty-four hours; I'm caught up on my paperwork; and there's an arrest warrant and an all-call out on a suspect. When I finish with this, I want to punch out and go home."

"Do tell." Ferris picked up the *Sun-Times* and made a show of reading it.

Thinnes filled his mug and headed for the conference room.

The album was still smudged with fingerprint powder. He got paper towels and cleaned it up, then studied it. Lewis English—Brother John—featured prominently in almost every picture. In some, his was the only face showing. There were several newspaper clippings on demonstrations involving the reverend's flock. One was accompanied by a picture with a woman's face clearly showing. And underneath it was the woman's name. Newspaper photographers usually got releases from the people they photographed. With addresses. Thinnes picked up the phone and rang the paper.

FIFTEEN

If he hadn't done a tour as a medic in Nam, Caleb would have found the bruises he'd developed overnight alarming. The exam at the hospital ER reassured him nothing was broken or seriously injured, but this morning everything ached. He inspected the damage as soon as he rolled out of bed. His shoulders, elbows, hips, knees, and forearms were a mass of blue and bile-yellow. And lacerations too small to have been noticed yesterday, while he was under the anesthetic of shock and adrenaline, made their presence painfully obvious every time he moved. After he'd finished in the bathroom and struggled into clothes, he dialed the office of his physician. A recorded message informed him that the doctor was on vacation. Emergency calls were being taken by another service; if he would leave his name, number, and a brief message . . . He left a message with his pager number. He had work to do and wanted breakfast first. Aspirin doesn't sit well on an empty stomach.

Dr. Martin Morgan's office was on Ridge Avenue in Evanston, just south of Evanston Hospital. Caleb found an open space for the Jaguar, mercifully near the door. He hobbled in and took the elevator up.

The doctor's hours were nine to five, Monday, Thursday, and Friday, but he'd agreed to see Caleb early. When Caleb entered the waiting room, the doctor himself greeted him and led him back to a small, tastefully furnished office. He was as tall as Caleb—six-foot-two, fortyish but fit, with gray eyes and auburn hair graying at the temples. His suit was expensive and conservative, except for the red paisley tie. His manner was reserved but not standoffish.

He offered Caleb a chair across from his desk and sat down. From a drawer in the desk, he took a blank chart form and a pen and began to elicit Caleb's medical history. He seemed to be in no hurry, waiting until he was sure Caleb had finished answering and noting the information in a kind of shorthand before asking the next question. Even allowing for professional courtesy, Caleb thought this extraordinary. He didn't miss, either, that when the doctor asked if he was HIV positive, he didn't record Caleb's response. "It's something I need to know for proper diagnosis and treatment," he told Caleb when he commented. "But if I put it in your chart, it becomes a matter of public record."

The leisurely pace gave Caleb time to observe the doctor and examine his office. He was left-handed and wore a gold wedding band. His hands were long-fingered and carefully manicured, but strong-looking, with fine, pale hair covering the backs. His voice was deep and melodious, but projected just enough to cross the space between them. It gave an impression of intimacy, though his reserve discouraged familiarity. He reminded Caleb of a cat. His credentials were displayed in the usual manner. He'd graduated with honors from Loyola Medical School, specializing later in internal and family medicine; and he'd been certified by the appropriate medical boards. There were medical tomes in the tall bookshelf behind him, and on the desk, a portrait of the perfect family—Dr. Morgan and his statuesque, blond wife; lovely, teenage daughter; and model-beautiful son.

When he seemed satisfied with Caleb's history, Morgan asked about the "accident" that was Caleb's presenting complaint. Caleb abbreviated the event as much as possible, but Morgan's eyes widened. "That was on the news! You're the Good Samaritan who saved the policeman!"

"I'd prefer to keep that between us."

Morgan returned his attention to the chart. "Yes, of course. Did they take X rays?"

"No. It didn't seem necessary, but they did have to suture some of the lacerations."

Morgan nodded. "And how are you feeling today? I notice you're limping."

"As if I'd been run over by a bus."

"What did they give you?"

"Tylenol with codeine."

"How's that working?"

"I haven't taken any yet. I thought I'd try getting by with aspirin first—fewer side effects."

Morgan nodded and made another note on the chart, then stood and said, "If you'll come this way, Doctor?" He led Caleb to an adjacent examining room and produced the ubiquitous paper gown. "Please take everything off but your briefs and put this on. I'll return in a few minutes."

The examination was as thorough as the history. Morgan peered into Caleb's eyes and ears and down his throat, giving the impression that he had nothing else to do all day. He felt Caleb's neck and throat with fingers as gentle as his voice. Caleb felt a little, involuntary thrill of pleasure at the touch, though there was nothing in the doctor's manner to suggest anything unprofessional.

As he listened to Caleb's heart, he lowered his gaze and seemed to focus his entire attention on what he was hearing. Caleb was reminded of a devout congregant, involving his whole being in his prayer. Morgan moved the stethoscope again, and as he concentrated, Caleb noticed how his long lashes lay against his cheeks. His expression gave no hint of what he was discovering about the state of Caleb's health, but Caleb had many times seen just such a rapt expression on the faces of symphony-goers—suggesting that all they needed for sustenance was what they were imbibing through their ears. The doctor's every movement was careful and deliberate, as if from long habit he moved in a way least likely to distress a nervous patient.

Morgan repositioned the stethoscope and said, "Breathe in slowly and deeply." Though there was nothing suggestive in his manner, Caleb felt himself responding as if to a lover's touch. He wished that he could meet someone like this, but someone who wasn't straight or married. And then he forced himself to think of borderline personality disorder and income tax audits.

SIXTEEN

At 8:30 A.M. Evanger invited Thinnes to come into his office and bring him up to speed; Oster tagged along. They left the door open so Evanger could keep an eye on the squad room. Unnecessary. Everybody was keeping busy.

"What've we got on this church?" Evanger asked.

"Established three years ago by the Reverend Lewis English," Thinnes told him. "Aka Brother John English, aka Rude Lewis—that was before he saw the light. Used to be a dedicated con artist. He bought up the church building at a tax auction and had it rehabbed. No information on how he financed either deal, but somehow he got it a tax-exempt status."

"Figures," Oster said.

"Carl," Evanger said. "Find out who gets the property now that he's dead, will you? See if he left a will?"

"Yeah, sure. . . ."

Viernes stuck his head through the doorway. "Thinnes, one of the tac cops just reported activity at the church. They're keeping an eye on things 'til you get there."

The sign on the door said DIVINE CONFLAGRATION CHURCH — ALL ARE WELCOME so Thinnes didn't think they needed a search warrant to enter. Besides Oster, he'd brought Swann, Viernes, Ryan, Ferris, three of the property crimes dicks, and three tactical officers—Azul and the team that'd been watching the building.

The cops stood against the back wall. The interior was dim. Except for rows of folding chairs instead of pews, and regular clear glass windows in place of stained glass, it was a pretty standard small church. The lectern was where the sanctuary would have stood if there'd been a sanctuary.

A service was in progress. The thin young man behind the lectern was lit dramatically by an overhead spotlight and didn't seem to notice as they filed in. He was Caucasian, and had thick, black hair with the odd strand of gray, and hazel eyes.

"An opal holds a fiery spark," he announced, "but *a flint holds fire.*" It was the kind of line amateur actors usually got off on. He should have shouted it. He was doing his best to imitate the speaking style of the late Brother John, without succeeding. He didn't have the confidence or polish. Or the practice. And he was reading his remarks, not reciting them.

"In the coldest flint there's hot fire. You must *be* flint. You must kindle the fire of belief in others. Then you'll see *how great a matter a little fire kindleth.*"

Standing next to Thinnes, Swann muttered, *"Kindle not a fire you can't put out."* Swann was the Area's resident expert on scripture. He obviously wasn't impressed.

"When your heart is on fire, sparks will fly from your mouth. . . ." He finally spotted the cops and trailed off. "Can I . . . what is it? . . ."

"Sorry to interrupt your service, Reverend." Thinnes had to raise his voice to carry across the space. "But we're conducting a murder investigation and we need your help."

"Er . . . sure."

An example of how a heater case burns up the usual objections to paying overtime, there were almost as many cops as there were worshipers—half a dozen men and eleven women. Thinnes used the standard divide-and-conquer routine for the interviews—separate the subjects and question each separately. They dragged the chairs around to make little conversation areas, and each interview team set up shop in a different spot around the room. The three church members Thinnes and Oster interviewed personally were typical of the group.

The preacher's name was Gary Oddman. He claimed he'd never heard of Officer Banks. He'd been preparing his Sunday sermon at the time she was being killed, preparing to deliver it while her remains were being dumped. He knew Brian Fahey slightly, but he hadn't seen him for a couple days. Fahey was one of several regular church members who'd been absent Sunday, the same members—excepting Charlie—who were absent today. He didn't know why. He didn't know Brian Fahey well.

"What's Fahey's part in the church?" Thinnes asked.

"He's the caretaker. And he runs errands. He used to be Brother John's chauffeur."

"Did he have any particular hatred for the police?"

"I don't know."

"Did you ever hear of him starting fires?"

"Only in a symbolic sense."

"The phrase 'Fire next time' mean anything to you?"

"It's from the Bible. God destroyed the world for men's wickedness by flood the first time. The next time it will be by fire."

"Who else is missing—your regulars?"

"Besides Brian, John and Abel Smith, and John Mackie, Ron Hughes and Sister Serena. But her attendance has been sporadic at best since Brother John passed away."

"Tell me about Serena."

"That's not her real name. I don't know her real name. She's schizophrenic—not that you'd have known it when

Brother John was alive, but she must've quit her medication. She's gotten real withdrawn—at first she wouldn't look at you when she talked to you. Lately, she won't even talk to anyone. And she hasn't been coming to services. . . ."

"How did you get to be minister?"

"I was elected."

Thinnes pointed around the room. "You mean they voted you in?"

"No, I mean *elected* in the sense of chosen."

"Who by?"

"Brother John, of course. He named me in his will."

"Any chance we could see a copy?"

Gary seemed suddenly at a loss. "I don't know. I don't have it."

"Who does?"

"The church's business manager."

"Where do we find him?"

"That's just it. I don't know. He called me up after Brother John's death and told me the church was to continue and I was to be acting minister until further notice. He said all the bills would be paid and everything taken care of. He sounded so reassuring, I didn't think to ask his name. And I didn't realize 'til he'd hung up that he hadn't left a number."

Thinness handed him his business card. "Next time he calls, you be sure to get his name and number. Then call me."

Next they interviewed a twenty-seven-year-old female Cauc who looked like a high school girl, down to her baggy overalls and platform shoes. Thinnes asked for her name and address—Gayle Slevin, Lakeview. Oster wrote everything down. She told them she was living with her parents and worked as a receptionist for a veterinarian, and she was supposed to be at work in twenty minutes, so could they please be quick.

"Tell me about the church," Thinnes said.

"We pray and fast and do good works." Thinnes waited. "We have meetings and vigils. Sometimes we do community work."

"Such as?"

"Well, we all have regular shifts at the soup kitchen. And we take turns working at the church store. Sometimes we rally for Jesus or picket godless businesses."

"Like when Brother John got arrested?"

"Yes."

"Have you ever been arrested?"

"No." Her answer seemed defensive—as if it was something to be ashamed of. "I wanted to be, but they wouldn't do it."

"The police wouldn't arrest you?"

"Yeah. They took Brother John away and told the rest of us to move along."

Thinnes waited. When she didn't elaborate, he said, "So you did what?"

"We went home to wait for further instructions." She pouted. "Brother John told us to. He said another would come to lead us into the millennium. It's only five years away, you know."

"This other that's s'posed to come," Oster said. "Who'd he be?"

She looked at Oster. "I don't know." She seemed genuinely puzzled. "That's the tragedy—he never told us."

The last girl made Thinnes think of an overeager waitress. He was almost surprised when she didn't say, "Hi, I'm Kathie. I'll be your server."

He asked her the same questions he'd asked the others. When he got to who, of those who usually attended services, had been missing yesterday morning, she told him Sister Serena, and brothers Ron and Charlie, the two Johns, and Abel. She didn't know any of their last names.

"What about Brian Fahey?"

"Is that his name? Fahey? He doesn't usually come to services, ya know?" She started to twist her finger absentmindedly in her hair. Habit.

"What does he do for the church?"

"He runs errands and, um, drives Brother John. . . ." They waited. "Used to drive him, ya know? Just stuff."

"He a believer?" Oster asked.

"Well, you know? What else would he be?"

Oster looked at Thinnes and didn't answer.

"What's he like?" Thinnes asked.

Her face went blank for a fraction of a second—she'd never really looked at him, Thinnes would've bet. Finally, she said, "I dunno. I mean . . . He's older, kinda quiet. Ya know? I used to think he was a dirty old man. I mean, before Brother John died he was . . . He used to stare, ya know? But since . . . he's been, ya know, kinda like almost scared of something."

Thinnes could feel Oster's irritation as he fought his own urge to strangle her. "So what do you think he's afraid of?"

She shrugged. "You got me. Ya know?"

"Who's been running the church since Brother John died?"

"Brian. Sort of. I mean . . . ya know? He said Greg should lead the prayers and, like, the business manager said we'd all get paid and whatever. Ya know?"

"What do you get paid for?" Oster demanded. His tone made it perfectly clear he couldn't see paying her for anything.

Thinnes shot him a look, then rephrased the question. "You work for the church, Kathie?"

"Yeah, I mean. We all do, ya know?"

Thinnes was getting tired of "Ya know?" If she wasn't actually clueless, she was a terrific actress. "One more thing, Kathie. Have you met this business manager?"

"Um . . . no."

"Know who he is?"

"You'd have to ask Brian. I mean, I'm not into any of that, ya know?"

"Where can I find Brian?"

She shrugged.

"Did you ever hear him threaten anyone?"

"No, I mean. I don't think I ever heard him say five words, ya know? Um, what's he done?"

"We're lookin' into that," Oster said.

Thinnes said, "Tell us about Brother John."

"He was special, ya know? He listened. I mean, he made you feel like he understood you better than anyone in the world. . . ." Her eyes began filling with tears. ". . . and, um . . . if you'd just listen, ya know, he'd give you all the answers."

SEVENTEEN

Sister Serena, aka Maria Cecci, lived in the first floor apartment of a two-flat that had JESUS LOVES YOU and JESUS IS ALIVE posters in the front window. She didn't answer when Thinnes rang the bell. After a couple minutes, he knocked, in case the bell was out. Still no answer. While they waited, Oster looked over the neighborhood.

They finally had the building super let them in. The apartment would've embarrassed a fraternity, and the super stood inside the door shaking his head in disbelief. Besides looking as if it had just been tossed by the DEA, there was garbage and dirty dishes everywhere, drug paraphernalia and a dozen empty wine bottles. "This ain't right," he said. "Maria's lived here five years. Last time I was in the place, you could've eaten off the floors. And she ain't a boozer. This ain't her."

"Well it's somebody," Oster said. He pulled on a pair of latex gloves and said, "Where do you start?"

Thinnes crossed to the bedroom doorway and looked in. Like the front room, it was filthy and disorderly. Except that the closet door was shut. Nothing else was closed—not the shades or dresser drawers. The bed was unmade. What's wrong with this picture? he asked himself. He took out his .38. He held it up and ready as he crossed to the closet door. His move caught Oster's attention. He followed Thinnes into the room, drawing his weapon, too. He covered as Thinnes stood to one side of the closet door and turned the knob. He yanked the door open.

A woman was sitting on the floor of the closet, with her legs drawn up and her arms wrapped around them. She gave Thinnes, or maybe his gun, a terrified look and let go of her legs. She buried her face between her knees. And she clasped her fingers together over the back of her neck with a sob.

No threat.

Thinnes holstered his weapon and said, "Maria Cecci?"

Oster said, "We're not gonna hurt you ma'am," as he put his gun away. "Get up. Now."

The woman didn't move. Oster took her by one wrist, Thinnes by the other. They pulled her hands apart and lifted her to her feet. Thinnes let her go.

A closer inspection showed a Caucasian, about five-three, brown-eyed and bleach-blond. She looked about forty-five, was wearing a dirty Salvation Army store wardrobe—white T-shirt under a camouflage flack jacket, and a full, mid-calf-length skirt. White socks showed above her combat boots. There was a rhinestone-studded crucifix around her neck. She pulled her hand from Oster's grasp and grabbed the crucifix, holding it out on its chain as if warding off a vampire. She didn't look at Oster as she said, "Don't touch me!"

"You gonna stand still and talk to us, Maria?" he asked.

"My name is Serena. I used to be someone else. Now I'm serene, serene, Serena."

"You ever been arrested, Serena?"

She started humming. Her fingertips beat a drumroll on the sides of her legs.

"Where were you yesterday morning, Serena?"

"Doin' the Lord's work."

"What would that be?"

She just looked away.

"We'd like you to come with us to answer a few questions," Thinnes said.

"No! You got no warrant! I mean no cause."

"We have probable cause to arrest you for conspiracy to commit aggravated arson," Oster told her. He took hold of one of her wrists and had it behind her and cuffed before she could react. Thinnes took her other wrist, holding on until Oster got the cuff around it. Then he radioed for a policewoman.

She didn't resist. But she kept up a steady drumming with her fingers against her backside. And she started singing, "Upon the wicked he shall rain snares, fire and brimstone, storm and tempest. Storm and tempest. Fire next time."

She was wound up so tight, Thinnes wondered if she was on speed. They left her "hanging"—cuffed by one hand to the wall in the Area interview room. Though alone in the room, she'd shake her head as if replaying an inner argument in her head and disagreeing violently. A couple of times, she started to get up and was stopped by the cuffs. She seemed startled, as if she'd forgotten them. Then she'd sit back down and drum against her thigh with the fingertips of her free hand.

While Thinnes watched, Oster came up behind him and said, "Speed freak."

"Or a manic."

"You been hangin' with the doc too much, talkin' like 'im."

Speaking of the "doc," Thinnes thought, it was too bad Caleb was a witness in the case. They could have used his opinion of Serena. Then again, they might be getting too dependent on the doctor's opinions. The idea pissed him off.

"The doc's here," Oster said.

Doctor Caleb was limping slightly but he was over the shakes he'd had when they sent him home yesterday—and he'd cleaned up nicely, traded his borrowed scrubs for a two-thousand-dollar suit and his Reeboks for Guccis. Even Thinnes was impressed. He'd make a terrific witness when they got to court.

They took him to the Area Three conference room they sometimes used for lineups. Sister Serena was there, flanked by a hooker and a female patrol officer who happened to fit the description. There was another hooker at the end of the line. The ladies of the night looked tired and bored, the cop looked mad enough to kill. All four women were wearing white choir robes that Ryan had commandeered from a nearby church. Serena was a dead cert to be ID'd. Though she was standing with her hands at her sides, she was calling attention to herself by muttering and tapping her thighs with the tips of her fingers.

Thinnes had his own theory about mental illness. Maybe some people were born with their wires crossed and some were damaged by their upbringing, but most of the "crazies" were just people who'd learned that acting goofy or violent got them what they wanted. They didn't need shrinks or medication, they needed society to take away the payoff.

It took only a minute for Caleb to pick the woman out. Number two, the agitated blond, was the one who'd handed her lighter to the pyromaniac. Caleb looked the others over carefully to be sure, then said, "Number two."

"Where have you seen her before?" Thinnes asked.

"She was one of the group trying to incinerate Officer Nolan."

Thinnes went into the room and pointed to Serena. "Put Sister Serena in 230, and keep an eye on her, will you?" he asked.

The uniform officer who was acting as matron nodded. "Sure."

Serena glared at Thinnes and said, "You sicko. Get my name outta your mouth!"

Thinnes ignored her, saying, "Thank you, ladies," to the other three women. "You can go."

Outside the room, he joined Oster and the doctor. As they watched the matron lead Serena away, Oster shook his head. "What's with her, Doc?"

"I wouldn't diagnose someone without a thorough workup, but based on what I see, I'd certainly consider schizophrenia."

"While you're here," Thinnes said, "maybe you could take a look at a video we have and give us an opinion."

"If it's not too long."

"Maybe twenty minutes?

After they'd screened Flyer's video, they waited for Caleb to comment. When he didn't, Thinnes asked, "What's your take, Doctor?"

"Marx wasn't far off when he called religion the opiate of the people, but I think what he failed to understand is that some people desperately need analgesics. Faith for them is laudanum—to paraphrase Thomas Blackburn—relieving *the pain of being human under inhuman conditions.*"

"Yeah." Oster said. "Well, for this bunch, I personally think their religion's more like PCP—makes 'em crazy an' unable to feel *any* pain." He switched off the VCR with an impatient gesture. "Why do they buy this shit?"

"People believe in God," Caleb said, "because He'll never fail them, never disappoint or betray them. True faith is resistant to challenge because nothing offered by critics can approach the comfort it affords. And God's like the hero in a romance—much better than a human being with human imperfections. Even though you can't get close enough to God to hold Him, by refusing—even theoretically—to examine His properties, you can keep Him perfect in your mind.

"Yeah," Oster said. "Okay. I can see believing in God. But what about listening to this nutcase?"

"Human nature. When their childhood religions fail them, people look elsewhere. If you were looking for certainty, this man's self-confidence could be irresistible."

"But why *this* shit?"

"It always fills some need. If they feel powerless, it gives them at least illusory power and the strength of numbers. If they're lonely, it gives them community and the feeling of being loved. If they're fearful, it promises safety; if they fear death, eternal life. It gives some the superiority or the comfort of certainty. . . ."

"But how can they be so sure? This stuff makes no sense!"

"Nothing's held with quite the fervor of an unexamined belief. And some people find the mere existence of alternative viewpoints threatening. They project the threat outward. It's also true that the more of himself a person invests in anything the less likely he is to examine it critically."

"Somebody oughtta set 'em straight about what century it is."

"True believers don't listen and don't need to debate. They may speak with the tongues of men and angels, but they don't dispute. To them, belief is self-evident, and their opponents are simply mistaken.

"Yeah?" Oster said. "Well, in my book, its a perfect example of what's the use."

The interview room barely had space for the three of them. That was the point—in-your-face proximity. Thinnes sat facing the door at a right angle to Serena. She kept edging away until she almost fell off the bench; the tips of her fingers beat a syncopated rhythm against her thighs.

Oster sat down across from her and read her her rights. "Do you understand these rights?"

65

For a minute she looked everywhere but at him, then said, "It's the contransfiguration of the dementable. . . ." Her fingers never stopped moving.

"How 'bout a yes or no?"

"Yes or no."

"Do you want a lawyer, wiseass?"

She glanced at Thinnes with her side vision and shuddered. "He's too jargonated."

Wondering if that was a reference to Oster's insult, Thinnes said, "Miss Cecci, would you like to speak to a lawyer?"

"No use. What good would it do?" She crossed her forearms over her chest and stuck her hands in her armpits, clamping her fingers into stillness with her upper arms. She still didn't look at either of them.

"What can you tell us about the policewoman who was murdered?" Thinnes asked.

"She was stoned." She stared intently at the floor in front of her and talked with increasing rapidity. "Flint's a stone—flintstone. The fire in the flint shows not until it's struck." As Oster's jaw dropped, she started singing, "Everybody must get stoned."

Thinnes recognized the line from a sixties song, but couldn't place it. Was she as crazy as she seemed or was this an Oscar-winning setup for an insanity plea?

Serena continued, faster. "Stone breaks scissors. Scissors cuts paper. Fire *burns* paper."

Oster scowled. "This is nuts!"

She shook her head without looking at him. "And he's in danger of hell fire that calls his brother fool. Or his sister, foolish." She looked at the ceiling and smiled, adding, "Fight fire with fire."

"You seem to be pretty interested in fire," Thinnes said. "Why is that?"

"Fire and water are good servants but bad masters. We had

fire and we had water—that's from the Bible. Or maybe it was James Taylor. That's the hell of it. My brain went dead when Brother John died."

"What does the expression, 'Fire next time' mean?" Thinnes asked.

She started singing, "God gave Noah the fiery sign, no more water, the fire next time."

Thinnes said, "Miss Cecci, do you want to make a statement?"

"Higglety, pigglety, my black hen, she laid down for gentlemen, sometimes ninety, sometimes ten—would've for women, to if they'd had the right equipment. Jim Jones was the Jones on his back. She was a hoarse whore. I was a whore of a different color. I was a whore for Jesus, only, we didn't call him that then. I was Mary Magdalen. Then I died, and he went to heaven. That was in my salad days. Now I'm in my word-salad days."

"What the hell does *that* mean?" Oster demanded.

"There appeared a chariot of fire and horses of fire, and parted them both asunder; and Elijah went up by a whirlwind into heaven."

That was from the Bible. Thinnes wondered who he could ask about the rest of the gibberish. He wished he'd asked Caleb to stay.

"And *you're* going up by squad roll into Ravenswood," Oster told her, "for a little head check." He glared at Thinnes. "How 'bout it?"

"I think we better book her and get her a lawyer first."

Serena gave another little grin without looking at either of them. "First what we'll do, let's kill all the lawyers."

EIGHTEEN

Later in the morning, Thinnes handed the photocopy to the Ford dealership sales manager and watched his expression change from mostly sunny to overcast.

"We're trying to get some information about a vehicle you sold," Thinnes said.

The man's name was Frank Gale. He was middle aged, fat and balding—he could have been Oster's cousin. "What did you want to know?"

"Who sold it, for openers."

"That would be Ed Limardi."

"He in today?"

"He's no longer with us." Gale sounded more cautious than regretful.

"Yeah? Why's that?"

Gale didn't answer right away. In fact, he seemed ready to never answer.

"This is a murder investigation, Mr. Gale."

"Maybe we'd better talk in my office." He led Thinnes into one of the glass-walled cubicles car dealers call offices and offered him a seat across the desk. When they were both settled, he said. "I . . . er . . . wouldn't want to be charged with slander."

"Anything you tell me that doesn't come out in court stays strictly between us." It was a standard line. It was also SOP.

Gale nodded. "Limardi was fired."

"Why?"

"Theft. Well . . . we found out he was giving terrific discounts to people to up his sales figures and then falsifying the paperwork to hide the bath the dealership was taking. That van was one of the ones he stiffed us on. And he was probably getting a five-finger commission from his customers on top of what he was getting over the table."

"So why didn't you prosecute?"

Gale shrugged. "It wasn't up to me or I would've. The state's attorney didn't think we had a strong enough case. And the owners didn't want any bad publicity."

"How long was he here?"

"Five years."

"You know where he went when he left?"

"No. And we didn't get anyone checking his references. He probably knew better than to even mention us."

"You got an address?"

"Yeah, sure."

"And how 'bout a list of the other sales he cheated you on?"

"I'll get it."

"And the name of the state's attorney on the case."

"Sure thing."

Gale was gone five minutes. When he came back, he handed Thinnes a sheaf of photocopies, with Limardi's personnel record on top. "You didn't get this from me," he said.

"No, it was that other guy—A. Nonymous. Thanks."

They shook hands and Gale handed Thinnes his card. "Let me know if I can help you with anything else. Of if you ever want a good deal on a car."

The lobby was busier than usual when Thinnes got finished briefing Evanger and the district commander, and there was an urgency bordering on ruthless about the way everyone was going about business. Thirty hours and counting since they'd found Banks and no arrests yet. Uniform and plainclothes cops were coming and going without the usual kidding or kibitzing; the few civilians seemed out of place. As Thinnes passed the District Nineteen desk, the sergeant told him, "Detective Swann asked me to tell you he's got your car salesman upstairs."

"Thanks."

Upstairs, Swann had his butt parked on the corner of a desk near the coffeemaker, where he could keep an eye on the door and the interview room. Thinnes ambled over and helped himself to coffee. "How's it going?"

"Can't tell with this guy. He asked me what was it all about. Once. Then he clammed up."

Thinnes took his coffee over near the interview room's two-way window and studied Edward Limardi—natural dirty-blond hair, blue eyes, six feet, 190 pounds, thirty-five or forty. He was alternately pacing the small room and sitting. Fidgeting. He'd obviously seen plenty of TV cop shows, because every time he looked at the mirror, he scowled and looked at his watch. It was gold—a Rolex, Thinnes would've bet—and matched his wire-rim glasses.

A cliché of police work held that guilty parties went to sleep while waiting to be questioned, but not all offenders were typical or that stupid. Still, Limardi didn't look like a man who was worried as much as a rich asshole who was pissed.

Swann came up to the window, and Thinnes asked him, "What've we got on this guy?"

"DOB March 12, 1953. No record of any arrests. No outstanding wants or warrants. Valid Illinois license. No recent moving violations, not even a parking ticket." Swann shrugged. "A regular citizen."

"What did you tell him to get him to come in?"

70

"That we needed his help in clearing up a matter involving a vehicle."

Thinnes finished his coffee and pitched the cup. Before entering the interview room, he asked Swann, "You want to watch, maybe take notes?"

"Okay."

Thinnes went in and introduced himself to Limardi, offering his hand.

"The other detective said you needed help in an investigation," Limardi said, "but he didn't say of what."

Thinnes took one of the Polaroids of the church van out of his pocket. Limardi looked at it and shrugged. "A Club Wagon. So?"

"Our investigation leads us to conclude it was used in the commission of a crime. And records indicate that you sold it to the group we think used it."

"I sell a couple hundred vehicles a year, Detective. I haven't sold a Ford since—I can't remember when. I don't see—"

"I think if you try, you can remember *this* Ford. The agency fired you for selling it below cost."

Limardi was good at hiding his feelings, but that got him. His smile disappeared. "I'd be very happy to find out who told you that. My lawyer could use the business."

"Lawyer?"

"He specializes in libel and slander."

"To win a slander suit, you'd have to be able to prove it wasn't true."

Limardi blinked several times, the only indication Thinnes had scored a point.

"It's not important," Thinnes said. "I'm not interested in any deals you made, just who you sold the van to."

"I'm surprised your informant didn't tell you that, too, and save us both the time and bother."

"Well?"

"The Reverend Lewis English. He was very persuasive."

"You don't strike me as a man who'd be persuaded by a religious type."

Limardi shrugged. "Car sales are quite competitive. Your informant should have told you that. Sometimes, when you're down for the month and running out of month . . ." He shrugged again. "So, maybe you salve your conscience by telling yourself it's for a church, so it's for a good cause."

"You talk to the reverend lately, or any of his church members?"

"No. I never saw the reverend after he drove away in his new van. And I never met any of his congregation."

"What can you tell me about the Conflagration Church?"

"Is that what he called it? I never heard of it." He looked pointedly at his Rolex. "I'd like to go now, if you don't mind. Sorry I can't be more help. But I've got a quota to fill. . . ."

NINETEEN

The modest bungalow was on Christina, in a neighborhood of similar houses. Many belonged to older people who couldn't keep them up; when the old folks died or got senile enough to be carted off to nursing homes, their houses were sold to young families with no time or money for major rehab jobs.

A light rain was falling, but it was too warm for the raincoats Thinnes and Oster were wearing as they climbed the porch steps. Oster's face and hair were damp; Thinnes couldn't tell if it was from rain or sweat. No one answered the bell when he rang, so Oster rapped on the door.

Linda Koslowski opened it. She had thick auburn hair and angry brown eyes. She was five-five and probably weighed 120 pounds. She opened her door with "What the hell's he done now?"

"Who?" Thinnes asked. They hadn't published Wiley's picture or given his name to the press.

The woman's anger softened in confusion. "You're not here about Terry?"

"Who's Terry?" Oster demanded.

"Easy, Carl," Thinnes said.

The woman said, "My ex, Terry Koslowski. I haven't seen him in a month, ever since I threatened to call the cops the last time he was here. If you're not looking for him? . . ."

"We're looking for your brother."

She waited. They outwaited her. "And?" She made a circle with her hand in an out-with-it gesture.

"And what?" Oster's tone had gone from belligerent to irritated. "We thought you might know his whereabouts."

"Their whereabouts," she said with a laugh. "I got five brothers."

"We're looking for Brian."

"I haven't seen him since I can't remember when."

"Mind if we come in and talk about it?"

She shrugged and stepped back from the door. "Suit yourselves." When she'd closed the door behind them, she waved in the general direction of an overstuffed sofa.

The living room was small and tidy, with barely enough room for the sofa, a chair, and a television. There was a starving-artist painting of flowers on the wall behind the sofa and a crucifix on the TV. Beyond the living room, they could see a small dining room with an open door to the kitchen.

They sat on either end of the sofa. She plopped onto the armchair across from it and leaned forward, putting her forearms together on her lap and cupping one upturned hand in the other. Oster pulled out his notebook.

Thinnes asked, "When was the last time you saw your brother?"

She thought about it. "Before Christmas he stopped by with two of his deadbeat friends—I'm not sure why. Anyway, when they started talking nasty, I told 'em to leave."

"What were their names?"

"Ah . . ." She chewed the inside of her cheek while she considered. "Ah . . . cough drops . . ." She raised and lowered her cupped hands. "Smith Brothers. Smith. I don't know their first names, but their last name is Smith. And they're brothers. And cons." They waited. She added, "Most of Brian's friends are cons. He's been—pardon my French—a fuckup since he was a kid."

74

"Why, exactly did you throw him out the last time he was here?"

"They were BS-ing about a girlfriend of one of them—Rosie, a mutual acquaintance. And one of these jerks says he was livin' with Rosie and she threw him out. He says he's gonna get back at her by settin' her on fire. Anyway, I said I wouldn't have that kind of talk in my house and he could leave. And I told them if anything was to happen to *my* house, they could count on some major trouble. I told 'em nothing better happen to Rosie, either. I think they were just blowin' smoke, though. But they left."

"Your brother ever set any fires?"

"Not that I heard of. Well, once. But not since he was a kid. And the old man whipped him within an inch of his life."

"So he didn't set any fires after that?"

"No. Funny. I'd forgotten about that. He kept whalin' on 'im, kept asking did he want to end up like his sister."

"What did he mean by that?"

"Our oldest sister died in a fire. Brian was only two or four, so he wouldn't remember. But he grew up hearing about it. Anyway, after my father whipped him, he didn't play with matches again."

"Your father beat him a lot?"

She thought about it. "Well, I guess he'd be locked up for it now, but then everybody beat their kids. Even the nuns at school'd haul off and crack us if we got out of line."

"Did your brother get singled out?"

"He got in more trouble than the others. And Pa never hit us girls. But he'd sometimes hit Brian if we did something wrong. He never hit my ma—he didn't have the guts."

"What kind of trouble did your brother get into?"

"Just the usual—cutting school, joy riding, shoplifting, like that. Like most kids. Only *he* didn't grow out of it."

"What did he go to prison for?"

"He got caught with a gun."

"Do you have any idea where he might be?" She shook her head. "Any idea who might hide him?"

Her eyes widened. "He's in that much trouble?"

"He tried to kill a police officer."

"Oh, Lord. He's done it this time."

"So it seems."

TWENTY

There was a deputy superintendent sitting in Evanger's office across from the lieutenant. Hiding out. Otherwise he'd have been downstairs in the district commander's office, or out front talking to the press. He didn't look happy.

Thinnes wasn't happy either. It was late Monday afternoon, and he'd had three hours sleep since Sunday morning. The anger that had acted on him like speed earlier had worn off, leaving him strung out, and fighting the sandman had left his eyes feeling gritty. He stifled a yawn. Outside Evanger's window, gray clouds hung above the acre or so of blue-and-white squad cars in the north parking lot. It had been raining off and on all day.

There was a *Sun-Times* on the desk, and the headline jumped up at him: "Arrest in Cop's Murder!"

The deputy pointed to it. "Where's the woman now?"

"We sent her to Ravenswood for a psych evaluation," Thinnes said. He repeated the details of Maria Cecci's arrest.

"How're we doing on getting Fahey?" the deputy asked.

"Pretty close to nailed down," Evanger said.

"We have an arrest warrant," Thinnes said. "And we searched his last known address." They'd also put out an all-call, interviewed every friend and relative he had—even cousins who'd never heard of him—and put his father's house under

77

surveillance. "We're following up on his known associates and fellow church members. It's just a matter of time."

"Were any of these people black?" the deputy asked.

Evanger answered. "Not that we're aware of. Why?"

"What's with this chant they were spouting—'the fire next time'? Isn't that from some black agitator?"

"James Baldwin," Thinnes said, "a writer." He wouldn't have remembered it himself, but Caleb had mentioned it.

Evanger continued, "As nearly as we can tell, it was lifted—along with a lot of other catchy phrases—by their crazy leader, Lewis English, aka Brother John. Seems he got religion, literally, during his last stay in Joliet. Did one of those mail-order conversions and was born again as a reverend."

The deputy nodded. "Go on."

Thinnes took up the story. "English spent time in stir polishing his act. The prison librarian said he read all the stuff they had on preachers and televangelists. And according to a guard I talked to, he had stuff sent to him on a bunch of others, including Billy Graham and Martin Luther King."

"So?"

"When he got out, he set himself up with a storefront mission down on Western and started practicing his fire-and-brimstone bullshit on anybody who'd stop and listen. He'd bought his own building and collected a bunch of lost kids and hard-core losers, including our torch, at the time of his death."

"Which was when?"

"A month ago."

"Cause?" Thinnes thought he detected alarm in the deputy's tone.

"Natural," Evanger said. "But we think some of his goofier followers blame the police, and Banks was retaliation."

"Christ!"

"Yeah."

"Guy from Bomb and Arson has another theory," Thinnes said.

The deputy frowned. "What's that?"

"He thinks some of these deadbeats may be using the church as a front for an arson-for-profit scheme."

The deputy looked skeptical. Why not? It *was* a stretch.

"Some of the surrounding business owners complained to the guys doing the canvass that the church has a very aggressive policy of soliciting funds. And there've been three suspicious fires in the area since the church opened. Also ten of the church regulars have extensive rap sheets. Two of those are so drunk most of the time, they don't know what state they're in, and another has an IQ of sixty-nine. But Fahey, and his best buddies—Ron Hughes, Lawrence Mackie, and John and Abel Smith—have all done time for arson or extortion."

"So?"

"Say the church is a front for something else," Thinnes said. "Whoever's behind this gets the church to solicit contributions from nearby property owners. Maybe they hint that having God on the payroll would be good insurance. Maybe they're also sounding out the owners about how convenient or profitable a little fire would be. Then they got this bunch of crazies stirred up to *set* fires. . . ." He shrugged. "If anyone finds out it was arson, the owner claims he was extorted and refused to pay. The church leaders claim they were misunderstood and can't be held responsible for all their loony followers. The crazies take the rap if they're caught."

"But if you're selling fires," the deputy said, "why call attention to yourself with all this publicity?"

"Advertising? Look, nobody said these guys were playing with a full deck."

Evanger shook his head. "Well, it's moot until we get the rest of them in custody."

"How're we doing on that?"

"We have Hughes," Thinnes told them.

They looked surprised. Evanger said, "Since when?" His tone implied, Why wasn't I told?

"About six hours after we found Banks," Thinnes said. "I just got word. He tried to rob a convenience store up in Twenty-four Sunday night, and was nailed by an off duty copper who'd stopped in to get smokes. Hughes gave the arresting officers a phony name, so we didn't connect him to Banks until he was booked and we ran his prints."

"I guess it's just as well," Evanger said. He didn't have to add what some of Chicago's finest would have done to Hughes if they' gotten their hands on him.

"What about the rest of the scum?" the deputy asked.

Thinnes said, "We've pretty much ruled out the sidewalk inspectors and the retard. And one of the others has an alibi."

"If my math hasn't failed me, with the woman that makes exactly the number that were in on torching the squad car."

Thinnes nodded.

"You talked to Hughes, yet?" Evanger asked.

"He's keeping quiet on the advice of his lawyer. The other three must've crawled into the same hole as Fahey, but we'll get the slugs if we have to turn over every rock in the city."

TWENTY-ONE

Things drift, really."

It was Tuesday morning. The young man sitting across the desk from Caleb paused. Caleb waited until the man continued. "Life seems to be going along on course, so you stop paying attention. Then you notice things going . . ." He shrugged. "Two years ago I had the best job in the world, the best boss. Then my boss got a new boss, and he's driving my boss crazy. And, you know, with gravity . . ." An oblique reference to the old chestnut: Shit runs downhill.

Caleb nodded.

"The job's not fun any more. I guess it's natural. Over time, things just drift."

"Even continents," Caleb agreed. "What did you hope to get from therapy?"

"Oh, I don't know." He was relaxed and betrayed none of the discrepancies between verbal and body language that signaled prevarication. "A course correction."

Caleb was going over the record of his last client for the day when, over the intercom, Mrs. Sleighton announced another visitor, "A Mrs. Noguerra."

Caleb's sister. Rosemary.

"Send her in."

The door opened before he could get to it. She entered and paused, obviously as uncertain as he about what to do next.

She'd been ten when he left for Vietnam. He'd been fond and protective of her while they were growing up, but he'd lost touch when he moved out of his father's house. And he'd transferred his affection to his friend Anita, he realized as he thought about it. The pretty woman standing before him was a virtual stranger.

Then they grinned in unison and hugged. "My God, Jack!"

"Ditto. Let me take your coat." He helped her off with it and was hit with the observation that she was very pregnant. Again. Her first child must be six by now.

"Congratulations," he said. "When?" He draped her coat over the back of the couch by the window.

She beamed. "Some time after Easter. We hope."

He gestured toward the couch. "Sit down. Can I get you coffee?"

She sat. "Thanks, but no. I'm making enough pit stops as it is."

Caleb took the chair next to the couch. "How are Victor and Jesse?"

"They're fine. Victor's . . . I was so lucky to find him."

"Are you sure it was luck? As I remember, you dated a number of *unsuitable individuals* before you met Victor."

"You mean before he decided I was ready for him? He's very logical. He told me he'd checked out all the available women and decided—on purely logical terms—that I was the best prospect."

"Victor seems to have unsuspected depths."

Victor also had money. Not that he'd had anything but a degree from Stanford when he married Rosemary. But sometime during graduate school he'd come up with a device computer companies now thought they couldn't live without. By age twenty-seven, he was wealthy enough to retire. Now he worked as a consultant—when he felt like it—and volunteered for things like Project Literacy and Habitat for Humanity.

She smiled. "He does." She took his hand. "I was going to call, but I was downtown and decided to stop and ask you in person. Victor and I would like you to come for Easter."

Caleb's felt a gladness bordering on giddiness. Then a sudden chill. "Will Robert be there?"

The joy vanished from her expression like sunlight when the day clouds over. "What is it you two fell out about? He's never told me. He used to worship you when we were kids."

"It was more of a falling off. He had me on a pedestal as high as the Sears Tower and he can't forgive me for failing to live up to his fantasy."

"Because you're gay?"

"Umhumm."

"What—horsefeathers!"

Caleb laughed.

"Who told him?"

"I did. I got tired of the when're-you-going-to-marry-and-settle-down business, so I told him. He didn't take it well."

Rosemary shook her head. "Well, he won't be coming. They've been invited to Marsha's parents'. But even if they *were* coming, you'd be welcome. Always. And if Robert doesn't like that, *he* can stay home."

"Is Victor of the same opinion?"

"Of course. I wouldn't marry a bigot."

"Then I accept. What shall I bring?"

"Bring a friend."

"Thank you. I'll see. What can I bring?"

"You don't have to . . ." She laughed and shrugged. They'd been well brought up—one didn't go empty handed. "Whatever you like. Dinner's at seven, but come early and visit."

She stood up and he stood, too. He gave her a hand with her coat. She gave him a him a quick, heartfelt hug. She was still nervous.

Caleb marveled. How had they become so estranged?

He rang up his friend Anita immediately, to ask if she'd like to go.

"Thanks," she said. But if I'm going to go through any heavy family stuff, I think it ought to be with my own family. I haven't spoken to most of them since I divorced Vincent. They may be ready to forgive me. I think I'll just go east and watch how the cattle fare."

"If you come back with any bruises, call."

"Thanks."

"What best friends are for—ice and liniment."

The frenetic activity he'd observed the last time he was at Western and Belmont had lessened, Caleb noted as he made his way up to the Area Three squad room. He'd read about Maria Cecci's arrest and that a second individual—already in custody—was being questioned in connection with the case. It didn't seem enough, though. He knew they hadn't arrested the ringleader, Brian Fahey, or they'd have asked him to come in and identify him in a lineup.

Thinnes was at his desk. Caleb walked up and didn't beat around the bush—"I want to help."

"Forget it, Doc." Thinnes was trying to annoy him. He knew Caleb hated *Doc.* "You're a witness in this case, and even an incompetent defense attorney would use that to get any evidence you helped collect thrown out."

"There must be something—"

Thinnes shook his head. "And don't get any ideas about snooping around on your own. You're also a department consultant. That brings the exclusionary rule into play. The best thing you can do is just go about your business and be ready to testify when we get these creeps in court."

TWENTY-TWO

The room was utilitarian—acoustical tile ceiling with standard fluorescent lights; semiglossed concrete-block walls; no windows; polished linoleum floor; metal wastebasket; electric wall clock—four minutes fast. Metal and plastic stacking chairs surrounded a wood-look Formica table.

The public defender sitting across from the assistant state's attorney was so short her head barely showed above the pile of legal folders in front of her—five-two and under a hundred pounds, dark-haired and brown eyed. She was wearing a public defender uniform, female version—suit, unrevealing blouse, unflashy jewelry, and matching heels. Attractive, but not a knockout. Four of the five men present, in their suits and ties, were sweating in the steam heat. Sitting to his lawyer's left, Ron Hughes shivered in his Department of Corrections uniform—tan short-sleeved shirt and pants. He was white, five-eleven, and sallow complected, with red patches over his cheeks that made him look like he'd been drinking. He had high cheekbones and forehead, blue eyes, and a prominent Adam's apple. His whiny, high-pitched voice sounded to Thinnes like fingernails on a blackboard. Fortunately, he was letting his lawyer do the talking.

"Here's the deal," she said. "My client pleads to murder-two and tells you what you want to know. If you get this other guy, he'll testify."

Thinnes lurched forward in his seat. "No way!"

On either side of him he could see Oster and Fuego copy his move. Fuego growled *caramba;* Oster muttered, "Christ!" Hughes put a finger in his mouth and started gnawing on the cuticle. He seemed to shrink into his shirt.

Across from the PD, the ASA didn't turn a hair. "Not acceptable, counselor. Your *cli*ent killed a *police* officer. We'll accept murder-one and forgo the death penalty."

"We'll take our chances with a jury."

"So will we. And by the time this case comes to trial, we'll have a pile of physical evidence and a roster of witnesses that'll make that circus in California look like a kids' puppet show."

"With the bereaved family sitting front row center," Oster added. He'd been watching too much of the O.J. trial himself.

The PD would've been a disaster as a poker player; Thinnes could see her think about it. But Hughes made the decision. He slid his hand along the table toward his lawyer, trying to get her attention. When that didn't work, he tugged on her sleeve.

"I think your client wants a word with you, counselor," Thinnes said. Looking at the others, he pointed to the door.

They stood in the hall talking until the PD called them back. When they were seated, she said, "My client's prepared to make a statement in return for certain guarantees." Hughes didn't look ready for anything.

"The only guarantee he's going to get," the ASA said, "is that we won't ask for the death penalty if he cooperates."

Hughes was staring at a blank wall, chewing on his finger. "Fine."

The PD made a gesture that was half nod, half shrug.

Hughes didn't look at any of them. "We didn't mean to kill her," he said. "We were all high. An' Wiley had us convinced the cops killed Brother John. He wanted revenge, to get a cop. That's what he said, anyway. We thought he was just blowin' smoke. Him an' the crazy woman." He looked up and apparently didn't like what he saw. He dropped his eyes and continued. "We drove around all night, drinkin' and doin' a shit-load of drugs. In the church van. Then we parked. In a alley. Wiley and the bitch got out. An' the next thing I know, Wiley's shovin' this woman in the back with us. They hit her in the head an' she was half out of it—bleedin' an' pleadin', let her go. Said she's a cop. Said she had family."

Hughes wiped his face with his hand, then began to worry his thumb with his teeth. He stared at the table as if seeing the event replayed on its surface. "Wiley told us to tie her up an' gag her. He said we weren't gonna hurt her, just keep her outta things a while. Then she started screamin' for help an' he hit her with her gun until she was quiet."

"Was she dead?" the state's attorney asked.

"I don't think so. But she was hurt bad."

"Where did this go down?" Oster asked.

"A alley. I'm not sure. I was drunk. Wiley had it all worked out, we just did what he said."

"Then what?"

"There was this cop car. Wiley drove it an' Mackie drove the van for—it seemed like—hours. Then we were in the park. An' Wiley had us all get out an' put on those stupid Klan robes an' chant. An' he started pourin' gas on the cop car. I thought he was just . . . ," he shrugged, ". . . burnin' the car. I didn't know there was cop in it. I mean that's crazy! I was too drunk to think. . . ." He glanced up at Oster as if trying to assess whether he was buying it.

"Just when did you observe that there was someone in the car?" Oster said. He pulled out a handkerchief and dabbed at the sweat beading his temples. It wasn't all that hot in the room.

"When the jogger came, when him an' Wiley got into it, that's when I seen the cop inside the car. Wiley was tryin'a set it on fire. That's when I started soberin' up. Real fast. When that jogger dragged the cop outta the car an' started runnin' with 'im, that's when I figured out that Wiley was really gonna torch it. I took off. I didn't even think of the woman cop 'til I sobered up. I heard it on the news. I figured Wiley an' the others must'a killed her to keep her from talkin'." Hughes stared at the clock.

Oster was squeezing the life out of his handkerchief, breathing as if he'd climbed a flight of stairs. "And like a good citizen, you came straight to the police with your information."

Hughes kept staring at the clock, refusing to look at him. The PD kept her eyes on her notepad.

The state's attorney finally said, "Then what happened?"

"I figured I better get some money together and leave town. I figured I was a dead man if the cops found out I was in on it." He glanced around at them.

Thinnes followed his gaze. The PD was still writing. Oster was treating his handkerchief like he'd like to treat Hughes's neck. Fuego was still as a cat stalking a roach. Hughes pulled the bottom of his shirt loose and wiped his face on it.

Go ahead and sweat, you asshole, Thinnes thought. He asked, "What did you get from this Brother John? What was his deal?"

Hughes paused before he answered. "At first, I thought he was just another con—what he was saying was crazy, really. But then—I don't know—he just wore you down. *He* believed it, you know? And he would sort of like—hypnotize you. I don't know how else to explain it. I mean, after a while I *believed* it. All that stuff. I couldn't even tell you what it was now. But I would've tried to walk on the lake if he told me to." He looked at them, maybe for confirmation that they understood, confirmation he didn't get. He shrugged. "You ever hear him preach?"

"No."

Hughes shrugged again. "I guess he was just a false prophet. Sometimes you don't know. . . ."

88

No, Thinnes thought, you don't. He remembered being moved by Martin Luther King's dream speech—even though he wasn't black or particularly interested in civil rights. "What made you choose Banks and Nolan?"

"Was that their names? I never thought about 'em having names."

"Doesn't look much like you *can* think," Oster said.

Thinnes was struck by how ugly anger made his partner. Was his own rage as obvious or off-putting?

"It's not necessary to be insulting, Detective," the PD said. She must be noticing, too. Oster's expression let her know what he thought of her interruption.

"Why Banks and Nolan?" Thinnes repeated.

"Wiley knew there were these two cops that always stopped for coffee at the same place and time every day. He said that if we did one of 'em, we wouldn't be seen and they wouldn't be missed right away—like they might be if we just flagged down a car in traffic."

"Go on," the ASA said.

"That's all. Afterwards, I tried to put the touch on Wiley; he laughed at me. Said they avenged Brother John without me, but if I went to the cops, I'd go down for felony murder just the same. What could I do? When I tried to pick up a few bucks so I could get lost for a while, I got busted. That's all I know."

"Why did Brother John keep Serena around?" Thinnes asked. "What did he want with a crazy woman?"

"She wasn't so bad when he was alive. When she was takin' her medicine, she was almost normal. She only started getting goofy after John died—must've stopped takin' her stuff." They waited. The silence made Hughes nervous. He squirmed in his chair and said, "An' she was real good at quotin' from the Bible. She helped John with his sermons—sort of a human Bible encyclopedia."

"Where's Wiley?" Fuego demanded.

"I don't know, I swear." Hughes stared at him. "Don't you think I'd try to cut a deal if I knew? I don't know."

Oster stood up and shoved his handkerchief into his pocket. "You're a pitiful excuse for a human being, you know that, Hughes?"

"People been tellin' me that all my life."

TWENTY-THREE

The cops put on a pretty good funeral. Impressive numbers of officers showed up in full dress uniform, marched in formation, saluted in unison. The superintendent showed, sometimes even the mayor. Full court press. And bagpipes—a real media circus. Then it was over. The family had a flag and a handful of newspaper clippings and could point to a star on the wall at Eleventh and State. That was it. A videotape of the show wouldn't be much comfort later when they were left with an empty house and a huge hole in their lives. Thinnes, Oster, Swann, and Ferris watched Banks's funeral on the TV in the conference room. For once, no one had any smart remark to make.

The funeral made Thinnes wonder how Banks's husband was doing without her, which made him wonder what he'd do without Rhonda. The closest he ever came to praying was to thank God for her. She was his heart and soul, his polestar. He understood perfectly the insane rage and despair that drove some men to kill wives who'd left them. Not that he could ever hate Rhonda that much. He might hate himself that much, though. If he ever lost her, he could see himself eating his gun. Or driving his car into a large tree.

During a commercial break, Ferris said, "Hey Thinnes, I heard you're letting that asshole, Hughes, plead."

"Saving the taxpayers the expense of the kind of media circus they got going on in L.A."

"Speaking of which," Ferris said. "You know what O.J.'s last words to Nicole were?" Oster looked disgusted; he shook his head. "Swann?"

Swann looked up from the paper. "I know what *my* last words to *you* would be—"

" 'Your waiter will be right with you.' "

Oster turned to Thinnes. "What was that definition of stress? The confusion in your gut when your head overrides the urge you have to beat the livin' daylights outta someone?"

"No, Carl," Thinnes told him. "Stress is having to work in the same Area with Ferris."

Swann said, "Aw, shut up, you guys. It's back on."

Thinnes walked into Evanger's office and closed the door. The day had turned colder and snow dusted the fleet of squad cars in the lot below the window. Afternoon traffic was building on Western.

Thinnes put the report on Evanger's desk and dropped into the rolling chair in front of it. "We haven't gotten near the bottom of this shit pile yet." He slouched in the chair, resting his right ankle on his left knee, and drummed with his fingers on the side of his shoe.

"You got guilty pleas from Hughes and Cecci. *She'll* never see the outside of a looney bin again. And it's just a matter of time before Fahey and the others turn up. What do you want?"

"A motive would be nice. I don't buy it that any of these assholes loved English enough to kill a cop for him. And Cecci's the only one crazy enough to think God put them up to it. Somebody had to be getting something else."

"But you didn't find any evidence of that. And Banks's family deserves some closure. Plus, we've got almost three homicides a day, citywide, and we're over budget on OT. I want you to go home and spend Easter with your family. We'll get the rest of these guys. And if we get them when you're off duty, we'll call you."

The Russian Tea Cafe wasn't the sort of place the cops usually held meetings. Which was precisely why Thinnes had asked Caleb to meet him there. It was close to the doctor's office—half a block west of Michigan Avenue, and it wasn't likely that word would get back to Evanger.

After they were seated and had their orders in, Thinnes said, "You remember how you felt the day you walked in and found Allen Finley's corpse?" He meant the victim in the first homicide they'd worked together, Caleb's patient.

Caleb nodded. "Outraged."

"I feel that way about Banks. We only got two of her killers; Fahey's still at large. And what if Cecci starts acting normal and they let her out? I don't like it."

"Didn't I read that she pled guilty?"

"Guilty but insane."

"She won't get out. What's really bothering you?"

Thinnes hated it when Caleb seemed to read his mind. But wasn't that why he'd come? "My boss wants me to drop it, take Easter off, then come back and get on to the next case. It sucks."

"Would taking a few days off ruin your chances of eventually making an arrest?"

"Probably not."

"Well then? . . ."

TWENTY-FOUR

Rosemary and Victor had bought the house in Kenilworth that Caleb grew up in—an ornate two-story Tudor-revival on Essex Road. He noticed, as he pulled up, that some of the oaks he'd climbed as a child were gone, but the survivors looked well cared for. Mature yews flanked the front porch; daffodils populated the flower beds still mulched for winter. Pulling in the drive was like coming home.

He parked behind the house and went to the back door out of habit. A short upward flight of steps led to a hallway off of which were the basement stairs, and the kitchen. Caleb turned right, toward the source of a wonderful aroma.

The room had been freshly painted and was cheerful if curiously old-fashioned, with the original, double-drain-board, cast-iron sink he remembered from childhood. Dried flowers and staples—pasta, beans, and rice—in mason jars continued the old-fashioned motif. The refrigerator was disguised as a pie safe, but when he opened it to put in the wine he'd brought, he saw that the inside was new.

He took his coat off and stood for a moment sorting the new from the former, Rosemary from Consuelo, approving that the two styles blended like succeeding generations.

A voice from the hall startled him as it echoed his feeling. *"!Bienvenido, hermano!"*

Caleb turned to greet his brother-in-law, flattered that he'd been called brother instead of *cuñado*. He answered, *"¿Que tal?"*

Victor Noguerra grinned. *"Bastante bien."*

Caleb's father, Arthur, was sitting in the high-ceilinged living room, playing cards with a dark-haired boy of six. They both looked up when Caleb and Victor entered. Arthur nodded and said, "James."

"Hello, Arthur."

Keeping one eye on his cards, the boy said, "Hi, Uncle Jack." Without looking at Arthur, he said, "Your turn, Grandpa."

Caleb said, "Hello, Jesse."

Arthur took a card from the face-down pile on the table, looked at it and put it down on the face-up pile.

Jesse picked up the card and said, "Gin, Grandpa." He laid his cards out for Arthur to see.

Arthur seemed startled, and unsure whether to be upset or pleased that he'd been beaten by the boy. Rosemary saved him by sweeping into the room to give Caleb a hug and ask for volunteers to set the table. She was accompanied by an energetic black-and-white dog that Jesse introduced as Pete the Mutt. Pete looked like a border collie.

"Millie's hiding," Jesse announced.

"Millie?" Caleb said.

"Millie's our cat." He patted the dog energetically.

"Pete needs to go in the family room while we're eating," Rosemary said.

"All right." He took the dog by the collar and half led, half dragged him from the room.

"Then wash your hands," Victor called after him.

"We weren't going to have a dog," Rosemary told Caleb, "but he was *so* cute . . ."

Victor, who was standing behind her, laughed and wrapped his arms around her. He was tall enough that her head just fit under his chin. "So after swearing for years that I would have to choose between her or the dog if *I* brought a dog home, she didn't even have to think about saying yes to Jesse." He punctuated his complaint by kissing his wife on the cheek.

"He's a vast improvement over that setter you used to have," Arthur said.

"When you were a child, *Querida?*" Victor asked.

"Yes," said Rosemary. "Poor old Bridget."

"She was a beautiful dog," Caleb told Victor. "But I'm sure there were goldfish with more brains."

They got almost all the way through dinner before Arthur said, "When are you going to marry that attractive divorcée you've been seeing, James?"

Caleb forced himself to hide his annoyance. He squelched the obvious: None of your business and said, "We've had this conversation before . . ." He fought the urge to add *Dad*, saying instead, ". . . Arthur. The answer is still never."

Arthur raised his eyebrows, then looked from Rosemary to Victor. For support? If so, he didn't get it. Rosemary looked at him as if he had just belched without apologizing. Victor could have been watching an exciting new game. This seemed to startle Arthur. He looked at Caleb. "I thought perhaps you'd grown out of all that nonsense."

"What nonsense, Grandpa?" Jesse asked.

"Jesse," Victor said, "Could you do me a huge favor and go see how much time is left on the stove timer? The pie has to come out as soon as it rings."

"Sure, Papa."

As soon as he was out of the room, Caleb said, "Arthur, to save us the tedium of rerunning this conversation, let me make something clear: I'll give up this *nonsense* shortly after I give up being right-handed. Or blue-eyed."

Either Arthur couldn't think of a response, or wouldn't make a scene by saying what he thought. There was an uncomfortable silence, before Victor said, "More mashed potatoes, Dad?"

After the pie—three kinds, with real whipped cream and hard sauce made with genuine bourbon—and coffee, they talked about Victor's business and Arthur's recent invitation to consult on a particularly difficult surgery. He couldn't resist saying, "I always thought *you* would've made a fine surgeon, James. Especially as you did so well as a medic in the service."

Caleb said, "Robert's doing a fine job of being the son that you wanted."

Rosemary suddenly stood up and started clearing the table. Caleb was aware that she was angry without knowing which of them had offended her.

Victor seemed unaware of the conflict. "Leave the dishes, *Querida*," he said. "I'll do them later. You cooked."

She looked at him and smiled briefly, then grabbed the coffee pot. "I think I'll make another pot of coffee." She hurried out of the room.

Caleb excused himself and followed her into the kitchen, where he found her leaning against the stove, blushing with fury. "How can he be so insufferable? How can you stand it?"

"I don't. When he starts to get on my nerves, I go home."

"It's not fair!"

"It hasn't bothered me since the day I realized I was a grown-up. Not only do I *not* have to do what he tells me anymore, I don't have to disobey him."

When Arthur had gone home, while Victor was showing Jesse how to wash dishes while watching TV, Rosemary and Caleb went into the family room to visit. They had the game on the TV, but had turned off the sound. Caleb wasn't even sure who was playing.

"Mother used to say Arthur had the sense of humor beaten

out of him as a child," Caleb told her. "When I was younger, I was too preoccupied with my own pain to understand. I guess I've healed. He doesn't make me angry any more—just sad. There's almost no chance of his ever being happy."

"Why do you say that? Isn't your whole life dedicated to helping people change?"

"People who want to change. And who believe change is possible. He's got too much invested in the status quo to even consider it. Change would be too terrifying."

As they thought about that, they watched one of the teams score. Pete the Mutt trotted up and plopped himself in front of Rosemary, and she rubbed his tummy with her foot. "I really can't recall Mother," she said. "When I try to remember her face, I see Consuelo's."

They'd called Consuelo *abuela*—grandmother—though she wasn't a blood relative.

"I don't think she'd want you to obsess about that. She chose Consuelo carefully. I think she knew she wouldn't live to see us grown, and that we'd remember her through Consuelo." Consuelo, too, had died.

Rosemary snuggled up to him and put her head against his shoulder. "Jack, are *you* all right?"

"I'm not HIV positive and when I'm not good, I'm careful."

Her obvious relief told him he'd answered the question she'd been afraid to ask. She blushed. "You must *hate* that." She stretched to put her arms around him, resting her head on his chest.

"You get used to it."

"Just like I got used to the macho shit-heads at work telling me I didn't have to worry my pretty little head about things."

Caleb laughed. "As long as you smile when you call me that."

"God, I'd forgotten! If you hadn't made me watch all those old classics with you, I'd probably have grown up to be like Marsha."

Marsha Caleb. Robert's wife.

"I'm sure underneath her fear and defenses, Marsha's human."

"Why are you always so forgiving?"

"To know all is to forgive all. Who said that?"

"I haven't the foggiest." They thought their own thoughts for a while, then she said, "Do you ever wish you could be different?"

"What would be the point?"

"No point. Just . . ."

"I used to wish I could be Mexican."

"Why Mexican?"

"I don't know. Maybe I was an *hidalgo* in a former life. I wanted to have black hair and dark eyes and speak Spanish."

"And you couldn't."

"Well . . . now I can speak Spanish."

"You're telling me to accept what I can't change. . . ." She squeezed him. "When *I* was little, I was so envious of you and Robert, especially Robert, because you were my big brother and I looked up to you. But I hated you, too. I was sure there'd been some terrible mistake, that I should have been a boy. I thought eventually things would straighten out and I'd grow up to be a man." She laughed. "Here I am telling a *shrink* about penis envy."

Caleb smiled. "You seem to have adjusted. What changed?"

"I met Victor. He made me realize it wasn't a penis I wanted, it was power. And I didn't have to be a man to have that."

"Ah, the transforming magic of love."

She pulled away from him then shoved him sideways with both hands. "Beast!" They both laughed, then she hugged him again and she was crying. "Oh, I've missed you! Only I've been so busy living day-to-day, I never noticed!"

It was like bad melodrama—her crying on his shoulder. He reached a tissue from the box on the coffee table and handed it to her. She blew her nose and sniffed. And laughed.

TWENTY-FIVE

Mid-May. Thinnes was sitting in the squad room, rereading his notes on a case he had to testify for the next day, when the sergeant walked up, coffee mug in hand. He waved it as he said, "Thinnes, aren't you still looking for a John Mackie for Arlette Banks's murder?" Thinnes was glad the mug was empty.

Nearby, Oster and Ferris, who were pointedly ignoring each other, stopped what else they were doing to eavesdrop.

"Yeah," Thinnes said. "Why?"

"Patrol just reported a shooting in an alley over near Broadway, somebody by that name." He switched the mug to his left hand and took a piece of paper out of his shirt pocket. The paper had an address scribbled on it.

Thinnes stood up and took his jacket off the back of his chair. "I'm on it."

"Lemme go with you, Thinnes," Ferris said. Why not? Every cop in the city would want to be in on nailing a cop killer.

"Forget it."

"C'mon. What if you need bodies to canvass the neighborhood?"

"You volunteering?" Oster asked. "There's a first."

"Okay," Thinnes told Ferris. "But come in your own car. I'm not going to listen to you and Carl bicker all the way over there."

The alley had been closed off with yellow police-line tape, backed up by a patrol car at the south end and a squad roll at the north. With Oster and Ferris in tow, Thinnes stepped past the car and ducked under the tape into a narrow, typical alley running parallel to Broadway. It was paved with old street bricks and decorated with gang signs. On the west side, scarred and weathered utility poles held rat's nests of intersecting wires above the roofs of detached garages and the fenced yards of two- and three flats. Facing them were the back walls and Dumpsters of Broadway businesses. Irregular patches of paint on walls and doors, and the occasional graffiti, testified to the ongoing turf war between property owners and the gangs. Fifty-five-gallon drums and the newer, rat-resistant wheeled garbage carts narrowed the passage; at one point an abandoned car stood opposite a half-filled roll-off box, closing the alley to just wide enough for a car to pass. The front end of a dark brown, late-model Ford Taurus was nosed in between the junk car and the Dumpster. To get by, Thinnes put his hands on the cars' hoods and vaulted over the space between them. Ferris was right behind him; Oster had to squeeze around the far side of the Dumpster.

Four feet in front of the Taurus, the body was facedown on the brick. A middle-aged Caucasian male, dressed in black kiltie tassel loafers, black twill slacks, and a gray knit shirt under a black windbreaker. Odd, Thinnes thought, that someone who dressed like that would hang with Wiley's scummy crowd. The dead man's salt-and-pepper hair was thick and cut short. His mouth and flat-gray eyes were open half way, and his tongue hung out as if he were trying to taste the brick beneath him. There was a .22-caliber hole in his nose, half way between the bridge and the base. Kate Ryan stood over the corpse, talking to a beat copper.

"This Mackie?" Thinnes asked. Ferris and Oster took positions on either side of him.

"What it says on his license." Ryan was wearing a Cubs cap and had her red hair tucked up under it. "Probably isn't *his* license, though."

"How's that?"

"The picture looks just like him." She said it straight-faced. The cop sniggered.

"What's the story?" Thinnes asked.

"It so happens we have a witness who's willing to talk. My lucky day."

"You oughtta buy a lottery ticket," Oster told her.

"Who's the witness?" Thinnes asked.

"The cook from that restaurant." She hitched a thumb toward a metal door twenty feet away, at the back of the closest building. "She was coming out for a smoke, just opening the door, when she heard something going down. She peeked around the door—which you will observe is relatively bulletproof—and observed our victim having a heated discussion with a young man of African-American descent. The word *honkey* was aired, as well as the n-word. When push came to shove—literally—the wayward youth pulled out a revolver and terminated the discussion, not to mention Mr. Mackie." Ryan sounded cheerful. Why not? One less cop killer in the world, and the cops weren't taking the rap.

Thinnes said, "Any idea what it was about?"

"Which one was going to back his car up and let the other go by."

Ferris peered down at the corpse. "Here lie the bones of John Mackay. He died disputing the right of way."

Oster scowled at Ferris. "*Mack*ie, not Mac*kay.*" He looked at Thinnes. "You *had* to bring him."

Thinnes just shook his head.

"Bendix is here," Ferris said, pointing north. As Bendix

joined them, he asked, "Got you working for Streets an' San now, Bendix?"

As much as he hated Thinnes, Bendix hated Ferris more. "I'd rather pick up garbage than smell like it," he told Ferris. He asked Thinnes, "Who'd you piss off to get assigned with him?"

"Thinnes's been working too hard, lately," Oster said. "Suffering brain farts."

TWENTY-SIX

Irene Sleighton, Caleb's receptionist, was a widow with an instinct for caregiving but no children. She divided her maternal energies between her church and the doctors she served. The office reflected it. It was always clean, but never compulsively neat. They'd had the same fish for three years, the same Boston fern for five. There was always fresh coffee on hand, occasionally donuts or sweet rolls, and she added homey, seasonal touches—like the understated Easter decorations. She herself was slim and silver-haired—though not old—fearless, compassionate, and discreet. And except for a penchant for muzak and tabloid news, she had no bad or annoying habits. When Caleb came in, she said, "Good morning, Doctor. You have a visitor."

"Good morning, Mrs. Sleighton. Thank you."

The man in the waiting room stood up and said, "Dr. Caleb."

Martin Morgan! He was as beautiful as Caleb remembered—thick auburn hair and gray eyes. Caleb felt an almost electric shock of physical attraction. He forced himself to cross the room and offer Morgan his hand as calmly as if he were Dr. Fenwick or Mrs. Sleighton. "Won't you come into my office, Doctor?"

Morgan shook hands, nodding, then followed him.

As he entered the room, Caleb found himself giving it a quick once-over for signs of dust or disorder. It was immaculate.

Bless Irene. He pointed to a chair and took his own seat. "Sit down, Doctor."

Martin sat. He was the antithesis of the cool person he'd been in his own office, where he was in his element and sure of himself. He clasped his fingers together, then unclasped them and rubbed his palms together. He seemed to notice that his hands were out of control because he made a fist with one and closed the other around it. All the time, his eyes wandered the room nervously, like those of a teenager sent to the principal's office.

"What can I do for you?" Caleb said.

Morgan glanced at him, then looked at his hands. "I came downtown today to talk to an attorney."

Caleb refrained from pointing out that *he* was a psychiatrist. He let his silence draw the problem out. Morgan would get to the point as soon as he could get himself together.

Morgan looked up and tried again. "My wife and I have been married eighteen years, but we're having difficulties." Caleb raised his eyebrows. "I'd like to see you professionally. I need to talk to someone."

Caleb felt suddenly overwhelmed, elated, then disappointed as he realized what that could mean in terms of future contact. But Martin was too damned attractive. Avoid the near occasions of sin. Caleb didn't trust himself. He wouldn't be objective, and objectivity was all. *Primum non nocere.*

He said, "I'm sorry, but I'm not in a position, at present, to take on any new patients." He tried to sound professional, but he sounded to himself like Dr. God pontificating. He wished he could think of a more plausible excuse for not accepting Martin as a client. The truth was, ethical professionals don't get involved with their patients, and at the moment, Caleb wanted desperately to get involved. He felt a strong desire to cross the intervening space and kneel at the doctor's feet.

Stop it! he told himself. Pull yourself together.

"I can give you several names," he said.

"Very well." Morgan seemed disappointed, but he had himself back under control, though he was such a controlled man, it was hard to tell.

Caleb pulled out a prescription blank, then fingered through his Rolodex. Margaret Thornton's name jumped out at him and he wrote it down. He added the names of others—two men and a woman. "Interview them," he said. "Go with the one you feel the most comfortable talking to."

Morgan took the paper and said, "Thank you." He rose to leave, hesitated, then held his hand out. "Thank you, Doctor."

Caleb took the hand. He felt an electric-like shock run through him and wondered if Martin felt it, too. If he did, he gave no sign. He gave Caleb a fleeting smile and walked out of the room.

TWENTY-SEVEN

Early in June, Thinnes got another break in the Banks case. At the request of a Detective Mark Fredd, he drove north, to the state's second most populous and crime-riddled city, to meet his Waukegan counterpart at the Lake County morgue.

Fredd looked like a candidate for office, from his expensive haircut to his Gucci loafers and matching briefcase. He was a big man—an inch taller than Thinnes and beefy—with coffee-brown eyes, sideburns, and dark brows and lashes. The corners of his mouth turned up naturally, giving the impression that he was constantly amused. Thinnes wasn't fooled; something about him brought Bendix to mind. His approach seemed political, too, but Thinnes didn't care. The detective was picking up the tab for lunch, afterward, at a place with excellent AC. That was an important consideration; the weather was hellish.

At the restaurant, their hostess led them to a table from which they could keep an eye on the door, the room, and—through the front windows—their cars.

Thinnes ordered steak and—to appease his conscience for the cholesterol—salad and iced tea. Fredd ordered a Caesar salad with his steak, and "the usual" to drink.

They had just come from viewing the remains of John Smith at the Lake County morgue. Thinnes didn't waste any sympathy on him. In a rare case of natural justice, Smith had gotten what he had coming. Now he was a run-of-the-mill crispy critter, fried in an arson fire he and his brother started. On the other hand, the morgue, which had just opened in April, was state of the art.

"So what did you think of our coroner?" Fredd asked, as a waitress appeared and put a scotch on the rocks in front of him.

Thinnes took a long swallow of his tea before he answered. The coroner was a woman in her sixties, silver-haired and energetic, and as sensible as anyone he'd dealt with. She'd given him a tour of the new morgue after he'd eyeballed the remains. "A class act."

"Isn't she? But don't let her grandmotherly appearance fake you out. Frank Bruno wouldn't last a round with her."

Thinnes smiled, then got to the point. "When do I see *Abel* Smith?"

"Disabled." Fredd laughed. "You don't. At least, not in this lifetime." As Thinnes opened his mouth to protest, he said, "Smith's chances of surviving the week are about zero."

"All the more reason! He killed a cop!"

Fredd held up both hands, pudgy fingers splayed. He had a wedding band on his left hand and a diamond pinkie ring on his right. "We got a statement from him, a deathbed confession." He lifted his briefcase onto the empty chair next to him, snapped it open, and took out a videocassette, which he handed to Thinnes. "The doctors got him so doped up he doesn't know his own name, but we were lucky. He didn't fuck up his lungs too bad so . . ."

"What's this?"

"A copy of his confession. At the very least it'll give you the names of his buddies."

"We've got them," Thinnes said, trying to keep his anger from showing. "Two of them copped a plea, one's in the ground, and *John* Smith's in the morgue. What we don't need is . . . What if he doesn't die?"

"He'll die, trust me."

"Even if he does," Thinnes said, "any public defender'll get this . . . ," he waved the tape, ". . . thrown out." He dropped it on the table.

"Give us *some* credit, *Detective*. Smith's a Catholic. He figured out for himself he hadn't got a prayer and asked for a priest. All we did was suggest to the padre that it would help us if Smith confessed to the police while he was at it. After they had their little private talk, Smith agreed to answer a few questions."

"And to let you videotape it?"

"That's right."

Thinnes swirled the ice around in his tea, then took a long drink to stall for time. To think of a diplomatic way to ask whether Waukegan had covered all the bases.

Fredd saved him the trouble. "We read him his rights and got him to say he knew he was a goner. We got what we needed on our case, and he was still with us, so we asked if he wanted to talk about anything else. That's when he said he helped off a cop—his words." He flicked his fingers dismissively. "You don't need to thank me. You can take me and my partner to dinner when we come to town to testify."

Thinnes tapped the cassette. "If it's everything you say, you got a deal."

The waitress interrupted at that point with their food. Fredd held up his watch, which looked suspiciously like a Rolex, and nodded, then winked at her. When she'd put down the dishes, she asked if he'd like another drink.

He smiled, reminding Thinnes of a crocodile eyeing a deer. "You betcha."

She turned to Thinnes. "Can I get you something, sir?"

"A refill?"

"Surely, thanks."

Fredd leered as she walked away. When she was out of

hearing, he saluted her with his glass and said, "To insure promptness." He held the glass toward Thinnes, in a hand that nearly buried it, and said, "Cheers." He finished it in one swallow.

"You have the right to remain silent. If you give up that right . . ." As the voice-over droned on, Thinnes studied what was left of Abel Smith—almost remains, in the usual sense. Not that you could have used the videotape of him without corroboration—lots of it. He was completely hidden by bandages, tape, and tubes. The camera paused briefly on the green-gowned, masked individual providing Miranda, then zoomed in on the slit in the bandages that served Smith for a mouth. Somewhere below the slit, a trach tube disappeared into the material covering Smith's neck and a gloved hand manipulated it so he could breathe up the air needed to work his vocal cords. Weird. Like a low-budget horror film.

"You understand these rights as I've explained them?" the voice asked.

"Yeah." Smith's voice was weak and breathy.

The masked interviewer asked a series of questions, beginning with, "Why did you agree to talk with us?"

"I'm checkin' out. Don't want to go to hell."

"Do you mean you believe you're going to die?"

"What I said." There was a long pause while the disembodied hand played with the trach tube, then a long Q-and-A regarding the Waukegan arson. "We got five hundred bucks for torchin' the place. Killed ourselfs for five fuckin' hundred bucks. . . ."

The voice led him through questions intended to positively identify the Waukegan businessman who'd paid the brothers to torch his building and asked, "Why are you telling us this?"

"Don't want that SOB to walk on this. Want 'im to fry in hell." He repeated the man's name "so there ain't no doubt."

"You got anything else you'd like to tell us about while you're at it?"

There was a long pause before he said, "Yeah. I . . . I helped off that cop down south. The broad. Helped beat her."

The masked man said, "Jesus!"

"We didn't plan it!"

Smith had to pause to breathe hard, whether from exertion or emotion wasn't clear. When he didn't' go on after that, the interviewer asked, "Who was we, Smith?"

"John'n me, an' Ron'n Mackie, an' the bitch, an' Wiley. Wiley put us up to it."

"What's Wiley's full name?"

"Brian. Brian Fahey."

"What are the others' last names?"

Smith had to think about that for a minute, or else he was running out of steam. The video mike picked up the rasping of his breathing in the meantime, and a muffled, unintelligible murmur of conversation between the interrogator and the cameraman. Then Smith said, "Ron Hughes, John Mackie. I don't know the bitch's name. The church bitch. Brotha John's whore. Fuckin' nutcase."

TWENTY-EIGHT

The heat took Chicago by surprise. Except for a tour in Nam, Thinnes had lived in the area all his life and he knew that a mild spring didn't mean a decent summer. April had seemed comfortable, May warmer than usual. June started at eighty degrees and went up. By the first official day of summer, the *Sun-Times*'s "Top of the News" caption said it all: "Temps Go Through the Roof."

By 2:00 P.M. the next day, it was ninety-three degrees, and Thinnes was on the ropes in a bout with the sandman. In spite of the AC, the squad room was warm, but he wasn't complaining. There were places all over the city with power outages. The others in the room, the sergeant, Len Swann, and Oster looked about as wide awake as Thinnes felt. The heat was taking its toll on Oster, too. His shirt was damp with sweat under the armpits and across the back. His face was as red as if he'd been drinking.

Thinnes stifled a yawn, then stood up and stretched. He sat back down, and as he tried to decide whether to go looking for something cold and caffeinated, Art Fuego came in. They hadn't seen him since the day Hughes copped the plea at Twenty-sixth and Cal. Fuego was in shirtsleeves, with his collar open. He was carrying a briefcase. He stopped halfway between the door and the coffee setup, then shook his head once and walked over to Thinnes's desk. Thinnes leaned back and hooked an empty chair toward him with his foot. "Take the load off." Fuego sat. "What brings you up our way?"

Fuego put his briefcase on the desk and opened it. "Funny you should ask." He lifted out a stack of case files and dropped it on the desk.

Thinnes looked through them. Five were aggravated arsons, one aggravated arson–felony murder—all by unknown offenders. "What've we got here?"

Fuego pulled three more files out of his case and handed them to Thinnes: fires of unknown origin—arson suspected. Well, why not? Fuego was an arson cop. Thinnes dropped them on the other pile and said, "So?"

"I think our old buddy Wiley Fahey is back in town," Fuego said, "I think he might be able to shed some light on these." He tapped the top file. "And these are in addition to the three I told you about in March."

Oster, who'd been listening in, pulled out a handkerchief and wiped his face and neck. "It's not bad enough we got the summer from hell with this weather," he said, "we gotta have a loony-toon runnin' around settin' fires. All we need is for the media to get hold of it that we got a cop-killing serial arsonist out there. We got chaos."

Thinnes let that go and said to Fuego, "I thought you said Fahey used a simple method of setting fires that anybody could copy. Apart from the fact that we don't have him in custody, what about these cases makes you think it's him?"

"It's more than just the incendiary device that's the same. Call it a hunch. The details are all identical—time of day, method of entry, . . . It's uncanny. In two of these unknown origin cases, the buildings belonged to the same guy—a sixty-two-year-old retired brick mason named Ronzani. Ordinarily, I'd have him in here fast enough to make his head spin, but he was the victim in the felony murder. Looked like careless use of smoking materials, only according to his housekeeper, since he lost a lung to cancer, he didn't smoke."

"Then it's got to be Wiley or someone he hung with," Thinnes said. "Maybe in Stateville. Or before he went in."

"I'll get started lookin' into that," Oster volunteered.

"And we'd better follow the money," Thinnes said.

"Ronzani's will leaves everything to his sister, who's got to be nearly as old as he is. Was. So even if we find her, I don't see her as much of a suspect."

"What about kids?" Oster said. "Disinherited? That'd be a motive."

Fuego sighed. "Lawyer said he didn't have any. Sister might not either. The guy didn't know, didn't even know how to contact the sister. His client hadn't seen her since they left Italy—at the end of World War Two."

"Maybe there's some other relative the lawyer doesn't know about who wasn't happy about being disinherited?"

Fuego shrugged. "We'll find out. The will hasn't been probated, but we'll see if it's challenged when it is."

"And you gotta have a list of offenders with the same MO as Wiley," Oster said. "Just in case it wasn't him."

"Yeah, but most of them have alibis or are in County or Joliet."

"Who'd know enough about it to do it?" Thinnes said.

Fuego said, "Firemen."

"You mean like in *Backdraft*?" Oster said.

"Nah. Anybody who could control all the variables like they did in the movie would probably be smart enough to make his fires look like natural causes."

"Yeah, you're right," Oster said. "What about heating contractors, demolitions experts, chemists, engineers . . ."

"How about stunt men?" Thinnes said.

"What?"

"The guys who set up explosions for the movies?"

"Yeah," Fuego said. "Them, too. What made you think of them?"

"I don't know. They always have great fires in the movies but you don't often hear of anybody getting hurt making them."

"Wait a minute," Oster said. "How come you're in here telling us all this?"

"I need help following up on it."

Oster pointed to the stack of files. "What's wrong with the dicks assigned to those cases working them?"

"I can't seem to interest any of them in my Wiley theory. He's been out of sight so long everybody thinks he's died or left the state." Fuego looked at Thinnes. "You said you didn't like the way we closed the Banks investigation. . . ."

Thinnes couldn't resist saying, "Maybe you ought to see if O.J. was in town when these fires occurred."

"Don't *you* start with that," Oster growled.

Fuego said, "All these open cases are making my boss nervous. He wants 'em closed."

"So what are *we* supposed to do? We don't have enough work with all the heat deaths?"

Fuego shrugged. "I've done the usual follow-up, and except for putting out a flash on Wiley, I'm out of ideas. I thought you guys might think of something. Maybe how to find Ronzani's sister?"

Thinnes said, "Try immigration?"

"No luck."

"Christ, Fuego," Oster said, "she could be anywhere . . . maybe went back to Italy, maybe dead."

"No, a neighbor I talked to said Ronzani'd heard from her once after he got here. She sent her folks a postcard after she got to New York, said she was moving to Chicago. Ronzani came here looking for her—never found her. The family never heard from her after that."

"We're talking fifty years ago! Who's to say she ever made it here? Or she could'a been murdered, or run over by a truck."

"Or married someone her family didn't approve of," Thinnes said. "In which case, there'd be a marriage certificate somewhere."

"Yeah," Oster said. "And since all the records are computerized, it'd just be a matter of seconds to check on that."

They all laughed.

"Italians are usually Catholics, aren't they?" Thinnes said. "At least, the new immigrants. What about calling all the Catholic churches and asking them to check their marriage records for 1945 to '49?"

Oster turned to Fuego. "There you go."

Fuego shrugged. "I got to be in court all afternoon."

Thinnes said, "Carl, why don't you?"

"Don't we have enough—?"

"Hey, if you'd rather drive around in the heat and look at stiffs . . ."

Oster scowled and reached for the stack of files. "Gimme those."

Fuego grinned.

At that moment, the sergeant came up with a slip of paper in his hand—another death investigation, Thinnes was ready to bet. "You guys free?" he asked.

Thinnes reached for the paper. "I got it."

The sergeant handed it to him. "Sixty-nine-year-old white male, probable heat death. Just make sure there was nothing funny about it before we transport 'im." He looked at Oster. "What're you doing?"

"He's busy," Thinnes said.

The sergeant looked annoyed. He took two more papers from his front pocket and held them out to Thinnes. "In that case, you can check these, too, while you're at it."

"Okay." Thinnes took his jacket off his chair back as the

116

sergeant walked away. "Carl, if you have time, you might also call Fahey's sister and run some of those arson victims' names past her—see if Wiley ever had a beef with any of them."

"Yeah. Okay."

"And check on the Conflagration Church—see if God's spoken to any of them lately."

"All right, already!"

TWENTY-NINE

All three of the victims Thinnes had been sent out to deal with had been murdered by the heat. One was already on his way to the morgue when Thinnes got to the scene. The other two were waiting on a detective's okay to transport. The beat cops had secured all three scenes, interviewed neighbors, and gotten the names of next of kin. They were getting really good at it. But then, they'd had enough practice.

Thinnes was on his way back to the Area when his radio crackled. He responded; the dispatcher announced, "Another dead body. Beat coppers think this might be the real thing." The real thing. Murder. The dispatcher gave him the address. Thinnes said, "Ten-four," and signaled a turn.

The heat slammed into him as he opened his door at the scene. It was already cordoned off—yellow police-line tape stretched across a rutted brick alley. The building to the north was boarded up; to the south, locked and shuttered. There was only one car. The copper sitting in it got out as Thinnes approached. He was in his late thirties or early forties—Thinnes's age, Irish, no safety vest, carrying a .357, not a 9mm. A veteran. He looked and smelled as if he'd just puked. Jerking his head toward the alley, he greeted Thinnes with, "Worst I've ever seen." He ducked under the tape.

Thinnes followed. "Yeah, it's been a hell of a summer."

118

The copper pointed to the end of the alley and said, "No. I mean *this*."

"What is it?"

"Dead body." He stopped and looked at Thinnes. "You got to *see* it." He shook himself.

They kept walking, approaching what looked like a brick factory built in the days before cheap electricity. It had large banks of windows, divided into one-by panes and covered with chain-link grids. In a better neighborhood, the place would have been under conversion into yuppie condominiums. In this one, it was empty. The door gaped. Long before they reached it, the scent of summer hit them—the unmistakable stench of ripe cadaver.

"What's the story?" Thinnes asked.

"Electricity was out for two days on this street. The owner of the building got a complaint from a neighbor about the smell. Neighbor figured a dog or maybe even a bum wandered in and died. Came over to check." The copper stopped in front of the door. "You mind if I don't go back in there?"

"That bad?" Thinnes said. He shrugged. "Long as nothing's gonna jump me if I go in without backup."

"Way past jumpin'."

"You call for a crime-scene team?"

"Yeah. Said it'd be an hour at least. DB's in no hurry."

Thinnes couldn't put it off any longer. "Okay." He forced himself to breathe despite the overpowering smell and stepped sideways through the door so he wouldn't have to touch it. The building looked about 60-by-120 feet with a 12-foot ceiling hung with banks of fluorescent tube lights. Afternoon sun glowed in through the grimy windows, hot and thick as molten plastic, slanting black shadows from the rows of columns holding up the roof. The concrete floor was webbed with cracks and stained, littered with small trash—McDonald's ketchups squashed like roadkill; crumpled cigarette packs and butts; a

119

cardboard box split at the corners and spread-eagled. The far end of the room looked like a wall of stainless steel interrupted by doors—walk-in coolers. The intervening space was filled with flies.

Thinnes pulled on gloves as he crossed to the door that was open, a left-handed door. Used, balled up, duct tape lay on the floor next to the door with a roll of the tape and bits of gray adhesive stuck to the door's edges and to the wall around the door.

Inside the cooler, he could hear the buzzing of a thousand insects. Light from behind him dimly lit the cooler's interior. Careful to avoid touching the adhesive, he gripped the edge of the door at a point where there was little probability of disturbing latent prints. He could feel the rotted gasket. He swung the door wide. The buzz got louder. The stench rolled out like invisible smoke. Hanging shapes materialized that for a fraction of a second looked like sleeping, man-sized bats. He took a step backward. Vicks and cigars weren't going to do it. Gas masks required.

Something was moving. His skin crawled. Keeping in mind that the beat cop had said it was safe, he leaned through the doorway and looked to the right for a light switch. Found it. Flipped it. The dim fluorescent, overhead, transformed the scene from shadow to really scary. It wasn't the worst he'd ever seen, but it was certainly the weirdest.

Inside, the cooler was ten-by-twelve feet, with a seven-foot ceiling that bristled with hooks. In the light, the giant bats were hanging animal carcasses, dressed—he guessed. He couldn't be sure because the carcasses were coated completely with insects and larvae. Other smaller objects, also hard to make out beneath the crawlies, hung among the carcasses.

The dead body—he could see why the cop had hesitated to describe it beyond that—was in the middle of the floor. Decomposition gasses had bloated it to a huge, shapeless mass covered in a living, squirming blanket of flies and maggots.

Under the wildlife, he could just make out denim, and athletic shoes, and a matted tuft of brown hair. It was obvious that the drain that serviced the cooler had been blocked by the remains. And fluid from the decomposition had collected between the treads of the diamond-point floor panels, creating the perfect environment for growing larvae. So the deceased seemed to be afloat on a shiny, milky, seething sea of worms.

THIRTY

Definitely unique," Thinnes told the beat cop as he pulled his gloves off inside out and balled them up.

The copper was leaning on Thinnes's car in the only shade this side of the street—under a half-yellowed elm tree. Dutch elm disease. Sweat dampened his hair and face and darkened circles under his arms and down his back. Thinnes opened the car, and the heat that had built up inside blasted him. He tossed his gloves in the trash box behind his seat, then rolled down the window and fished out his cell phone. He rang HQ and asked whether a crime scene team had been dispatched "Not yet," he was told.

"Is Bendix on today?"

"Yeah, why?"

"This is a really unusual case," Thinnes said. "We need your most experienced team." He called animal control next—let them deal with the Conservation cops. When he hung up, he hawked and spit into the gutter, but he could still taste the smell of death.

Bendix had ditched his jacket and tie but was still drenched with sweat. He ambled toward the cooler, puffing his cigar, fighting the flies and god-awful stench with a toxic cloud of his own. When he got to the doorway, he stopped and took the cigar out of his mouth.

"Holy Mother of God!" He stood with his mouth open for a full fifteen seconds, disregarding the flies. It seemed like thirty seconds more before he could bring himself to talk again. He turned to Thinness and said, "What a fuckin' waste of good venison."

They'd figured out from the feet that the larger hanging carcasses were dead deer. Poached, probably.

"Yeah," Thinnes said.

Bendix hawked and spat into the moving carpet of maggots, well away from the human remains. "What the fuck am *I* doing here?"

"Gathering evidence."

"Of what?" Thinnes shrugged. "You even got a crime here? All I see is a dead guy. City's full of 'em. ME's up to his asshole in dead bodies. So what?"

"He died under suspicious circumstances. I gotta do a death investigation. You gotta collect evidence."

"Fuck you! I'm filing a grievance!" Bendix shoved the stogie in his mouth and stalked out.

That left the technician who was carrying the camera with a clear view of the scene. He swallowed and asked Thinnes, "What do I do?" He couldn't take his eyes off the maggots.

"Get as many pictures as you can stomach. Documentation."

"Do I hafta . . . go in?"

"No, but try to get good shots. This has to be seen to be believed."

There wasn't much useful evidence—a few fingerprints on the cooler door and a cigarette pack on the floor next to it. When the tech had lifted the prints and bagged the package, and had run off two rolls of film, they went back out to wait for the meat wagon.

The afternoon had slipped below the tops of the buildings across the street, though the resulting shade didn't offer much relief. Bendix was sitting sideways in his open car, watching the smoke rise from his cigar. The beat copper had been joined by his partner—a young, male Hispanic—and a civilian, a tall, old man, bowlegged with arthritis, with a beer gut like nine-months-pregnant. He was dressed for the occasion—T-shirt, cutoffs, and work boots with his socks rolled down over the tops. He hadn't bathed or shaved in too long, and he had no teeth. The coppers introduced him as the neighbor who'd made the complaint to 911 about the smell. Mr. Al Linsky. Linsky was toting a tube dispenser of four-ounce paper cups and a fifth of Jim Beam. "Figured you guys could use a little splash of some-thin' to settle your stomachs."

He sloshed the whiskey into a cup and offered it to the Irish copper, who looked as if he desperately wanted it. He looked at Thinnes, who shrugged, then at Bendix.

Bendix gave Thinnes a long, appraising look, then walked over and took the whiskey and slugged down. He nodded at the old man, crumpled the cup, and walked back to throw it behind the seat of his car. The other three men looked at Thinnes, who shrugged, and the old man gave a cup to each, and to Thinnes.

As he took it, Thinnes noticed Linsky had the fire department logo tattooed on the inside of his forearm. Thinnes waited until the old man had filled the cups and poured one for him-self before saying, "Cheers." He downed the whiskey as fast as Bendix had and watched the others do the same. The old man offered them all seconds—all declined—before refilling his own. Thinnes collected the empties, nested them, then crushed them, stomping on the debris, before throwing it in the box behind the car seat. The technician put his gear in his own van and took off. The beat cops got in their car and started the engine. Thinnes pointed to his Caprice and asked Linsky if he'd like to talk in the AC. "I need to hear your story."

"Just as soon stay out here," the old man said. "Not much of a story." He sat down on the curb in front of the car, with his back to the alley and its barrier tape. He refilled his cup and put the bottle against the curb. In spite of his arthritis, he managed to bring his knees up almost to his chest and rest his elbows on them. All the better to bend the elbow, Thinnes guessed. He parked his own tail against the front of his car.

"Not much of a story," the old man repeated when they were settled. "Widow owns that." Without looking, he hitched his thumb over his shoulder toward the crime scene. "Been tryna sell it eight or nine years now. Someone's been takin' down the signs; lettin' the air outta people's tire's when they come lookin'; an' like that." Again without looking, he swung his thumb over his shoulder to point, this time from north to south, at the buildings flanking the alley. "Probably one of these bastards hopin' to get their hands on it cheap when the old lady croaks. Anyway, when I smelled it—I live downwind, in case they didn't tell you—I figured maybe some animal wandered in there and died. Never figured it for anything like this. . . ." Again he indicated the alley with his thumb. "The door wasn't locked, so I went in and looked. . . ." He shrugged.

"Was somebody using the cooler?"

"Seems so. Wasn't s'posed to be."

"So who'd use it without permission?"

Linsky took a sip of his booze and thought about it. "Bout anybody from the neighborhood might know it was empty. The stiff, maybe?"

The squad roll driver had come equipped—high-topped rubber boots and long-sleeved gloves. He and his partner had bagging stiffs down to a science: lay the bag out next to the remains, roll the body in, zip. In the case of maggot man, they grabbed him by the pants and pulled him out of the cooler first. They ignored the maggots.

"We *love* Levis," the driver said. "We could do commercials."

125

"Yeah," his partner said, "You wouldn't believe how often a stiff's clothes'll come apart before we get it loaded. Not Levis."

"I'll try to remember that," Thinnes said, "If I ever plan to get murdered. As long as you're at it, mind checking for an ID?"

Oster was still in the squad room when Thinnes got back. "Thinnes," he said, "Bendix is beefin' you. For harassment. What the hell d'you do to him?"

"You know how he's always bragging that he's seen everything?"

"Yeah."

"Now he has."

"What?"

"You had to be there."

"Glad I wasn't. You stink." Before Thinnes could be hurt, he added, "I'm not kiddin'. Go take a shower."

THIRTY-ONE

Thursday night Caleb had dinner with friends at the Palmer House. It had been nearly a year since he'd been there, and the oppressive heat made him reluctant to hurry out when his friends called it a night. He told them he'd have a nightcap in the hotel bar and take a cab home.

Forty-five minutes later, he noticed a man across the room who seemed to be alone and who'd had too much to drink. Caleb watched him for a full minute before he realized that he knew him. It took another thirty seconds to place him. Martin Morgan. With recognition came disappointment, disappointment that Morgan failed to measure up to Caleb's standards of appropriate behavior, as well as that he, Caleb, had so misjudged him.

Caleb was ordinarily repulsed by drunks, but the doctor's state of inebriation was in such contrast to the controlled individual Caleb had met previously, that the psychiatrist was fascinated. And Morgan wasn't sloppy or maudlin, only ineffably sad. As the physician tried to cross the room without staggering, Caleb wondered whether he was a controlled binger or in some state of crisis. It was in case the latter situation obtained—and out of long professional habit—that Caleb walked over to where Morgan had stopped to steady himself against the back of an unoccupied chair. Caleb beat the bouncer by two steps.

The muscular black man was dressed in a blazer with the

hotel's logo. He carried a discreet radio. "You know this gentleman, Sir?"

Caleb nodded.

Apparently ignoring their exchange, Morgan seemed to be trying to place Caleb. He swayed on his feet. "Do you know me?"

Caleb said, "Martin," as if they were old friends. No use compromising the man's reputation by title-dropping. "You seem a bit under the weather. Perhaps you should sit down and let me call you a cab."

The bouncer seemed relieved.

Morgan considered Caleb's suggestion a long time before he said, "Yes." His whole body swayed as he looked for somewhere to sit.

Caleb pointed toward a vacant chair near the door to the men's room, then took Morgan's arm. "I'll take care of him," he told the bouncer.

The man's "thanks" sounded sincere.

Caleb seated his charge.

Martin announced, "I'm drunk."

"Yes."

For a moment Morgan stared at him, then said, "I'm sorry." And after a pause, "I don't remember you."

"Jack Caleb. We met last March." Martin still seemed at a loss. "At your office?"

"Oh, Lord! A patient. I *am* sorry."

"Don't worry about it."

Remembering the family portrait, Caleb wondered what sort of woman Morgan's wife was and decided he could find out. "May I offer you a ride, Doctor?"

"A ride? Where?"

"Where do you live?"

"Kenilworth."

Small world. Caleb pushed the rush of associations out of mind and said, "Let me take you home."

"I can't." He shook his head and looked at Caleb as if expecting Caleb to provide clarification. When none was forthcoming, he added, "Go home."

"Why can't you go home?"

"You can never go home."

An echo of the Moody Blues' melody came to mind like déjà vu. What else did he and Morgan have in common? He waited.

Morgan put a hand, fingers splayed, over his face and sobbed. "My wife threw me out."

"Ah."

"I think I'm going to be sick."

Caleb pulled him to his feet and hurried him to the men's room. After they'd flushed the remains of his dinner, Caleb helped him clean himself up. "Come on," he said, finally. "You sit down while I call a cab."

Twenty minutes later he steered his charge to the registration desk of the North Loop Hotel. The clerk on duty—a Ms. Lennox, by her badge—was a café au lait black woman with almond-shaped, obsidian eyes that gave her an exotic appearance.

Morgan folded his arms on the counter and rested his head on them.

Caleb caught a glimpse of disgust from Ms. Lennox, then the display of her public service smile. "My associate needs a room."

"Does he have a reservation?"

"No."

"I'm sorry. With all the visitors in town for Taste . . ." Taste of Chicago, the city's annual food fest . . .

Caleb handed her his business card and watched her attitude adjust for the better. He often put guests and visiting colleagues up at the hotel and even more frequently patronized its restaurant.

She obviously recognized the name. ". . . Lucky to have a room available. Single or double?"

"A single will be fine," he said. "No bar."

She nodded and checked her available rooms. "I have one near the elevator?"

A toss-up. Noisy, but nearby. In any case, if Morgan's sleep was disturbed, it was no more than he deserved. "That'll be fine."

"I'll need a major credit card. . . ."

Caleb turned to Morgan, who was shifting his weight from foot to foot and sagging floorward like a child falling asleep on his feet. "Martin?"

Morgan didn't answer.

Caleb patted him down like a cop looking for weapons. He located a wallet in an inside jacket pocket and extracted it, then extracted a Visa Gold card. "Will this do?"

Ms. Lennox didn't seem to find the procedure unusual. She nodded and ran the card through her machine, which in no time produced a receipt with a signature line. She handed the paper and a pen to Caleb.

Caleb said, "I need a signature, Doctor." He put the pen in Morgan's hand and the paper under it.

Morgan produced a scribble on the paper, a reasonable facsimile of the scribble on the back of the credit card. For the first time in his life, Caleb could see some use for the system of internship and residency that produced men who could sign their names when they were too drunk or drugged or psychotic from sleep deprivation to know what they were doing. He gave the receipt back to Ms. Lennox. "He'll need valet service for his suit. I'll bring it down." She nodded, then typed information on

130

her terminal. "And a wake-up call at eight. Breakfast . . ." She looked up. Caleb added, "Eggs—over easy, whole wheat toast, tomato juice, coffee. A *Tribune*. Oh, and an emergency kit."

"What size?"

Caleb looked at Morgan, who was close to his own size, and guessed. Ms. Lennox disappeared through a door behind her post, returning shortly with a small, glitzy shopping bag that she put on the counter. Inside, he knew there'd be pajamas and a terry cloth robe, toothbrush and toothpaste, mouthwash, deodorant, razor, trial-size shaving cream, and an assortment of trial-size after shaves.

"Thank you."

She nodded. "How long will Mr. Morgan be staying?"

"One night. Or, he'll let you know in the morning."

Caleb had to half carry Morgan up to the room. In the elevator, he dropped the bag on the floor and propped Morgan against a front corner holding him there with one hand while he pushed the button with the other. He wished he'd waited for a bell hop.

I need to get a life, he thought, as the door opened on the seventh floor. He shook Morgan awake and maneuvered him toward the room, leaving the bag in the hall. Morgan's eyes were open, but Caleb was sure nothing was making an impression. Playing the hero was getting to be a neurotic habit, Caleb reflected. He needed an appraisal of his own mental faculties. However, as he thought about it, his physician wouldn't have referred him to a man whose professional and moral credentials were less than impeccable. So Morgan must have redeeming qualities. Caleb leaned him against the wall while he unlocked the door. Morgan closed his eyes.

"Martin, wake up."

"I'm so tired."

"I know. Come in and you can go right to sleep."

Morgan swayed forward, nearly falling on his face. Caleb

caught him, turned him around, and pushed him into the room. As soon as Caleb let go, Morgan sank onto the bed, closing his eyes and curling into the fetal position. Caleb retrieved the bag from the hall and closed the door. He checked Morgan's pulse and pupillary response, then took the pajamas and robe from the bag, laying the latter across the room's only chair and the former on the bed. Dressing and undressing helpless adults was a task for which his years as a hospice volunteer had prepared him. He removed Morgan's shoes, socks, and suit jacket, then everything else—down to his wedding ring. He emptied the pockets onto the dresser top. He couldn't help noticing that Morgan had a beautiful body, well formed and well developed. He looked like a runner—long muscular legs and narrow hips. His genitals were well proportioned; he'd been circumcised. His abdomen was flat, and he had a sprinkling of auburn hair running up his midline and across his chest.

Though he was a licensed physician, Caleb usually confined his examinations to mental states and motives, referring his patients to their own physicians or to hospitals, HMOs, or clinics for physicals. He blushed and hurried to cover Morgan with the pajamas.

Through it all, Morgan slept like an exhausted child, and only the alcohol vapor he exhaled suggested he was other than an innocent.

Caleb rolled him to one side of the bed, pulled back the covers, then rolled him over on his side in the center. After covering him, he took the emergency kit into the bathroom and emptied the rest of its contents onto the vanity. He checked his new patient a final time, gathered up his clothing, and left him to sleep it off.

Down at the desk, Caleb handed Morgan's clothes to Ms. Lennox. "Do you still have my card?"

She put it on the counter in front of him.

Caleb turned it over and wrote on it. "This is my home phone number. Call me if you have any problems."

She smiled and nodded.

As he passed from the air-conditioned lobby into the sweltering summer night, Caleb considered the story of the Good Samaritan and its modern corollary: No Good Deed Goes Unpunished.

THIRTY-TWO

You'll have to speak up." Irene Sleighton's voice was muffled as it came through the door.

Caleb said, "Excuse me," to the woman sitting opposite, and crossed his office to see what was going on in the reception room.

Two small boys—seemingly identical, about four years of age—were circling the room with plastic aircraft, bombarding each other with imaginary but very noisy artillery fire. Irene was on the phone and—by the look of her—nearly at her wit's end. A man stood facing her, ignoring the chaos, with his back to Caleb. Even from behind his body language signaled plainly that he was not involved with the children.

Caleb clapped his hands together twice. The boys froze and turned to face him. Irene put a hand over the receiver and said, "I'm sorry Doctor." Caleb was dimly aware of the man turning his way.

"Where's their mother?"

"With Doctor Fenwick." Fenwick was Caleb's partner; his office across the waiting room from Caleb's.

Caleb said, "I see." He squatted down to make himself less frightening and fixed the nearest child with a serious expression. "What's your name?"

The boy looked terrified. "Bobby."

Irene returned to her phone conversation.

Caleb pivoted without rising and looked at the other child. "And your name?"

Tears filled his eyes; he curled his right index finger and put it in his mouth. Caleb waited. Bobby said, "Sean."

"Well, Bobby, you and Sean need to play more quietly." Neither responded. Caleb said, "Do you like stories?"

Sean opened his mouth, then shut it. Bobby nodded.

"If you pick out a story . . ." Caleb pointed to a neat stack of children's books on the table near the fish tank. ". . . Mrs. Sleighton will read it to you when she gets off the phone."

After a fractional delay, during which presumably they considered this proposition, both boys dropped their toys and charged toward the books.

"Stop!" They froze again. Caleb stood up to ease the strain on his legs. "You need to walk."

They started off again, more sedately. They selected books with a minimum of shoving and hurried to show him what they'd chosen. "Read mine," Bobby insisted. "No, mine!"

Caleb glanced at the clock above Irene's station. It was going to be a very long hour. "Mrs. Sleighton will read them both if you're very quiet."

Irene hung up the phone and hurried across the room, picking up the abandoned toys as she passed. "I'm sorry," she said again. She started herding the boys toward the couch.

"It's quite all right." He remembered the other visitor and turned to find Martin Morgan watching him. He felt an odd shock with the recognition, though after last night's events, not surprise. He forced himself to cross the room and offer Morgan his hand, as if nothing untoward had ever happened, and to suppress his involuntary shiver when the doctor took it.

Morgan blushed, seeming at a loss. After a pause, he said. "Thank you." There were bags under his beautiful eyes, and his face seemed to have aged fifteen years since Caleb had first seen him. Hangover.

135

Caleb said, "You're welcome." He glanced at Irene, too oc-cupied with the children to notice them.

After a long, awkward pause, Morgan said, "I wonder—I know it's an imposition but—could I have a word with you?"

"I'm with someone right now."

"How thoughtless of me—"

"I'll be free in half an hour. You're welcome to wait. Or come back later."

"If you don't mind, I'll wait."

Caleb felt the same disconcerting thrill he'd felt in their pre-vious encounters—purely physical, but unsettling. It'd been many years since he'd felt the sensation—not since he'd fallen for Christopher Margolis. So long that he'd forgotten . . .

Looking for signs that Morgan realized the effect he was having, Caleb nodded. The man was too immersed in his own troubles to notice Caleb's. "Make yourself at home in the mean-time." He recrossed the room and reentered his office. He told the young woman who was waiting patiently, "I apologize for the interruption."

When he escorted the patient out through the waiting room, he was pleased to see the Katzenjammer kids still settled quietly on the couch, on either side of Irene. Across the room, Dr. Mor-gan also seemed to be listening intently. Caleb didn't believe in love at first sight, but he could appreciate instant infatuation—lust at first sight, intended by nature to overcome our ingrained xenophobia. But Morgan was straight, so there was no point in even fantasizing. Caleb sighed inwardly and said, "Doctor, will you come in?"

"I don't know how to thank you." Morgan was wearing the same clothes as last night. Thanks to the valet service they were pressed and fresh. Morgan wasn't. "I can't think what came over me," he said. "I haven't lost control like that since high school."

"Think nothing of it. You mentioned you were having marital trouble. People react strongly to that as a rule." He didn't add that he'd seen far more bizarre behavior.

"I'm seeing one of the counselors you recommended, but I don't feel I'm progressing very fast. My wife and I are separated, did I say?"

"Not specifically. I gathered . . ."

"My wife's in love—not with me, of course." He dropped his eyes and blushed as he added, "She's having an affair, and the sight of me drives her into rages."

"A man?"

If Morgan found the question odd, he didn't show it. "Yes. I've filed for divorce."

"Do you know his name?"

"No. I don't want to know."

"Guilt?"

Martin nodded. "It's my fault, really. For years she's accused me of being cold and unfeeling, of not loving her." He studied Caleb's face for a moment. "I've tried to be a good husband, but some things—like nonexistent passion—can't be faked. And she won't settle for support, fidelity, and affection." He looked to see Caleb's reaction. Caleb kept his face neutral. "She's become a—a shrew—due to frustrated needs, I'm sure, but it's alienated me to the point that I no longer *like* her, also not something I can fake. I've loved her as much as I was able. But I'm realizing—therapy's helping me to see—that she's right. I haven't loved her as she wanted. I . . . I can't. And she's become like a mad woman. As her passion for this man increases, her hatred for me becomes more passionate."

Hatred. Not the opposite of love, its dark side. It wasn't over until indifference replaced the hatred, or—if you were lucky—friendship did. Mrs. Morgan didn't sound indifferent, but Morgan seemed resigned. If he were Caleb's patient, Caleb would have asked about it. There was in his narrative a suggestion of the understanding that precedes forgiveness. But Morgan wasn't a patient, so Caleb only listened.

"This isn't going to be a *War of the Roses*—we'd never fight about money—but there're similar elements. Did you ever wake up one day and suddenly notice someone you'd admired was all warts and clay feet?"

Caleb gave him a noncommittal gesture. In truth, except for the years with Chris—which hadn't lasted long enough to get old—he'd never lived with anyone long enough to become bored. He quoted John Fowles:

> *Old friends. One has them.*
> *They help one grow up,*
> *One knows them more and more;*
> *One knows them more and more*
> *And suddenly too much.*

"That's it! Is it even possible to live with someone without getting bored?"

How much of what we perceive as boredom or loathing for another or his habits, is clinical depression, or sublimated anger, or projected self-loathing? Caleb wondered. "I don't know."

"I don't know why I'm telling you all this," Morgan said. "I've always been suspicious of instant intimacy—the slobbery drunk who bares his soul, then doesn't remember your name the next day. I've been with Helen for twenty years and I don't feel I know her. I *know* she doesn't know me."

"What makes you feel she doesn't know you?"

"Don't do that shrink thing with me."

"Sorry. When I first graduated from medical school, I was

138

full of advice and encouraging feedback. I've had to train myself to just listen. It's become a habit."

"What I *want* is advice."

Caleb shrugged and twisted his mouth to express the irony he perceived. "I'd stay in therapy. And give yourself time. It took you how many years to establish this habit of withholding? You're not going to change overnight. It sounds as if you have a lifelong habit of non-self-disclosure to overcome. Put your house in order with respect to your wife. And be patient."

THIRTY-THREE

The DB's name was Dino Ori; the autopsy was the next afternoon. Thinnes and Oster didn't bother to attend. Late the following morning, they stopped by the morgue on their way to lunch.

"What brings you here today, Detectives?" Dr. Cutler only looked up for a second from the body he was dissecting.

Thinnes could see his point. Unless there was evidence of foul play, detectives didn't have to attend the autopsies of heat victims, and Thinnes couldn't think of a single dick who'd come in to watch a PM for fun.

"Maggot Man."

The usual smell of the morgue—meat and bleach—had been overpowered by the odor of putrefaction. Cutler didn't seem to notice. "You could've hosed him off before you shipped him."

"What, and wash away all that valuable trace evidence?"

"Spare me."

"So, what did he die of?" Oster said.

"God knows. Maybe."

"You're supposed to be God around here."

"Well, there's no sign it wasn't natural—no gunshot or stab wounds, no bruises or contusions; hyoid bone's intact. He had a bad heart, but there's no clear evidence of infarct. He might have suffocated. But if your cooler was really airtight, he prob-

140

ably wouldn't have been found yet. Officially, I'm going to go with undetermined, but my best guess is he froze to death."

"You're kidding!"

Cutler shook his head.

"Fuckin' hottest summer in the history of the world and this SOB froze to death!"

"That's about it."

"Can't you just see the press gettin' hold of it? Christ, Doc! I'm glad you're calling it undetermined."

THIRTY-FOUR

By the time Thinnes was nearly through proofing his report on Maggot Man, the heat and exhaustion had started to catch up with him. The report blurred; he began nodding off. He came wide awake as Swann, who was sitting at the next table, elbowed him.

"Thinnes, wake up." He pointed toward Evanger's office.

Evanger filled up his doorway. "Thinnes."

Thinnes couldn't tell from his tone whether he was happy or pissed. But then, neither could anyone else in the squad room. Thinnes didn't borrow trouble by worrying about it. "Yeah, Lou?"

"Guy named Fuego, Bomb and Arson, is holding for you. They got a fire over on Division Street—looks like arson.

Thinnes said, "Thanks, Lou," and picked up the phone. "Thinnes, Area Three." He stifled a yawn.

"Art Fuego." His voice sounded far away—cell phone. "We just found a crispy critter that might interest you."

"Anyone I know?" Thinnes said. He was suddenly wide awake.

"Could be. He had Banks's piece."

"Where are you?"

"Don't bother. We're almost done here and there's *nothing* left that would interest a layman. Why don't you meet me at the morgue, bright 'n' early? And see if you can locate Wiley

142

Fahey's dental records in the meantime. With luck, we can close the Banks case *and* some of these old arsons."

It took two hours and sixteen phone calls, but Thinnes managed to save himself a trip to Stateville Prison, the last place Wiley was known to have had his teeth looked at. Two sheriff's deputies were bringing a prisoner to Twenty-sixth and Cal, to testify in an upcoming trial. One of them agreed to bring Wiley's dental records along, too. When he signed the receipt for them, Thinnes didn't forget to ask what the deputy liked to drink. And he made a note to pick up a fifth of Glenfiddich after the autopsy.

The postmortem was almost over by the time Thinnes handed the dental records over to the forensic dentist. He was the one dentist none of the cops minded going to see, which was why they called him Painless. He didn't look anything like John Shuck and had probably been in grade school when *MASH* came out. He was already set up for the comparison. He took the X rays out of the envelope and put them up on the viewer, below films made earlier of the arson victim.

"Looks like we've got a match here, Detective." He stared at the films half a minute longer, then looked at Thinnes. "I should have my report ready sometime this afternoon."

Down in the autopsy room, there were a lot of jokes going around about barbecues. Nothing Thinnes hadn't heard. The black humor never got old because the subject never got less serious. The roast—Thinnes winced at the pun—was more savage today because "the victim cooked his own goose." There was a crack about "burned on the outside, raw on the inside," and Fuego said, "What'd you expect when the cook's a turkey?"

They kept up a steady banter until the AME announced the cause of death—"smoke inhalation"—and showed them the victim's blackened, cooked airway. When he got to Wiley's heart, Fuego said, "Sure he didn't die of a heart attack, Doc?

His MO was a no-brainer, even for him. He should been home in bed by the time there was enough smoke to inhale."

They went to a place near the morgue for lunch, it had decent AC and a quiet booth in the back. While they ate, they confined their remarks to Fuego's salad and Thinnes's and Oster's steaks. They didn't talk shop until the waitress had cleared away the plates.

"So," Fuego said, "where's this turkey been roosting all these months?"

"More to the point," Thinnes said, "why does he conveniently turn up dead when he finally turns up.

"And who's been payin' him to torch these places?"

Oster said, "If it *was* him."

Fuego shook his head. "I'd say no question of that. The only question is, did he work alone?"

Oster wiped his face. "And for who?"

"I got something," Fuego said. "Wiley had a buddy in Stateville by the name of Terry Koslowski."

"Where've we heard that name before?" Oster asked.

"Fahcy's sister's Koslowski," Thinnes told him.

"Bingo," said Fuego. "Both of 'em listed her as next of kin. I was reading Koslowski's rap sheet; it gets better."

"He blows things up for the movies?"

"No. He's a licensed electrician. He got nailed for rigging the wiring to torch a building for a contractor who ran out of money before he ran out of project. They let Koslowski plead out in return for testifying against his boss. He's been keeping out of sight since he discharged his parole."

"Let's see if he still belongs to the union," Thinnes said. "They may have a current address. I take it the one his PO gave you is bogus."

"He moved the week after his parole was up."

"Figures," Oster said.

"He's got no directory listing," Fuego added. "No vehicle registered with the DMV, which has him at his old address. No water billing. And he doesn't own property in Cook County."

"Well, If I remember correctly," Thinnes said, "there wasn't any love lost between him and his ex. She might know where to point us."

"If he's still in the city, we'll get him," Oster said.

"Yeah." said Fuego. "If it's not him, it has to be someone else Fahey hung with."

Thinnes said, "We still need a motive. What about the financial status of the property owners?"

"We're still working on that. Preliminary indications are one's in Chapter 11, the rest vary from shaky to very well fixed. Ronzani may have even been holding paper for someone else."

"That could be your motive."

"Did you locate Ronzani's sister?" Fuego asked.

"You gotta be kidding," Oster said. "You got any idea? . . . Naw, you couldn't. Let's just leave it at I got fliers out for a woman born Ronzani at all the parishes that had a lot of Italians come in during the late forties to midfifties. One lady told me she'll announce that we're lookin' for this woman at the next bingo game."

"What we know is that out of nine fires we have eight different owners; six different insurance companies; three zoned commercial, two multi-family, and four single family; and six different mortgage lenders in three different neighborhoods. Apart from the MO, there's nothing to connect them."

"Any of 'em connected with the Conflagration Church?"

"No. That still up and running? I thought all the movers and shakers were dead or locked up. And you didn't think their substitute preacher was gonna hold it together."

"According to the CAPS cops, they been holding weekly services."

"I'll be damned."

THIRTY-FIVE

Bennigan's was crowded for two o'clock in the afternoon and seemed freezing compared to outside. Thinnes and Oster both put their suit jackets on while they waited for a table. The hostess finally showed them to a small one in a window bay facing Michigan Avenue, where they could watch the sweaty crowds parade past. Across the street, tourists swarmed between the bronze lions on the steps of the Art Institute. Everything looked faded in the hazy sunlight.

Oster said, "Thinnes." When Thinnes brought his attention back from across the boulevard, Oster jerked his head toward their waitress.

"Would you like something to drink, sir?"

Thinnes had missed her canned greeting. He said, "Iced tea."

"Would you like to order now?"

A cold beer and a game on TV, he thought. Any game. He said, "Maybe in a couple minutes. We're expecting someone else."

Smiling brightly, she nodded and departed.

Their chairs backed up to the partitions between the window bays so that they faced each other across the table, with the window on one side, the room on the other. They sat and stared past each other, not talking except to thank the waitress when she brought their drinks. By the time Caleb arrived, they were ready for refills. He borrowed an empty chair from a nearby table and sat down. It didn't seem to bother him to have his back to the room. When the waitress had come and gone again, he said, "What can I do for you?"

"We found Brian Fahey," Thinnes said. "What's left of him. And the States Attorney let Sister Serena cop a plea. Officially the case is closed."

"You could've said that on the phone."

"This case is driving me nuts," Thinnes admitted. "I thought you might be able to help us sort it out. There's got to be more to it than just a bunch of losers getting stoned out of their heads and killing a cop, but I can't figure out what. As far as we can tell, none of 'em had anything to do with Banks or Nolan before the day they killed Banks."

"What *do* you know?"

Thinnes told him what they'd found out about the Conflagration Church and its founder, finishing with, "You saw the tape. The guy was a con, but there was something there."

"He was charismatic. And he had self confidence. You can scarcely overestimate how seductive that is to the uncertain."

"Okay," Oster said. "That might explain Brother John and his Jesus freaks, but where do Fahey and the rest come in?"

"Criminals are opportunists. They probably saw a way to exploit the situation."

"But a little storefront church with, at most, two dozen members," Thinnes said. "What's to exploit?"

"You're the one who said there was a connection."

"Looks like Wiley Fahey set a bunch of fires," Oster said, "besides Nolan's car." He told Caleb about the cases Fuego had brought them. "It'd look like do-it-yourself land clearance if any one party was benefiting, but . . ." He shrugged. "And how do you connect a cult with excons and arson?"

"Jim Jones," Thinnes said.

"The asshole that took nine hundred people with him when

he checked out?" Oster didn't look convinced. "Brother John was a deadbeat, but nothin' like that."

Thinnes looked at Caleb. "Besides, he's dead."

Caleb sat back and said, "Cults are about power. And so is arson, in a slightly different way. By the way, why did Mr. English call himself John? If I recall rightly, his given name was Lewis."

Oster shook his head. "You got me."

Something stirred below the surface of Thinnes's memory and he held a hand up to stop the distracting back-and-forth while he tried to grasp it. "I have to check my notes—but one of them said John told them another would come."

"But he didn't say who or you'd have followed up on it." Thinnes nodded. "Not Brian Fahey."

"No. Everyone we talked to, even his sister, seemed to think Wiley was a perfect example of What's the use."

Caleb raised his eyebrows. "An unnamed other could explain the name John. John the Baptist prefigured Christ. John the Beloved was His most faithful disciple."

"C'mon," Oster said. "You suggesting we got a nut running round thinks he's Jesus Christ?"

"And if that's the case," Thinnes said, "where does the arson fit?"

"To answer that, you'd have to know what purpose it serves."

"Maybe it's like Carl said, urban renewal."

"Then someone's profiting."

"Or it could be a pyro," Oster added.

Thinnes and Caleb both shook their heads. "Not according to Fuego," Thinnes said. "Wrong profile."

Caleb said, "I agree. From what you've told me, your arsonist is methodical if unimaginative. And it seems businesslike in a macabre way, so he may be setting fires to order."

"Okay," Thinnes said, "we have a hypothetical Svengali

running a storefront church by proxy. The proxy drops dead. Svengali disappears. The church members go off the deep end and kill a cop. One of them lays low for three months, then starts setting fires—for no apparent reason—until he accidentally torches himself. . . . It doesn't make any sense."

"You could just give up trying to connect the dots and call it a number of curious random events."

"That's even crazier."

Caleb smiled.

"All right," Oster said. "Supposing there *is* somebody behind *all* of this. What kind of mutt are we lookin' for?"

"I'd say someone brilliant, narcissistic, and charismatic. Enough of a talker to convince Lewis English of his election. And he's probably someone who doesn't let anyone get close; who has followers but no peers; who loves no one unconditionally. Any affection he bestows would be dependent on absolute acceptance and obedience, in return for which he offers certainty."

"Sick," Oster said.

"Symbiotic," Caleb corrected. "Pathological relationships often are."

Thinnes finished his iced tea and signaled the waitress for a check. "I guess we better have another look at the church— see if we can find the money."

THIRTY-SIX

The overnight *low* had been in the upper seventies, so it was already muggy Sunday morning when Thinnes parked around the corner from the Conflagration Church. He'd timed it to get there just after the service started. He wanted to see how the new reverend was doing without a police presence throwing his game off.

The dark church interior camouflaged him as he slipped in and took a seat in the back. He estimated a 300 percent increase in the congregation—mostly white and Hispanic, and young—since last March. Oddman's performance had improved, too—voice or acting lessons, probably. And he must have studied some of Brother John's old speeches because he was using most of the same lines. He said, "*We* have been *elected* to bring God's message," and Thinnes got the impression he meant *we* the way queen Victoria did in "We are not amused." The sermon was full of catchy quotes and hellfire and brimstone generalities, but short on advice for peaceful coexistence. It sounded great if you didn't think about it too much, but the congregation was amening in all the pauses.

"God has a plan!" Oddman intoned. No doubt. "I *know* it! And if you *refuse* to hear that *plan,* you will *burn* for it!"

Thinnes remembered what Caleb had said about religion giving power to the weak. Oddman seemed like a newly minted bully, a might-makes-right thug who'd just found a weapon mightier than pen or sword.

Thinnes sat through the whole service and waited until the lights came up and the congregants had started to drift away before he approached the minister. "Morning, Reverend."

"Good morning. Detective? . . ."

"Thinnes."

"What brings you to our humble service?"

Thinnes could've called it a lot of things—humble wasn't one.

Oddman continued. "I read in the paper that those responsible for the police officer's death pleaded guilty. So does this visit mean you've gotten religion?" No mention of the fact that *those responsible* had been church members.

"Not quite. We're still looking into it."

"What can I do for you?" He seemed more eager to appear helpful than actually help.

"You never got back to me about your business manager."

"I must have been mistaken on that." Thinnes waited. "We don't have a business manager. I must've been thinking of the church's counsel. But I understood you spoke with him. He said he'd been contacted by the police."

"I'm sure he was, but I didn't talk to him."

"Well, he takes care of Caesar, if you get my meaning."

He almost didn't. He decided, when he'd made the connection, that it was too cute. He tried to recall the first impression he'd had of Oddman. He'd seemed a lot more timid. Comparing then to now was like looking at a cocaine user before and after. Or watching a bully with a new sap.

Thinnes asked him a half dozen more questions about leadership, membership, and church business. Might as well ask a car salesman the dealer's cost on a car. Oddman avoided straight answers by going off on tangents. Thinnes said, "You getting any pointers from other preachers?"

"Just 'It Pays to Increase Your Word Power.' " When it was obvious Thinnes hadn't a clue what he was talking about, he added, "You know, in *Reader's Digest*. Why? Do you think I need pointers?" It was the first sign of the insecurity Thinnes remembered.

"Actually, you seem a lot more sure of yourself."

"Practice makes perfect. And I believe I've discovered my forte."

No doubt. Not faith, but the power to manipulate with words. But it wasn't a total transformation. There was a certain nervousness in the way he said, "Overall, Detective, how did you find the service?" He blinked and his jaw sagged when he got the implication of Thinnes's answer:

"Educational."

Thinnes took comp time on Monday morning and slept in. When he walked into the Area, Oster said, "What time zone're you workin' out of?"

"Nice to see you, too, Carl."

"The state's attorney's been trying to get you all morning. He took our theory about the Conflagration Church's mysterious business manager to a judge to try'n find out who the new owner of the church property is." Lewis English, it turned out, hadn't left a will. His church "and all its appurtenances" had been transferred by some legal hocus-pocus to a real estate trust. And the attorney handling the paperwork was invoking client privilege to avoid telling anything to the cops. "The church's attorney called our warrant application unwarranted interference by government in church business. The judge is callin' it a crock."

"So we're SOL"

"Yeah. But I'll keep diggin'. Somebody's gotta know somethin'."

"Tell us about Terry," Thinnes said. They were sitting in one of the tiny District Nineteen interview rooms. Linda Koslowski was hunched forward in her chair with one leg crossed over the other and her arms together—elbow to wrist—on her thigh. She straightened and ran a hand through her auburn hair. She didn't look at them.

"We got married right out of high school. Back then, getting married was all I thought I could hope for. He started knocking me around almost from the beginning. I took it fifteen years, then told him I wanted out. It was ugly. He wouldn't agree to a divorce or anything else. When he went to prison for setting that fire, I got my chance. When he got out, he tried to get me to take him back. I had to get a court order to keep him away."

"When did you see him last?"

"February."

"Were he and your brother friends?"

"We all went to high school together, Brian and Terry and me and some others."

"What happened to the others?"

"One of the guys was killed in Vietnam. Two went to college and never came back. Three of us girls married and lost touch. Brian'n Terry went to jail." She shrugged.

"Do you have any idea where we can find Terry?"

"No, but his mother might. I think she still lives in Jefferson Park. Part of the reason we all drifted apart was the old neighborhood was integrated—ethnically speaking. I mean, most everyone was Catholic, but we had Irish and Italians and Poles all living together in the same parish. But then things started to go to hell. I . . . I mean, I'm not prejudice or anything, but the neighborhood started changing and everyone moved."

He understood. White flight.

"What's Koslowski's mother's name?"

Stella Koslowski turned out to be no help at all. The two-flat she'd lived in after she moved away from the "old neighborhood" was occupied by renters who paid a management company every month. The management company deducted their fee and expenses, then sent the balance to a bank. The bank held it in a trust set up to pay monthly installments at an upscale nursing home. All arranged by Koslowski senior, before he passed away, when Mrs. K. was already getting forgetful.

Just to be on the safe side, Thinnes and Oster drove to the nursing home and interviewed the management. No, Mrs. Koslowski's son didn't visit his mother, not since she stopped recognizing him. Yes, they'd be happy to give the police his address and phone number, although the person they were supposed to notify in case of emergency was her lawyer, not her son. The address was the same one the parole officer had given them.

They found the old lady in the facility's day room, strapped into a wheelchair so she wouldn't fall out. She was dressed in a clean, cotton dress and mismatched socks and slippers. After watching her stare into space for five minutes they decided that they'd hit a dead end.

THIRTY-SEVEN

Caleb had refined his talent for reading body language to an art, but it was sometimes a dubious gift. At times he could only turn it off with sleep, or isolation, or alcohol, or by running to the point of exhaustion. Friday, after he'd seen his last patient out, he felt melancholy, which boded ill for isolation. And it was too hot to run, so he headed for his favorite watering hole. Gentry's was on Rush, less than a mile north and only a block west of the office. He took a cab.

Inside, he sat where he could watch the bartender and ordered a Bass.

He was enough in tune with his own psyche to know what being out in the scene meant. Faced with the prospect of dating again, everyone was thrown back to age thirteen, with all its anguish and insecurities. He sometimes read the singles pages of the paper, but always found something wrong with the petitioners—too young, too old, too narcissistic—so he wouldn't have to respond. Sour grapes. It was harder to do that in here where the men were uninhibited or desperate enough to walk up and introduce themselves, sometimes too quickly to allow for the invention of an excuse. Still he enjoyed the show.

Today the press of gorgeous bodies made him think of Martin Morgan—Martin!—though the doctor wasn't as beautiful as some of those present. Walt Disney—paraphrasing Freud—had had it right: A dream is a wish your heart makes.

Then Martin was suddenly there, at the far end of the bar, sipping a mixed drink, looking exquisite if uncomfortable. When you're thinking of someone and he's there suddenly, it's as if your wish had conjured him up. For a full minute, Caleb wondered if he was hallucinating, if the heat and the intensity of his loneliness had combined to drive him round the bend.

The only way to find out was to confront the problem. He picked up his glass and walked over to the space Martin had left between himself and the man next to him. He said, "Good evening."

Martin blushed and stammered, "What are you doing here, Doctor?"

"My question precisely."

Morgan reddened, shrugged.

They were both embarrassed; each made a clumsy attempt to set the other at ease. Both laughed.

It was only human, Caleb reflected, to choke in situations where the outcome of the encounter is too important. "What are you doing for dinner tonight, Doctor?"

"Martin, please. I hadn't any plans."

Was it Caleb's imagination, or did he detect an undercurrent of excitement? He felt his own pulse accelerate. "Would you join me?"

Martin seemed pleased. He nodded.

"Excuse me for a moment." Caleb put his beer down and headed for the men's room. Giving him a chance to bolt or hoping he would take the opportunity to vanish discreetly? Or was the latter possibility wishful thinking on Caleb's part?

On his way back to the bar, he helped himself to several of the free condoms the establishment provided. Martin was still there, looking anxious.

They dined in the Chicago Athletic Association members' dining room with its spectacular view of Michigan Avenue and the park beyond. During the main course, they discussed life, art, and Martin's children. During dessert, Caleb gave a TV guide version of his own life and love life. He got the check and told Martin he could get it next time. After dinner, they took a cab to Gentry for a nightcap.

When they'd installed themselves at a tiny table and were sitting with knees almost touching beneath it, Martin said, "One of the reasons I'm seeing a shrink is that . . ."

The pause was anguished. Caleb couldn't help. Though the suspense was murderous, pressing him might kill the embryonic confidence.

Martin continued. "When you came into my office last March, I felt—for the first time in my life . . ." He looked away, ". . . sexually attracted." He glanced at Caleb, then wiped his face with his hands. "No, that's not true. It was the first time in my life I freely admitted to myself being attracted to a man and wanting desperately to act on the feeling." He glanced at Caleb and must have been reassured by what he saw because he went on. "I renounced my nature when I took my marriage vows, the way a priest renounces sex." He smiled ruefully. "Like many priests, I've discovered I have no vocation. But I have my children. . . ."

Caleb nodded. People outside his profession might have found the story incredible, but Caleb saw it often enough to think it commonplace. He limited himself to resting a hand on Martin's forearm though he wanted to take him in his arms, to try with all the skill he'd acquired over the years to ignite the passion he suspected Martin harbored. Common sense and self-control prevailed. "I understand. Many of us are so desperate for affection that we latch onto the first semipresentable person who pays us any attention. We stop looking for a better fit. But ultimately, our grip on our unsuitable lover becomes a stranglehold because we know, on some level, that there's nothing else to keep us together."

"I've felt that. When we were first married, I was afraid Helen would find another man more appealing. And she'd be like a mad woman when she saw me even talking to an attractive woman."

Caleb nodded. "But no intelligent adult believes for long that jealousy or possessiveness is love. And no sane person will accept either one as a substitute. They may be flattering at first, but they become stifling."

"Eventually we came to our senses."

Caleb thought about that during the ensuing pause; Martin studied the ice cubes in his glass. A lock of his hair had fallen over his forehead and gently kissed his lowered lids with their long lashes. Strange how a particular constellation of features could capture one's imagination but leave another's cold. How could Helen Martin resist him?

But he knew. A love eroded by indifference or incivility was almost impossible to rehabilitate. An unrequited passion could quickly turn to hate.

"A penny for your thoughts," Martin said.

Caleb wondered how candid he should be. Martin wasn't a patient, but he was—technically—still married. On impulse, he said, "Frankly, I find you very attractive."

It was obvious that made Martin uncomfortable. He said, "I'm sorry. I didn't mean to put you on the spot."

It seemed like a non sequitur; Caleb knew it wasn't. He sat back and made himself sit perfectly still, willed himself to seem neutral and nonthreatening. He felt his professional persona taking over. He said, "Go on" before he could even think whether it was an appropriate response.

Martin took another sip of his drink and put the glass down. Swallowing, he looked at Caleb, then looked away. "I don't know if I can love anyone."

It might have been a subconscious ploy or a brilliant pickup line to catch a shrink.

"Why did you agree to dine with me?"

"I thought . . . I hoped . . ."

"That I'd seduce you?"

Martin nodded without looking at him.

"Look at me, Martin." He looked. "Would you like me to seduce you?"

"God help me. I don't know."

"That's honest."

"Yes, I think so."

"Have you *ever* made love with a man?"

"No. Are you? . . . Do you? . . ."

"Am I HIV positive? You know I'm not."

Morgan blushed.

"But it's one question you never trust anyone to answer honestly." He reached into his pocket and took out one of the condoms he'd put there earlier. He slipped it into Martin' jacket pocket and repeated, "Not anyone. Not even once."

For a fraction of a second, Martin looked ready to cry. Then the sense of what Caleb was telling him must have penetrated, because he nodded.

A relationship of any worth or substance was built up over time, with each encounter revealing more, friendship growing by accretion as each successive layer of the personality was revealed—the cliché of the onion came to mind. Caleb knew that the electricity he felt was principally infatuation. Yet without it, no one would ever get close enough to bond. He finished his drink and put the glass down. He studied Martin's face, trying to memorize every line and lovely feature. He smiled and gently touched Martin's cheek. "I think we need to take this slowly."

THIRTY-EIGHT

According to Oster, the Mrs. Ori who owned the factory with the cooler was the dead man's aunt, and even though she'd had a poor opinion of Dino Ori, his death was a shock. She couldn't help them, though. She hadn't given her nephew permission to use the cooler. She hadn't seen him in a month or more.

When you thought about it, Thinnes decided, it was amazing how many people you met postmortem whose lives and personalities you pieced together from other people's reports and impressions and from the kind of trouble they'd gotten into that got them killed. What was even more surprising was how real some of them became, so you could almost swear you'd met them. And how some were never more real than a poor newspaper photo. Like Dino Ori. Even though he had a color photo of the guy—antemortem, as the ME called it—Thinnes couldn't get the picture from the cooler, of the bloated, maggot-covered Ori, out of his head. Other people's impressions of him didn't help much either—deadbeat, failure, fuckup, disappointment to his long-dead mother, God rest her soul.

Oster said he'd get with Animal Control and contact the Conservation police about the poaching angle. Thinnes was happy to let him deal with it. The ME had left the manner of death up in the air pending toxicology results, which was fine with Thinnes. He had plenty of other cases to work. Besides, he admitted to himself, he was hooked on Art Fuego's arson mystery, particularly as solving it promised to answer his unresolved questions about Arlette Banks's death.

Before he took off, Oster said, "Oh, yeah, Thinnes, Fuego said he'll stop by this afternoon and bring us up to speed."

After lunch, they assembled in the Area Three conference room, where Fuego laid his notes and case files out on the conference table. "What do you guys know about fire?" he asked.

"I know when somebody yells fire, if you got any sense, you get out," Oster said.

"Didn't you ever want to be a fireman?"

"Never."

"Well, did you ever see the movie *Backdraft*?"

Thinnes nodded. Oster said, "Yeah, so?"

"Well just about everything in that movie is bunk. *I* was never in a fire you could see farther ahead in than six inches. The only accurate part was what DeNiro said about fire being alive. That was right on—it *is* alive. And it eats people and houses and anything else combustible. And it breathes air."

"Tell us about arson," Thinnes said.

"It's an equal opportunity crime—females do it just as easy as males, whites, blacks, Hispanics, young and old. Doesn't take any special brains or talent."

"So where do you start with it?" Oster said.

"You walk around the outside. Look for signs of forced entry. Unless he's gonna lob a Molotov cocktail at his victim, an arsonist is like any other criminal. He has to gain entry first. So you look for windows broken in, not out, jimmied doors, things like that. You make diagrams, take pictures—document everything. You work from the least burned areas to the most burned. You save what you think is your point of origin for last because once you've determined that, you've got no justification for poking into less involved areas. You don't talk to anyone and you don't let anyone into the scene until you've worked it all out.

"You've got to document everything with pictures and physical evidence, just like any other crime. Only for arson, you're looking for the remains of incendiary devices and traces of foreign combustible materials."

"Foreign?"

"Yeah. Stuff you wouldn't ordinarily expect to find in the premises—like gasoline in the kitchen. With a real pro, you won't find anything—they use whatever's available."

Oster nodded.

"Then, to prove arson, you have to eliminate sheer stupidity, accidents, and acts of God. Usually it's not easy."

"Okay," Thinnes said. "So where are we with these cases? What've we got for a common denominator? Just the MO?"

"The Ronzani fire totally destroyed his apartment and left the building a virtual loss. His estate collected exactly thirty-seven thousand dollars, about one-third what the building was worth. It was sold to . . ." Fuego consulted his notes, ". . . a real estate developer named Michael Wellman."

"Who handled the sale?"

"You mean the realtor?"

"Realtor, lawyer, whatever."

"Don't know." Fuego made a note on his things-to-check list.

"Let's find out what kind of commission the realtors got—on all of these."

Fuego picked up another file. "This one did $50,000 worth of damage to a building worth $75,000. Owner says he's arguing with the insurance company about whether they'll fix it or write it off."

"Same insurance company?"

Fuego looked in the file. "No."

"Same agent?"

"No."

"Same realtor?"

"Nah. Wait. Same as for four of the others, but it's a neighborhood firm so it could be just a proximity thing."

"I think maybe we'd better bring Evanger up to speed on this thing. And then we'll check out Mr. Wellman."

THIRTY-NINE

Caleb was making notes in the file of the patient who'd just departed when his intercom buzzed. Irene Sleighton's voice said, "Dr. Caleb, there's a woman here to see you."

Caleb smiled. "Woman" was Irene's code for a rude or pushy female person who didn't have an appointment. He thanked Irene and finished his notation. When he'd put the file away, he crossed to the waiting room to inspect his visitor.

She was an expensive if not a natural ash blond, and her eyes were an even more unnatural shade of violet. Her makeup was flawless. Her clothes and accessories said money even more definitively than her hair. They were flattering though too obviously expensive, and the simple gold and diamond jewelry underscored the dollar signs. Tasteful new money.

She walked across the waiting room like a queen taking possession of a new territory, and said, "I'm Helen Morgan." She held her hand out at a slight angle, as if giving him a choice—to shake it or kiss it.

Caleb shook it firmly enough to give an impression of strength without causing discomfort.

She rewarded him with an appraisal verging on a leer.

"Would you like to come into my office, Ms. Morgan?"

She smiled, as if that was exactly what she had in mind. "*Mrs.* Morgan."

Caleb nodded, then stood aside to let her precede him into the room. He closed the door. "Won't you sit down?" He didn't indicate a particular seat, preferring to let her tell him about herself by her choice.

She looked the room over quickly but—Caleb was sure—thoroughly. Then she walked over to his desk, and behind it as if to sit in his chair. She was watching for his reaction. He hid the annoyance he felt and waited. She moved to the conversation area, sat down on the couch, and crossed her legs.

He sat opposite. "What can I do for you, Mrs. Morgan?"

She put her purse on her lap and started digging through it, though he was certain she knew precisely where everything was inside. Eventually she pulled out a box of Virginia Slims. "Got an ashtray?"

Caleb produced one from a drawer in the small table next to his chair. She made a production of taking a cigarette out of the pack, tapping it on the box, then making a V-for victory sign with her hand to hold it between her index and third fingers. She shook it back and forth at him.

"Got a match?"

"Sorry."

Caleb crossed one leg over the other and clasped his fingers together over his kneecap. Then he leaned back to watch her reaction.

She put her free hand on her thigh, just above the knee, and the hand with the cigarette on top of it. She leaned forward and said, "My husband's seeing you, isn't he?"

"What leads you to believe that, Mrs. Morgan?"

She leaned back and laughed, then waved the hand with the cigarette. "Just like Eliza."

"The computer program that mimics a therapist?"

"Answer a question with a question. It must be a stitch when a bunch of you shrinks get together." Caleb waited. "That tactic won't work with me. I want a straight answer."

"I repeat, what leads you to believe Mr. Morgan is seeing me?"

"It's *Dr.* Morgan. I found your card in his wallet."

"I see. Well, if you *are* a doctor's wife, you know that confidentiality concerns would prevent me from telling you even if your husband were my patient."

She laughed and started to put the cigarette back in its package. "Were? So he's *not* your patient. What's your business with him?"

"I think you better ask *him.*"

"As if he'd tell me."

Caleb stood up. "I'm sorry I can't help you. If there's nothing else . . ."

She didn't budge. "What if *I* wanted to—what's the word—hire you?"

"I'm not taking on any additional patients at this time, but if you'd like a referral . . ."

She stood up and said, "Forget it," then shoved the cigarette pack into her purse. "*I'm* not the one who can't get it up."

FORTY

The patient was a woman in her early forties. She was wearing wire-rimmed glasses; gold Laurel Birch earrings; a man's white shirt—open at the neck—with a World Wildlife Fund tie featuring big cats; black slacks; and black leather shoes. She had silver rings on all but her left ring finger and on both thumbs. "Do you realize," she said, "how hard it is to concentrate when you're in love?"

It took Caleb a full ten seconds to notice it wasn't a rhetorical question, and another ten to process the question. He looked down at his notepad where he'd inscribed the name "Martin" and enclosed it with a heart. He felt himself blush.

"I'm manic," the woman continued. "I can't sit still. I feel like turning cartwheels, but I'd probably break my neck. I can't think of anything but him. When I'm with him, I babble. When I'm not with him, I'm lost in space."

"The technical term for it is infatuation, and I'm afraid it's incurable. I can't even offer any symptomatic relief. Fortunately, it's self-limiting."

"Meaning?"

"An emotional state neither the mind nor the body can sustain indefinitely. You'll get over it."

"What am I supposed to do in the meantime?"

"I'll bet you can answer that yourself."

"Take it slow. And be sure he's not married, or a psycho or

167

serial killer before I get too involved." She frowned. "How do I know if he's what he seems?"

"What's your gut feeling?"

She twisted the ring around on her right middle finger. "All my feelings are centered lower than that these days."

She slid the ring up and down. No ambiguity there. Caleb smiled.

"It's catch-22," she said. "If he doesn't try to get in your pants by the second or third date, you think he's gay or something's wrong with him. But if he does offer to jump in the sack, he probably never heard of safe sex. You have *any* idea? No, you're probably happily married. . . ."

Caleb laughed, ignoring the invitation for self-disclosure.

". . . And even if he doesn't jump your bones the first date, how many are enough? How do you know when you *know*?"

"Those may be the central questions of the human comedy. But we'll have to work on them next time. . . ."

After he'd seen the patient out, Caleb dialed his attorney. "I'd like you to make some discreet inquiries," he told him, "about a Dr. Martin Morgan."

"What is this?" Harrison asked when Caleb had given him Martin's basic statistics.

"He's hinted at a future partnership. He seems too good to be true."

"He probably is if you don't trust him."

"No. It's more my own objectivity I don't trust. I like Dr. Morgan very much."

"Okay. How deep do you want me to dig?"

"I need to know if he has any dangerous vices and whether he's been unfaithful to his wife."

Caleb's last phone call was to an internist he knew who practiced at Evanston hospital, Dr. Athens.

"Do you know Dr. Martin Morgan?" he asked him.

"Family practitioner?"

"Yes."

"Sure, why?"

"I was thinking of using him for referrals."

"You could use me for referrals."

"The man who recently complained he didn't have time to speed-dial his broker?"

"Touché." Caleb waited. "I've never heard anything bad about him. His patients seem devoted."

"But?"

"He doesn't play golf."

"Unquestionably a character defect."

Athens laughed.

"So what does he do with his spare time if he doesn't play golf?"

Athens had lost interest. "Oh, I don't know. You can't shut him up about his kids if he gets started so maybe he's one of those cheerleader dads who goes to all the Little League games and recitals. Or maybe he actually spends time with his wife."

Having met the wife, Caleb really doubted that.

FORTY-ONE

They checked out Michael Wellman before they went to see him. On paper at least, he didn't seem like the type who had to torch buildings for folding money. And it didn't make sense that a man with so much would commit murder—though he might not think of hiring a torch to "clear" valuable real estate that way—just to get property he could afford to buy at ten times the price. At any rate, there were none of the usual flags—no outstanding debts or judgments, no upcoming divorce, no record of compulsive gambling or heavy drug use. The only odd thing they found out about him was that he'd never had a driver's license. He had an office suite in the Sears Tower.

The marble, glass, and chrome reception area was standard and pretty much a variation on the main lobby off Franklin—plush carpet, decorator art, designer receptionist. Wellman's personal office was like a kid's playground, complete with big-screen TV and a telescope trained on the lake front. He also had a Habitrail populated by gerbils, a pinball machine, and a pool table with the model of a development project set up on it. The walls that weren't glass were decorated with posters of Michael Jordan, Walter Payton, and Ryne Sandberg—autographed—and The Grateful Dead. The Gateway, fax machine, and copier sported rows of dancing teddy bears, and the shredder had a rose-and-skull decal.

Wellman was as tall as Thinnes with thick, graying black hair, hazel eyes, and an extensive tan.

The chairs he offered them were office variety, just like the one he took on the other side of the conference-size table he was using for a desk. It was piled with papers and blueprints, as well as a remote for the TV and a Chicago Monopoly game in progress.

He sat back in his chair, which rocked and swiveled, and laced his fingers together behind his head. "What can I do for you guys?" Before they could answer, he straightened up and said, "Would you like something to drink? Ice tea or pop or something?"

Oster shook his head; Thinnes said, "No, thanks."

"Then what can I do for you?" Wellman crossed one leg over the other, resting his ankle on his knee, and jiggled his foot.

"We're investigating an arson fire in the neighborhood where we've been informed you own property. We'd like to know how you came to buy the Ronzani place and get some history on the area and the situation there."

Wellman leaned back in his chair and laced his fingers behind his head as he thought about it. "Sure thing." He rocked back and forth, jiggling his foot. He didn't seem nervous as much as hyperactive. "I tried to buy it while the old man was alive, but he wasn't interested. Afterward, a realtor who knew I was interested contacted me."

"How important was that property to your project?" Thinnes asked.

Wellman got up to pace back and forth along his side of the table. "It's not really a project yet. It's like the west side was a while ago. There's still some viable housing stock that could be rehabbed, as well as plenty of vacant lots and buildings that are beyond hope. What's going to happen hasn't quite sorted itself out yet, but when it does, I'll be in a position to move on it."

"Has anybody come to you with an offer to expedite the process?" Oster asked.

"No. And I'd certainly send him packing if he did."

"How's that?" Thinnes asked.

"It would encourage the wrong element to take an interest."

"But it *would* speed things up," Oster said.

Wellman laughed. "As if that were needed. Advance planning in this game, Detective, is twenty or thirty years. I have enough projects on the front burner to keep me busy for ten. By that time, this region will be . . ." He shrugged. "The question will be settled, and I'll be on top of it, whichever way it goes. I don't need to cut anyone in or share the profits."

"What can you tell us about the realtor who handled the Ronzani property?" Thinnes asked. "What's his name?"

"Cox. He's been in the area forever and has a good reputation. And he had the property I wanted at a price that wasn't out of line with my long-range projections. I probably could've gotten it for less by holding out, but it doesn't hurt to let the locals make something as well. And there was a hint that someone else was interested, so it seemed prudent to move on it."

"What was the name of the agent who handled the sale?" Wellman's pacing was getting on his nerves, and Thinnes felt like telling him to knock it off.

"Helen Morgan. She's supposed to be one of Cox's top people."

"Supposed to be?"

"I wasn't impressed with her. She didn't seem to be very hungry for a sale."

"This the first time you dealt with Cox?"

"No. Just my first dealings with Mrs. Morgan. Cox is okay." Wellman stopped pacing and shrugged. "Maybe she's just better at condos. Listen, would it help if I offered a reward for help on this case?"

Oster made a face. "Actually, sir, it wouldn't. What a reward would do is bring every creepy crawler in the city out of his hole."

FORTY-TWO

Thinnes was scheduled for court the next morning; the case was continued. Driving back to the Area, he called in on his cell phone.

"We got another aggravated arson," Evanger told him. "Swann's on it. Go over and see if it might be related to that string of fires you and Oster are working. And in any case, give Swann a hand with the canvass." He gave Thinnes the address and hung up.

Urban renewal was nibbling away at the near north side and developers were eyeing the Green—Cabrini-Green—like rats scoping out a garbage can, pulling strings to get the vertical slums pulled down. Thinnes had always thought it was just a matter of time before a sniper in the project took aim at one of the nearby upscale high-rises, or a stray bullet took out one of the yuppie Sandburg Village residents barbecuing on his balcony. All hell'd break loose, and after mop-up operations, the land around the Green would be primo real estate. Whoever owned it—besides Michael Wellman—would become very rich. Thinnes didn't really care. He could sympathize with the Cabrini residents who didn't want to move. No one in an upscale neighborhood was going to invite them in, and where did you go from down? Refrigerator boxes on lower Wacker Drive? What he *did* care about was how the land was being cleared. Attrition and eviction notices were one thing, arson something else.

The two-flat he pulled up in front of was surrounded by police-line tape and TV news trucks. A female reporter rushed up as he got out of the car and shoved a microphone in his face. Sweat beaded her upper lip and trickled down her cleavage. Her expensive shoes were soaked from the water all over the street. Thinnes would've bet the hydrant was open before the fire trucks arrived.

His "No comment" was reflex. He ducked under the tape and strolled down the gangway between the fired building and its neighbor. The back porch was mostly missing. The alley behind the scene was crowded with fire trucks and firemen stripping off their rubber suits.

Swann, who was talking to one of them, waved his arm toward Thinnes. "This looks like a pretty straightforward grudge fire," he said. "Victim's boyfriend threatened to kill her, and it looks like he did."

"So we need to find out if anyone saw him?" Thinnes said.

"Yeah."

"What was her name?"

"Guadalupe Mendoza. She was sixteen. The firemen told me it was probably a Molotov cocktail—the preferred method for conflict resolution among some of the local gangbangers. They're supposed to be sending someone over from Bomb and Arson to confirm."

"He's here now." Thinnes said, pointing to the plainclothes Caprice that was squeezing past the firemen.

The driver was a thin, light-complected black male, who parked facing against traffic with his door just inches from a utility pole. Art Fuego got out the passenger side of the car. The driver slid across the seat and was right behind him.

"What's happening, bro?" the driver asked Swann. He was way overdressed for the occasion, in a trendy suit.

Swann slapped his hand and said, "Same old same old,

Jimmy. This is Thinnes," he added, pointing. He nodded at Fuego and said, "Art. Who's on?"

Fuego said, "Jimmy's show. I'm just another warm body." To Thinnes, he said, "Can I bum a ride from you when we're done here?"

" 'Pends on where you're going."

"Clark and Addison, but I've got something that might make it worth your while to go out of your way."

Thinnes shrugged. "Why not?"

"What do you think, Jimmy?" Swann asked, waving at the wreckage. "Think you can figure out the cause?"

Jimmy looked up at the charred remains of the building's back porches and shook his head slowly. "It's incendiary, man. There're only three causes of incendiary fires—men, women, and children."

Fuego lived in a white limestone three-flat. Thinnes didn't ask, but he knew that condos in the area went for figures in excess of $300K. Fuego's wife must work.

They parked in the alley in front of his garage and went in through the back gate. The yard was tiny and nearly filled by a vegetable garden. A trellised patio extended out from the house with a picnic table and barbecue.

Inside, two small, reddish brown and white dogs waited for Fuego by the door. They had silky hair, long ears, and docked tails. Together, they weren't as heavy as Toby; they wriggled with delight at the sight of their master.

"Cause and Origin," Fuego said. "Brittany spaniels." He let them into the yard and told Thinnes, "Follow me."

They went through a neat, bright kitchen, not unlike Thinnes's, to a small room serving as an office. There was a state of the art computer with a killer commercial printer. The walls were decorated with three-foot-square, computer generated maps of Districts 17, 18, 19, and 23, with streets, District and Area boundaries, utility and property lines, structures, and major landmarks indicated. Zoning districts were printed in different colors. Tiny red flames marked various properties on the maps—fire scenes, presumably; large black question marks designated others.

"I'm hoping to sell the Department on buying one of these systems," Fuego said, booting up the computer. "It's a little more sophisticated than ICAM." The Information Collection for Automated Mapping program that kept statistics on various types of crimes in the city's 279 beats. "But I got a feeling they won't buy it 'til the City gets all its utilities computerized." He used the mouse to zoom in on and highlight the area with the most question marks and fire markers. A couple more clicks of the mouse and a query box appeared on the screen. He typed in an address, and one of the little fires began to burn on the screen. "Ronzani's house," he said. He highlighted another property using the mouse and a few keystrokes. "This is the factory building where you found Maggot Man. The building south of it belongs to a trust."

"How do you know?"

"I looked it up—along with all the other parcels on this grid. This is just a square mile, and it took me six months of my spare time to enter the data, but I think you can get the idea." He clicked, and half the properties in the middle of the screen turned red. "These belong to Michael Wellman." Another click and half the rest of the map's center turned blue. "These belong to a Dr. Martin Morgan, the rest to individuals and trusts. It's like a Monopoly game, only with the land trusts, it's hard to know who's playing."

Thinnes was impressed, but it was a pretty expensive setup for a detective, even if his wife worked. "You a big gambler?"

"No." Fuego dragged out the *o* to let Thinnes know he understood the implication of the question and resented it. "For the record, there's an eighty percent markup on computer hardware, and I've got a brother-in-law who gets me good used equipment for cost."

"For the record, I'm happy for you."

Back at the Area, Swann had fired up one of the squad-room computers and spread his notes out on the table next to it.

Viernes, who was just winding down with coffee and the Chicagoland section of the *Tribune,* pointed to a paragraph in the back pages.

Thinnes read: "Twenty year old Angelo Ortiz lost his life yesterday at 3:30 in the afternoon, on the steps of his family's home in Pilsen. He was shot to death by gang assassins. No one knows why."

"Most of the time," Viernes said, "you feel like a Band-Aid on a shotgun wound. You just go along telling yourself it's a job, just do it and forget it. Until, one day, you've had too much."

Swann looked up from his work. "Yeah, man." He said it very softly. "The way I see it, there're cats burning all over the city, burning with every kind of fire and desire known to man. And there's cats dead and dry inside as tinder, ready to explode at the first little incendiary suggestion—*that* kind are fucking terrifying! There's so many, so much hate and rage, it's a wonder there's a stick left standing."

Viernes shook his head. He stood up and pushed in his chair. "I'm calling it a day." He handed the newspaper to Thinnes and walked out.

Reluctant to start his own work, Thinnes paged through the paper from back to front until a caption caught his eye. He read the accompanying paragraph, then threw the *Trib* in the nearby wastebasket. To no one in particular, he said, "Get the body bags ready—somebody just hijacked a truckload of fireworks!"

FORTY-THREE

You know what this city needs more than any single thing?"

It was one of those questions people asked when they were trying to sell you something. Thinnes could think of plenty of things—jobs, decent schools, a cure for the disease that made people solve their problems with drugs and their differences with guns. . . .

The speaker was William Cox, an older guy who'd lost some weight, but was probably still 190 or so, and six feet tall. He had gray hair—long for a guy his age but combed and slicked back—a receding hairline, and sagging jowls.

Thinnes said, "What's that?"

"Affordable housing." Cox pushed his wire-rim bifocals further up on his nose. He was wearing a white summer suit with a Snoopy tie and was sweating in spite of the AC.

There were pictures of wife, kids, and grandkids on his desk, a kinetic sculpture—a whimsical wire affair run by pulleys and clock gears—and one of those oil-on-black velvet-paintings of a clown that made Thinnes think of John Wayne Gacy.

Cox's real estate agency was in a brownstone in Lincoln Park, south of Fullerton. A pleasant, middle-aged receptionist had shown him and Oster in, and Cox had told them to make themselves at home.

"We're looking into an arson fire that killed a man, Mr.

Cox," Thinnes said. Oster said nothing. Cox looked surprised and waited. "The building belonged to an Aldo Ronzani."

"Ah, yes. When I heard Mr. Ronzani had passed away, I offered my services to his executor. We were able to arrive at a mutually beneficial arrangement."

I bet you were, Thinnes thought. He said, "You found somebody to buy a burned-out building?"

"It was so badly damaged by the fire that the gentleman who bought it had it razed. I believe he's planning a new development."

"His name?"

"Michael Wellman. It's a matter of public record—when property's conveyed."

"Unless it's put in a blind trust."

"Ah. Yes. But in this case there's no mystery. No problem, I hope?"

"Did you handle the sale personally?"

"No. That particular sale was handled by one of my sales associates, Mrs. Morgan."

Thinnes shrugged. "She any relation to a Dr. Martin Morgan?"

"I believe her husband is a doctor. Whether he's the Dr. Morgan you're interested in, you'll have to ask her."

Thinnes asked about the other properties on his list and a few more questions about Wellman. Cox's answers backed up what he knew already. "How long has Mrs. Morgan worked for you?"

"Three years. I can't believe . . . She's an exemplary employee."

"She a good salesman?"

"Very successful. My associates work on commission; she's one of the highest paid."

"Michael Wellman didn't seem too impressed."

That news seemed to genuinely upset Cox—his mouth sagged open and he blinked several times before saying, "Well, he never said anything to me. . . ."

Helen Morgan was built. And she knew it.

When Cox told her over the intercom that two gentlemen were waiting to speak to her, she called back, "Certainly." She sounded like Sally Kellerman, who does the seductive voice-overs for TV commercials. Thinnes wondered if she practiced it.

She walked into the room like a model walking down a runway. As far as he could tell, she was naturally blond, but her eyes were an unnatural blue—almost purple. He would've bet her clothes cost a bundle—not that he was an expert on women's clothes—and that the gold-diamond jewelry was the real thing. She was modeling an ivory-colored linen suit that showed off her assets: traffic-stopping cleavage and legs almost as perfect as Rhonda's. Once they'd been introduced, she invited the two detectives into her office.

Following close behind Thinnes, Oster whispered, "She's so plastic I could hold a lighter up to her and she'd melt."

"Shut up, Carl."

When they got there, she gestured to chairs and said, "Have a seat, gentlemen." She sat at her desk, really an expensive table that showed off her legs as she crossed them. Straightening in her chair, she slipped her hands into the side pockets of her skirt, making the front of her jacket fall open. Her blouse was silk, or something like it, and left no doubt as to what she had underneath. Thinnes could hear Oster take a deep breath.

She took her hands from her pockets and straightened the things on the desktop: pictures of two children in a molded Lucite frame, a gold lighter encased in a chunk of cut glass, a notepad with the company letterhead, a gold pen. Then she seemed to give Thinnes her full attention.

"If I wanted to get started investing in real estate," he said, "say, buy something run-down to hold until urban renewal caught up with it, how would I get started?"

He could see her adding up his haircut, watch, and suit and deciding it wasn't worth her time. While she thought about it, she raised her chin and looked at him along her nose, from under half-mast eyelids. It was almost funny but, hey, it worked for Lauren Bacall.

"I'm afraid that's not my area of expertise," she said, finally. "I'll have to turn you over to one of my colleagues."

A junior associate, no doubt, but she made it sound as if she was terribly disappointed, even as she stood up to show them out.

"Never mind." Thinnes took out his star and held it up. "I was just wondering. We're actually here on official business."

"How can I help?" She was good at concealing her feelings but didn't quite manage to hide her surprise. Before he could answer, she reached under her chair for her purse and started digging through it. He waited. She pulled out a pack of Virginia Slims and waved it at him. "Mind if I smoke?"

"It's your office."

"So it is." She made a production of taking out a cigarette, putting the pack away, and reaching for an ashtray from the shelf behind her—waiting for one of them to offer her a light. Neither of them smoked; neither reached for the lighter on the desk. She finally picked the glass chunk up herself. After she'd fired up the cigarette and had a long drag, she repeated, "What can I do for you?"

"Tell us about Michael Wellman."

"Who?"

"The man you sold the Ronzani property to."

"Oh, him. A thirty-five-year-old child. I handled that sale as a favor to Mr. Cox. It was the first time I'd dealt with Wellman." Her tone implied the last time, too, if she could help it. She leaned forward. "What *is* this about?"

Thinnes glanced sideways in time to see Oster redden and refocus his attention on his note-taking.

It must be habitual with her, Thinnes thought, to use an aggressive come-on as an offense. Some people did it with anger or rudeness. He wondered if she could turn it off at will. He could see where Wellman, who hadn't mentally reached puberty yet, would be unimpressed.

"You ever heard of a Brian Fahey?"

"No."

He couldn't tell if she was lying. "Terry Koslowski?"

She shook her head. "Should I?"

"You know a Dr. Martin Morgan?"

"I used to think so."

"Could you clarify that?"

"He's my husband."

"Does he own any real estate near the Ronzani property?"

"I'm not telling you anything more about anything until you tell me what this is about."

"Aldo Ronzani's death resulted from an arson fire—that's felony murder."

She laughed. Another Lauren Bacall rip-off. "You're wasting your time and mine. Martin doesn't have the balls to commit murder."

"What about you?"

"I don't have a reason."

It was cold in the building, but Oster was sweating by the time they walked out. He loosened his tie and said, "Whew!" Then he turned his head as if easing a stiff neck and added, "Nice tits."

FORTY-FOUR

Thinnes's car didn't have AC, so they took Rhonda's. Thinnes drove. In a summer like this, the number of open hydrants in a neighborhood was as much a measure of its residents' income as the condition of the buildings—as accurate as the presence or absence of graffiti. Thinnes would've bet there weren't many open hydrants in Lincoln Park. There weren't any in this part anyway. The Conroys lived south of Belden, in a two-flat on the west side of Dayton. They'd bought the building when they were married in the early seventies. Now it was worth so much they couldn't afford to sell—capital gains would've killed them. Thinnes started looking for a parking spot as soon as he turned off Webster. When he was nearly to the end of the block, he turned west, then south into the alley between Dayton and Freemont. He pulled behind the Conroy's garage and parallel-parked six inches from the door, facing the wrong way.

"John!" Rhonda said. She pointed down the alley at the sign that threatened illegal parkers with towing.

"It's okay," he said. "They won't tow a cop."

She frowned but didn't say what he knew she was thinking. She hated double standards. She got out and stood with her back to the car while he climbed across her seat. He paused, before getting out, to dig his Official Police Business sign from under the seat to throw on the dash. She stiffened as he took her arm and steered her toward the Conroy's back gate. It wasn't locked. He pushed it open and waved her in. He closed the gate behind them, and they started down the walk.

He felt the adrenaline-rush almost before he recognized its cause. He grabbed Rhonda's arm hard enough to make her gasp, and stepped between her and the danger. "Don't move!"

In the center of the path, the biggest Doberman pinscher he'd ever seen stood at attention. Black and tan, ears up, panting with excitement or expectation. The dog's teeth seemed at least three inches long.

Rhonda started to say "What—?"

A voice said, "Miata, sit!" The dog sat as if operated by a switch. "Stay."

Thinnes looked past the animal to see a small, dark-haired woman in black. She had piercing eyes behind large glasses. "She's quite friendly," the woman said. She had an East Coast accent. Not New York, not quite Boston—the only accents he would have recognized.

Thinnes stayed put. The dog looked as friendly as a canine cop ordered to watch.

The woman stepped around her dog. "You must be John and Rhonda." She held her hand out. "I'm Deen Kogan."

He took the hand, tiny compared to his. Her handshake was as firm as Rhonda's.

Rhonda, meanwhile, stepped around them and knelt beside the dog. "Hello, Miata. Aren't you a beauty?"

The dog sank down and wriggled with pleasure, then licked Rhonda's face. Next to Rhonda, it seemed much smaller. She rubbed the sides of its face and stroked its head. Then she stood up and offered her hand to Deen. "How do you do?"

As the women turned toward the house, Miata fell in behind. Thinnes was left bringing up the rear.

Rhonda's friends were like Rhonda—moderate, liberal, and sensible. Their hostess, Jeanette, was an artist. A tiny white

184

woman, she must be eighty-seven pounds soaking wet. She had blue eyes and prematurely gray hair. Her husband, Harry, sold insurance.

The other guests were Howard, a high school shop teacher, and Deen. Within ten minutes of meeting him, Thinnes decided that Howard was the kind of guy who got on with kids because he'd never really grown up. As for Deen, Thinnes thought about the axiom that people were like their dogs. On the surface she certainly wasn't anything like a Doberman—he'd have pegged her for a miniature schnauzer or small greyhound type. But on second thought, he saw that she watched and listened like a cop. And when Jeanette told him that Deen ran a theater in Philadelphia and directed its productions, he understood. Anyone who could stand up to actors and nutcases and some of the I'm-God's-gift-to-the-world new-money types that financed a theater had to be tough as a drill sergeant and have the tactical skills of a field marshal. She wouldn't bother with some fussy little yap-dog.

While they were winding down after dinner, Deen asked Harry about the insurance implications of the heat. He seemed to know his stuff, so Thinnes asked about fire insurance fraud.

"The most obvious and easiest type to catch is filing multiple claims—take out policies with more than one company, then torch the building."

"But they have to prove a loss," Deen said.

"Well, usually, when the police ask the name of the insurance company, the guy says, 'I must really be upset, I can't think of it. I'll get back to you.' Only he never does. He gets multiple copies of the police report and fills in the blanks with different company names. Or, if the cops are smart enough to put something like "none given" in the blank, or to find out a company name, the guy gets some White-out and doctors the forms."

"How do they get away with that?"

"If they don't get too greedy, nobody notices. The sheer volume of claims precludes checking every fact. They usually check that a police report was made—a loss actually occurred—and send an adjuster out to estimate the damage."

"So how do you check whether somebody's insuring property with more than one company?"

"Check the information services insurance companies subscribe to—NICB, IRC, and PILR. Get the insured's name and DOB and call around."

FORTY-FIVE

Caleb had been sitting on a golf cart-like vehicle parked in the cloister on the south side of the Chicago Botanic Garden's main complex of buildings. The cloister surrounded a fountain consisting of numerous jets of water rising from a floor of overlapping concentric rings of square stones. The sound it made as it fell back down was too high-pitched to be a roar—more of a constant white-noise, a mantra that stopped thought and calmed obsessive ideation. Surrounding the fountain were ferns and low-growing junipers, yew bushes, cut-leaf silver maples and white pine trees arranged to give the serene feeling of a Japanese garden without its formality. It was early enough for the heat to be merely uncomfortable; unbearable would set in in an hour or two. He was thinking of Martin, as he had many times since the night they'd met at Gentry's, daydreaming. As before, the thought of Martin seemed to conjure him from the humid air . . .

"Jack!" Martin seemed to glow with pleasure, a little guilty, perhaps. "*You* come here, too!"

They'd discussed many things at their last meeting, though not Caleb's substitute for church. He refrained from saying, obviously. Meeting Martin by chance for the third time in a single summer was mind boggling. Karma, or an amazing congruence of interests?

"Do you come often?" Martin asked.

"Two or three times a month. And for some of the programs."

"We always come on days when Helen doesn't feel like going to Mass—that's every Sunday lately."

"We?"

"My children are with me. They went to get a drink. We've been coming early to avoid the heat."

Caleb nodded.

Martin stared at the cascading water and continued. "I was a devout Catholic once. I think it was the music. The Mass used to be in Latin, and if you didn't understand it, you could imagine the words were magical incantations that had the power . . ." He blushed as he trailed off. "This must sound crazy."

Caleb had been thinking of *Carmina Burana* as Martin spoke. When he'd first heard it, he'd been moved to almost orgasmic bliss. "Not in the least. Why do you suppose so many of us pay dearly for season tickets to the Lyric?"

Before Martin could respond, a girl's voice said, "Martin, Josh needs to go to the washroom and he's too old to go in the ladies room with me." A statement of fact without emotional expression. If the speaker was annoyed to be saddled with a small boy, it wasn't apparent.

Caleb stood as she got nearer.

She was in her teens. The boy was much younger, an early frame, Caleb was sure, from a time-lapse of Martin's life. His baby-blond hair hadn't darkened yet; it would. But his eyes were already gray and serious.

"Over there," Martin said, pointing.

The boy put his hands in his pockets and headed in the direction Martin had indicated.

"You're not going to let him go in by himself?!" the girl demanded.

Martin opened his mouth as if to reply, then closed it. By

188

way of an answer, he stood and said, "Excuse me," to Caleb, then hurried after the boy.

The girl turned to Caleb and met his gaze squarely as she held her hand out to him. "Hi. I'm Linny." She had blue-gray eyes and long lashes—though perhaps that was mascara—her mother's beauty and confidence, her father's height and coloring—though she'd dyed her hair black, the auburn roots showed. Rows of earrings adorned the edges of her ears, and there were silver rings on every finger. "Martin's my father."

Caleb shook her hand. "How do you do, Linny? I'm Jack."

"I'm pleased to meet you." She sounded pleased. "My mother was sure my father'd be meeting a woman. She asked me to spy. Now I won't have to." He raised his eyebrows slightly by way of a reply. Linny tilted her head. "Oh, she didn't say *spy,* but that's the translation."

"Well, your father and I didn't arrange to meet, but since we did and we're acquainted, we said hello."

"She didn't say what to do if he met a man."

Caleb didn't know what to say to that so he said nothing.

"I'm fourteen," she said, as if he'd asked. "My brother's only eight. There's just two of us—my parents don't have sex much."

He had to work hard to avoid showing his surprise, though as he thought about it, Helen Morgan's daughter would have learned the value of an ambush with her first words. She seemed disappointed when he wasn't shocked. "Where do you know my father from?"

"I'm also a doctor."

"Oh, yeah? What's your specialty?"

"Psychiatry."

Her eyes widened and she smiled. "What do shrinks do for fun?"

"We sit around watching for Freudian slips." The joke was older than she was, for that matter older than he.

She grinned. "So you can point to them and say 'Your Freudian slip is showing'?"

"Precisely."

"Very good! Very punny. How did you know I would know what a Freudian slip is?"

"Lucky guess." She gave him a skeptical look. "Your father's bragged about how smart you are. I figured if you didn't know, you'd ask. Besides, I understand you watch *Star Trek*."

"He told you that?" Caleb nodded. "He never tells anyone that!" He shrugged. "You're more interesting than most of my parents' friends."

"Why is that?"

She shrugged. "Maybe because you're not easy to shock."

"Perhaps because I remember being a teenager."

"Did you give your parents gray hairs?"

"No doubt. You?"

"My *moth*-ther. Giving my dad a hard time would be cruel."

He realized she was flirting, trying her budding sexual power out on the semi-safe ground of her father's middle-aged friend. He was flattered. "Interesting."

When Martin and Josh returned, Linny announced that it was time to go to the cafeteria and cool off. Josh's eyes widened and he said, "Ice cream!"

Linny rolled her eyes and shook her head. "You're such a child."

"Race you," Josh challenged.

"Josh, no running!" Martin yelled.

It was strange to hear. Caleb had begun to believe that Martin was too controlled—or maybe the word was repressed—for a public display. Josh apparently hadn't heard; he kept running.

"I'll get him," Linny said. "Meet you there," she told Martin. "You, too, Jack. You can entertain my dad while we spend his money in the gift shop."

"Please come," Martin entreated.

Caleb got up, and they followed the children in companionable silence. When they reached the perennial garden, Caleb asked, "Does your wife know about your proclivity?"

"Good God, no! I mean . . . she'd use it if she did. She's asking for the moon and the children." He paused thoughtfully. "I'd die for my children."

FORTY-SIX

Thinnes?"

"Yeah." Thinnes wedged the receiver between his ear and shoulder and reached beyond the phone to turn the digital clock so he could read the time. Two o'clock. It was dark in the room. Must be A.M.

"Does the name Morgan ring a bell?"

"You wake me at this hour just to ask that?" He kept his voice low. No use waking Ronnie. "Who *is* this?"

"Art Fuego."

"God! Don't you ever sleep?"

"I got rousted for a car fire."

"And misery loves company."

"Thought you might be interested. Car was registered to a Martin Morgan."

"And?"

"A woman was driving it."

"Was?"

"She's toast."

The witness was in shock, sitting sideways in the backseat of Fuego's car with his legs hanging out the open door and his feet planted on the gas station drive. He was facing the mop-up activities on the street. He kept hyperventilating. After every few sentences, he had to stop to breathe into the barf bag the paramedics had given him. Fuego was telling him to slow down and take it easy, but he was having trouble. He'd already given a statement to patrol and complained about having to repeat it.

"I stopped to get gas . . . and make a phone call," he said. "I parked there." He pointed at the remains of the pay phone mounted at car-window level at the edge of the lot, across the road from the smoldering wreck of Martin Morgan's car.

"Why'd you pull in like that?" Thinnes asked. "The logical way to pull in would be the other way, so you wouldn't have to get out or climb across the seat to reach the phone."

He swallowed. He took a deep breath and let it out. "I like to keep an eye on things."

"Ahuhn."

"Ah. Actually, I was s'posed to meet someone." He swallowed again. "I didn't wanna miss 'im."

"So where is this guy?" Fuego demanded.

"I dunno. I guess—" He breathed in, held it a long moment, and breathed out. "When he saw all the ruckus, he must'a decided to keep goin'. Didn't wanna get involved."

Thinnes said, "Go on."

"Well, after I park . . ." He wiped his forehead with his palm. "I see this broad drive up. I notice . . ." He swallowed. ". . . cause she stops practically in front of me, in that pay-attention car. Right under the street light there." He pointed to the blackened skull of an overhead light dangling above the wreck. "It was workin' fine before."

"Yeah," Fuego said.

"An' you don't see many white broads out alone this time'a night—'less they're hookers, and then they're in a cab or with a pimp."

They waited while he paused, looking ready to puke. He swallowed and took a deep breath.

"Then I get into my conversation an' forget about this broad 'til I hear some asshole leanin' on his horn." He breathed in and out. "I look up an' see the light's green, but the broad's just sittin', yackin' on her phone. What looks like a pretty involved conversation—wavin' her hand an' all.

"And there's this guy right up on her ass in a brown car, leanin' on his horn. She just gives him the finger." He shook his head. "He puts it in reverse and backs up to go around. When he gets up even, he leans on the horn. She looks up. He flips her the bird. Then he flips his cigarette butt at her. Right out his window and over the top of his car. An' he floors it and takes off.

"It musta lit the gas before it even hit the ground. I mean— it happened so fast. Just Boom!"

And his aim wouldn't have to be perfect, Thinnes thought. Judging by the burn pattern on the street, the gas tank had leaked quite a bit while the car sat at the light. Any spark within a couple feet would be close enough.

The witness shook his head. "One minute she's talkin' on the phone, the next . . .

"God! When I seen that fireball I hit the deck!"

"What?"

"I mean, I dived right for the floor. Then there was this huge explosion—just like the movies only . . . It musta been the gas tank exploding. When I look up, it was just all fire. Everything on fire—the street, the tires, her . . ." He put his hand over his mouth and swallowed hard.

Thinnes distracted him. "What did you do next?" He said it with a hard edge to his voice. The witness seemed to come back from his private rerun.

"I . . . I slid over and put the damn car in reverse and got the hell outta there!"

"That when the receiver came off the phone?" Fuego asked, pointing at the remains.

"Yeah, I guess."

"Didn't you smell gas before?"

"Yeah, sure. But what the hell. At a gas station you *expect* to smell gas." He seemed to be drifting.

"D'you get a look at the torch?" Fuego asked.

"Huhn?"

"What did the guy look like?"

"White. He was white. I didn't see him real good. He didn't stop under the light. He didn't stop at all. Christ! He just flipped his butt at her like he was flickin' a booger off his finger!" His eyes widened like a kid's at a horror film.

Fuego grabbed his forearm and shook him. "Snap out of it! You got to help us ID this bastard."

"Yeah, sure . . ." He put his hand over his mouth and stood up unsteadily. He barely got the rest out before he started to heave. "First I'm gonna be sick. . . ."

FORTY-SEVEN

After they'd sent the witness to the Area, Thinnes and Fuego watched the major scene team pack up their van and the squad roll team pack the remains into a body bag. Remains. Accurate term, this time.

"Wanna bet we'll find the gas cap was loosened, too?" Thinnes said, "Just like Nolan's car?"

"If we find enough of it to find anything," Fuego said.

"Well, it wasn't Wiley Fahey this time."

When the tow truck—a flatbed rig—backed up to the charred wreckage, Fuego said, "Hard to believe that was a hot white Mercedes two hours ago."

"It wasn't *this* hot two hours ago."

"Bad, Thinnes. Even for this early in the morning."

"Guess we better go wake up the doctor and ask who was driving his car."

"First we'd better clear your working this one with the watch commander."

The watch commander turned out to be Rossi, Thinnes's nemesis. He listened while Fuego reported on the fire and the possible connection to Banks's murder, then he turned to Thinnes. "I suppose you want me to authorize this so you can have the OT?"

Thinnes yawned. "Yup, I love giving up half a night's sleep to give bad news to some suburban yuppie."

Rossi actually sneered. "Glad to hear that. You can call Kenilworth and coordinate with them." He stalked into his office and slammed the door.

Thinnes thought, Gotcha!

"What's *his* problem?" Fuego asked.

"It was heads I win, tails he loses, whatever he decided. Among other things. Let's get going before he changes his mind."

Just before sunup they pulled up behind a Kenilworth squad parked in front of Morgan's house. The house was east of Sheridan Road and seemed pretty ostentatious—just the sort of place you'd expect to find a Mercedes.

The reaction of the man who opened the door was right for someone rousted before dawn by the cops. He was in pajamas and robe. His face was puffy and lined with imprints from the pillow he'd been using. His hair was a mess.

"Dr. Morgan? Martin Morgan?"

"Yes?"

"Do you own a Mercedes 500, S class?"

"My wife does."

"But it's titled in your name?"

"I suppose so. What's this about?" He was beginning to sound worried.

Because Thinnes's in-laws lived in neighboring Wilmette, he knew something about the kind of people who lived in Kenilworth. Innocent residents weren't panicked by a visit from the cops though they sometimes carped about the inconvenience. Most people would've bitched about the hour. Morgan was either guilty of something or unusually cooperative for a yuppie.

"Is your wife home?"

"My wife?" He actually had to think about it. He half turned and looked behind him, toward the stairs Thinnes could see on the far side of the room. Morgan finally said, "I thought so. But I don't know. I'll have to check." He started to close the door on them, then stopped and said, "Come in." He waved them toward a white couch with matching chairs in the center of the room. "What's this about?"

The Kenilworth cop let them do the talking.

"Maybe you'd better see if your wife's home first," Thinnes said.

Morgan nodded, then hurried up the stairs.

"What do you think?" Fuego asked, when Morgan was out of earshot.

Thinnes looked around. The room was all white—ceiling, drapes, deep plush carpet, and furniture—except for the bright, silk Georgia O'Keeffe poppies on the glass tabletop. "I'd say Dr. Morgan makes a pretty good living."

"That's not what I meant."

Thinnes glanced pointedly at the Kenilworth cop and told Fuego, "Too soon to tell."

After a few minutes Morgan was back. "She's not here. What happened? Where is she?"

"Your car was involved in an accident," Thinnes said. "The blond woman who was driving was killed."

Morgan said, "Helen's blond," then seemed to realize the implication and drift away inside his head for a moment. "Where *is* she?"

"The Stein Institute," Thinnes said, using the formal name. It somehow sounded less brutal than the morgue.

Morgan shuddered. "You'll need an identification. I'll get dressed."

"I'm sorry, Dr. Morgan. You can't identify her. We'll need to get the name of her dentist."

Morgan went white and his eyes opened wider, as if he'd

just been shocked wide awake. He said, "Oh," and rested his forehead on the palm of his hand. He stared at the crook of his arm for a long time. He finally took a deep breath, half hiccuping, the way people do when they've been crying. His eyes brimmed with tears that didn't spill over. He sniffed once and said, "As a physician I've had to break this sort of news many times. It's not like anything I could have imagined."

Thinnes tried to imagine what he'd do if someone told him Rhonda was dead. Probably take out his service revolver and put a .38 slug through his head.

FORTY-EIGHT

Rossi'd gone home by the time Thinnes and Fuego got back to Area Three. They got themselves coffee, and Oster joined them when they went to report in.

"The witness was a washup," Evanger told them. "He didn't get enough of a look to make an ID. Go over and interview the guy that called it in."

"Name," Thinnes said.

Evanger handed him a sheet of paper. "For all the crying they do about the good old days, no one ever mentions how the modern gadgets save our butts. Safety vests, enhanced 911, cell phones, and caller ID . . ."

"Yeah," Oster said. "And junk mail, junk calls from autodialers, and—"

"Quit yer bitchin'," Fuego told him.

Thinnes, who'd been half listening as he read the information on the paper, said, "Hel-lo."

Oster said, "What?"

"Edward Limardi. Where've we heard that before?"

The Mercedes-Benz dealership where Limardi worked was small and exclusive. The shiny cars in the showroom were reflected by spotless windows and polished terrazzo floors. The two salesmen wore suits that hadn't come off any rack. Both had styled, blow-dried hair and neat mustaches. Thinnes would've bet money the older one was a poster boy for a hair replacement outfit, and the younger man—Limardi—spent lots of time or money at a health club. Fuego held his star up and said, "I need to talk to you, Mr. Limardi. Privately."

"Yeah, sure," Limardi said.

The other salesman excused himself nervously and hurried away.

Limardi pointed to one of three glass-walled cubicles along the far wall of the showroom. "I've been expecting you. How 'bout my office?"

"I'd really rather talk in *my* office."

Limardi nodded. "You traced my call." When Thinnes didn't confirm or deny this, he added, "Is Helen all right?"

To the best of Thinnes's knowledge, Limardi hadn't made any attempt to check on Helen Morgan after he'd called 911. Even if she'd only been an acquaintance, that was odd. And the preliminary investigation indicated that they'd been an item. Which made it all the odder.

"She's dead, Mr. Limardi."

"My God!" Limardi tried to looked shocked, but didn't pull it off.

Thinnes held his hand out in the direction of the door. "Shall we go?"

He put Limardi in the Area Three interview room and let him cool his heels for twenty minutes while he thought about how to proceed. Most of the techniques that worked on novice offenders were probably invented by flimflam artists like car salesmen. And whatever else he was, their investigation of him back in March indicated Limardi was a pretty good car salesman.

When Oster came back from inspecting the plumbing, Thinnes asked him, "Have we worked out Mrs. Morgan's itinerary last night?"

"Yeah," Oster said. "We got lucky. Her appointment book

was in her purse, which got charred on the outside but didn't burn up. She had a date for dinner with this clown. . . ." He pointed through the two-way mirror at Limardi. "We checked the restaurant. The waiter remembered them—seems *he*'s a big tipper. Car sales must be good."

"What better way to get remembered by the help?"

"Yeah. Well, the waiter said they only ordered one bottle of wine with dinner, so he was surprised when the woman seemed like she'd had too much to drink. He's sure they split the bottle. 'Said 'the broad was all over the guy'—his words—and the guy seemed embarrassed. They left about eleven."

Ryan, Swan, and Ferris came into the squad room at that point and naturally gravitated toward the interview room. Curiosity *is* a common vice in detectives.

"What've you got here?" Ferris demanded. He'd shed his tie and suit jacket; his face and graying hair and shirt were soaked with sweat.

Thinnes ignored him and asked Oster, "Where do you s'pose Mrs. Morgan spent the time between eleven and when she was torched?"

"*I* can tell you that," Swann said. He, too, was damp with sweat but he was still in "business attire." He was sipping coffee. It made Thinnes hot just to watch.

"Well?"

"With the guy you sent us out to check on."

"Limardi," Ryan added. She'd tied her fire-red hair up in twin pony tails which made her look sixteen.

"Where?"

"His place," Swann said. "He's got a condo on Sheridan Road."

"The doorman saw them go in?"

"Naw. He doesn't have a doorman, *but* the building across from the entrance to his parking garage does. And *that* doorman hates him. Claims to have lost money on a car deal. Anyway, he said he saw Limardi park a white Mercedes S500 in the bus stop in front of his building at about eleven-thirty and get out with a blond woman, a looker. Approximately an hour and a half later, he escorted the same woman—he thinks—back to the car. She left; he went back in the building."

"So our own 911 tape and this guy who hates his guts are Limardi's alibi. Neat."

"Tell us about Mrs. Morgan," Thinnes said, sitting close enough to be in Limardi's personal space.

Limardi pretended not to notice but he was sweating and it wasn't *that* hot. "Safe sex," he said.

"What?" This from Oster who was sitting across from Thinnes, taking notes.

"Safe sex," Limardi repeated. "She was married. You know—MD husband, 1.7 kids, house in the suburbs, nice car, nice dual income. She wasn't going to give that up for a car salesman, not even a Mercedes salesman. So there wasn't any danger she'd be expecting me to marry her."

"She was getting a divorce."

"Yeah, sure. Married men use that line a lot, too. She wasn't serious."

"Maybe she wasn't," Thinnes said, "but her husband was. He filed."

Limardi shrugged. "Then maybe he decided to save the cost of litigation. You looked into that?"

"Maybe we're looking into what the two of you were doing last night," Oster said.

"Fucking. What do you think?"

"Cut the crap, Limardi," Thinnes said. "And just tell us what happened."

Limardi leaned back on the bench and said, "We went to dinner—but you knew that. I'm sure you talked to our waiter, and the maître d', and half the other customers in the restaurant.

Then we went to my place for a little dessert. Then I put her in the car and sent her home. That was the last time I saw her."

"How is it you came to call 911?"

"She called me on her car phone, said there was something wrong with her car. She wanted me to come fix it on the spot. I was in bed already. I was trying to get her to call a tow truck when she started screaming. I hung up and called 911."

"So what'd you do then?" Oster demanded.

"I told the 911 operator what happened and hung up."

"And?"

"There was nothing else I *could* do. I tried calling her car phone back and got that out-of-service message. So I went back to bed."

"You never thought of getting up and going to see what happened?"

"Yeah. And then what? Hold her hand until her husband showed up to claim her?"

"You're a real piece of work, aren't you?"

"Look, am I under suspicion here? If I am, I want a lawyer."

"At the present time, Mr. Limardi," Thinnes said, "we're just trying to establish what happened before our witnesses forget the details. If you wouldn't mind, we'd like you to write down everything, exactly as you remember it, in as much detail as possible. When we get this guy, we don't want him getting off because of some detail someone forgot."

"I can do that."

"Thanks." Thinnes turned to Oster and tried to sound mad as he said, "Carl, could I have a word with you?"

They went out and closed the interview door. Ferris was still there, watching. "You guys didn't even make him break a sweat."

Oster said, "Don't you have something to do?"

"Ferris, why don't you go get us a couple of Cokes?" Thinnes said, "as long as you're hanging around?" To Oster he said, "I'll get him started on his statement, Carl. You go get hold of that 911 tape."

"Right."

Forty-five minutes later, Thinnes and Oster witnessed Limardi's signature on the last of the pages he'd carefully filled with details.

Thinnes said, "Thank you, Mr. Limardi. We appreciate your cooperation on this." He offered Limardi his hand.

As Limardi took it, Oster smirked and said, "But like they say in the movies, don't leave town."

FORTY-NINE

Bill Cox had come in to the Area, as requested, and Thinnes took him to the conference room. If he'd looked old the first time they met, now he looked like an ME's case. Thinnes figured he'd finally come up against a problem he couldn't solve with the right property.

After asking him a series of questions about Helen Morgan's activities the previous day, Thinnes said, "Did her husband have anything to do with why you hired her?"

Cox looked like a man who's been caught in a lie. But then, he *had* given the impression he didn't know Dr. Morgan.

"It's true," he said, "that I hired Helen because her husband was a doctor, and I thought she might persuade him to invest in real estate. That's why I hired her. But I kept her on because she was good. She grossed more her first year than either of my most experienced salesmen."

"Had she been having trouble with anyone lately, a dissatisfied customer, or maybe someone who asked her out and wouldn't take no for an answer?"

"Not that I'm aware of. But then, I doubt she would've confided in me."

"Why's that?"

"She'd have been worried it would get around."

"So?"

"It would be—Ah . . . my sales people are quite competitive. Of course they wouldn't give anyone an advantage by admitting there was something they couldn't handle, if you see what I mean."

"Just how competitive *are* your sales people?"

Cox's eyes widened as he considered the implication of the question. "Nothing like that!"

"I'll need their names anyway, and addresses and home phone numbers. You can fax them to me here." He wrote the Area fax number on the back of his business card and handed it to Cox.

Cox said, "She was being sued for divorce."

"We're looking into that."

"Her husband seemed decent enough, the one time I met him, but . . . Those who're closest know which buttons to push, and Helen could be difficult. And who knows what a man has in his soul."

FIFTY

Oster and Thinnes were halfway through a hurried lunch when Thinnes's pager went off. When he answered it, Evanger told him to beat feet back to the Area. They had an irate citizen chewing the ears off the community relations officers. Thinnes's case. "Which one?" The Morgan murder.

When he walked into the community relations office, the cop on duty, a veteran female, looked relieved. She didn't sound at all sarcastic when she thanked him for getting there fast. Before she could introduce him to her visitor—a woman sitting near the door—*she* jumped up and said, "Martin Morgan killed my daughter! I'm sure of it."

"Who?"

"Helen Morgan."

"Who are you?"

"Helen's mother. Eileen Kerrigan Seely."

"I see." He did see. If they put a photo of Helen Morgan in the computer and aged it the way they did with missing kid pictures, it could be the spitting image of this woman. "Maybe we should go talk about this in private, Mrs. Seely. Would you please come with me?"

That took some of the wind out of her sails. She followed him meekly upstairs, and through the squad room—where he took Oster in tow—into the conference room. Before they took up where she'd left off, she accepted a seat and declined coffee.

"Do you have any evidence to support your accusation, Mrs. Seely?" Thinnes said. He hadn't bothered to bring Oster up to speed. He was a quick study.

"He was the only one who would benefit from her death."

"That you know of."

"He was divorcing her!"

"And?"

"He wanted her dead."

"That's not the same as killing her."

"Did you check where he was?"

"He said he was home, asleep. We don't have any evidence to contradict that."

"Have you looked?"

Oster cut in. "If Dr. Morgan were implicated in his wife's death, Mrs. Seely, wouldn't you be first in line to get custody of his kids and control of her estate?" Bad cop.

"I resent that implication!"

"What implication?"

"That I'd unjustly accuse Martin to get the children."

Thinnes said, "What can you tell us about your daughter's business?" Good cop.

Seely seemed pacified by the change in tack. "She was doing very well. She was a superb saleswoman."

Oster said, "Mightn't she have stepped on a few toes on the way up?"

"Nonsense!" She looked at Thinnes. "Martin loathed her. He hadn't slept with her in years."

Thinnes raised his eyebrows. She reminded him of his own mother-in-law, Louise Coates. He couldn't imagine Rhonda telling Louise something as intimate as how long it had been since they made love. But then, Rhonda wasn't Helen Morgan.

Seely seemed to realize she'd gone too far. She blushed. "He had her heavily insured," she said less adamantly.

Thinnes nodded. "I'm sorry for your loss, Mrs. Seely. I

know it won't bring your daughter back, but we *will* get her killer. You have to let us do our job."

She wavered but her eyes stayed dry. What had Rhonda said about women who can't or won't cry? A hard woman?

"Can you tell us anything about her boss?" Oster said. "Did she get along with him?"

"Yes, of course."

"And the man she was seeing the night she died?" Thinnes said. "Did she ever mention him?"

"Edward?" Thinnes waited. "She said he wanted to marry her. When her divorce was final."

"How serious were they?"

"He'd given her a ring. She showed it to me. It was quite beautiful, quite large. She had it appraised. It was worth ten thousand dollars."

"Had she ever mentioned any fights with him, or a disagreement?"

"No."

When Thinnes got back from escorting Mrs. Seely to her car, he told Oster, "Get hold of that waiter—see if he remembers Morgan flashing a big ring."

Oster scowled as he nodded. "Why are we bothering with all this? It's almost always the husband."

"Too obvious."

"Well, in all the books and movies, it's real estate developers that did it, so why don't we just go snatch up Wellman, read him his rights, and get it over with?"

"No, Carl. In this case, I think O.J. did it."

FIFTY-ONE

Violent crimes detectives went to a lot of funerals—to see who seemed sorry, who acted indifferent. Thinnes had seen every sort of reaction except the one favored by TV writers. He'd never seen anyone get overcome by guilt and confess, but he was always open to the possibility. You never knew. You could never safely say, now I've seen everything. He figured Helen Morgan's funeral was pretty standard for a white, upper-class, Catholic funeral. It was held at Sacred Heart Church, in the north suburb of Winnetka, and was what his family—who weren't Catholics—would've called "High Church," with vestments and candles and a Mass. He recognized the music— Mozart's *Requiem*—from the movie *Amadeus* that he'd seen to pacify Rhonda and had liked in spite of himself. There were a surprising number of people—many of the same he'd seen at the wake the night before. He was also surprised to see Jack Caleb. Even though both Caleb and Morgan were MDs, Morgan practiced out of Evanston Hospital and was an internist, not a shrink. He would have to ask Caleb about him later.

During the service, at opposite ends of the church, Martin and Caleb stood and knelt and sat with the rest of the congregation, but neither took communion. Thinnes didn't think Caleb was Catholic, but he wondered if Morgan held off because he had something on his conscience—like murder. His kids were a girl who looked about fourteen and a boy of seven or eight. The girl was red-eyed and stiff, the boy spaced out. Morgan was stone-faced through the service, caring for the kids—handing out Kleenex or hugs like a robot—reminding Thinnes of O.J. He wondered what other parallels there were to the Simpson case.

Thinnes buttonholed Caleb out beside his car. "I didn't know Morgan was a friend of yours."

"I was referred to him after the incident in Lincoln Park last spring. We've met socially on a few occasions since."

"I'm surprised you're talking to me about it."

"He's not a patient. And I'm not revealing anything told to me in confidence. On the other hand, you have a job to do, and you'd be remiss if you didn't consider the victim's husband."

"You think he had anything to do with his wife's death?"

"No."

Thinnes was glad there was no trace of righteous indignation in his answer, no 'Of course not!'—just no. "Did you know they were splitting up?"

"Martin told me."

So they were on a first name basis. "Did you know the wife?"

"I met her once."

"What was your impression?"

"She seemed ferocious."

"As in man-eater or bitch?"

"Either. Both. She thought her husband was seeing me professionally and wanted something she could use against him."

"And if he was, you wouldn't be mentioning it to me now."

Caleb raised and dropped his eyebrows as he said, "Precisely."

"How'd she know about you?"

"Martin had my business card. Apparently it never occurred to her that I might be *his* patient."

"Morgan talk about her much, or about the divorce?" He

212

could see that Caleb was uncomfortable, but he wasn't going to let him off the hook.

"He mentioned that they were divorcing." Thinnes waited. Caleb finally said, "Martin is my friend. If I come across evidence that he was involved in his wife's death, I'll call it to your attention immediately. Barring that, I prefer not to discuss him with you."

Thinnes felt a flash of emotion. "Is he gay?"

"You'll have to ask *him*. It's not something I could tell you."

Thinnes thought of Dean Olds—who'd never been charged with killing his wife, though his male lover had been tried for it. There wasn't any suggestion of a woman in Morgan's life, but no one had thought to ask about a man. And it would suggest a beauty of a motive. In a custody fight, a straight woman—even an adulterous one—would get the kids over a gay man. The courts were funny that way. Which left him wondering where Caleb came in. If they were just colleagues, Thinnes knew Caleb would do the right thing, even if he made himself a huge pain in the ass in the process. But if they were lovers . . .

Thinnes suddenly felt ashamed. Caleb wouldn't cover for a murderer, no matter how attracted he might be to him, any more than Thinnes would if the killer were an attractive woman. Would he?

FIFTY-TWO

After the Mass the funeral cortege proceeded to Calvary Cemetery on the border between Evanston and Chicago. The drive gave Caleb time to think.

His friend Manny was buried at Cavalry. He'd died the day before Easter a year ago. His friends had taken up a collection for the gravesite and the stone and had collaborated on the epitaph, a variation on Edna St. Vincent Millay's poem, "The First Fig."

Caleb's belief in God had been formed in Vietnam. The childhood edifice inherited from his parents, to which he'd paid lip service in his youth, had been blown away by the first hostile fire, when an enemy round tore a life-ending hole in the chest of the first comrade. But a journalist he'd subsequently been pinned down within a foxhole had given him a kind of palliative substitute for his lost naïveté.

"If He follows His own rules," the writer had said, "God's as powerless to stop this as we are."

"How can you say that?"

In his mind's eye, Caleb could see his sardonic grin.

"God gave us free will. You're not really free if you're not free to fuck up. And He gave us history and Machiavelli to learn from. You're also not free if you're not allowed to forget, or to ignore the lesson in the first place. So don't blame God. *We* fuckin' did this."

Caleb thought of that whenever something occurred that seemed senseless or ironically tragic.

Free will.

Free will and accident could account for all the misery laid at the feet of God. In the beginning, God had created accident. It was an oversight that it wasn't mentioned in Genesis, but the authors probably hadn't been as thoughtful or as imperiled as Caleb's journalist. And God was stuck with it.

The insight made Him fairly irrelevant for Caleb, but it also made him stop blaming God for things, let him stop hating Him.

The graveside service was brief—mercifully—because of the heat. Caleb was surprised to be invited to the house afterward. As he'd already rescheduled his afternoon patients, and hadn't anything urgent to do, he accepted. Curiosity, he told himself. In fact, an excuse to be near Martin, no matter how unaware he was of Caleb. After the cemetery, the limo took the family back to the house; Caleb followed in the queue.

The house was east of Sheridan Road and was far more ostentatious than Caleb would have expected of Martin. Parking restrictions on the street had been suspended, and Cadillacs, Mercedes, and Lexuses crowded the curbs on both sides. Caleb's Jaguar seemed in its element as he eased it between a Lincoln and a BMW.

Inside you could see the lake from the antiseptic living room. There was an open bar, and people who'd pressed around the grave at Calvary stood in aimless groups as caterers passed hors d'oeuvres and white wine. Caleb recognized a few of the guests—mostly overlapping medical staff from Northwestern Memorial and Evanston Hospitals. Martin's lawyer was there, and Helen's. They seemed on friendly terms. There was a large contingent in real estate, and a few whose occupations and avocations never came up. Caleb introduced himself to others as he circulated unobtrusively, eavesdropping. Almost everyone was talking shop. No one mentioned the divorce. He felt like a spy.

When he was introduced to Helen Morgan's mother, he thought immediately of the adage, To know all is to forgive all. Eileen Seely perfectly explained her daughter. She worked the room like a politician and accepted condolences like a queen. She spent a good deal of time supervising the caterers, though— to Caleb's mind—they were performing competently. And she seemed to seek out Martin and the children frequently to offer comfort that they seemed to find unhelpful.

Martin, Caleb noticed, had drinks pressed on him from every side, which he accepted graciously but put down untouched. He seemed exhausted, but he didn't fail to notice when Linny helped herself to a glass of wine. He made excuses to the couple he was speaking with and hurried to relieve her of it. There was no anger in his body language. He might have been taking a lighter from a toddler. Sitting across from the little skit, Caleb could tell from their gestures that the girl wasn't angry with her father, just bored and unhappy.

Caleb looked around for Josh. The boy was sitting cross-legged in the space between the huge windows that faced the lake and the heavy drapes that partially covered them. Caleb walked over and squatted next to the boy, saying nothing.

Josh turned. "Oh, hello. I forget your name."

"Jack."

Josh nodded; Caleb waited. "I wish I was grown up. Then I wouldn't have to come to stuff like this."

Caleb nodded. "Bored?"

"I guess. What are these for, anyway? Funerals?"

"When someone dies, people are very hurt and unhappy. They often hurt so much they can't think. They forget how to act. So there are customs to tell them what to do until they start thinking straight again."

Josh looked dubious. "I miss my mom." Caleb agreed that he should. "And I'm bored."

"I doubt if anyone would mind if you read a book or played a game."

"Games are no fun by yourself. And there's no kids here except my sister." His tone spoke volumes about how much fun his sister was. "Would you play with me?"

"Sure."

"Checkers?"

"If you like."

"No. Monopoly. I'll go get it." He looked around. "This wouldn't be a good place."

Caleb pointed to an open door—off the living room—to an unoccupied office. "How 'bout in there?"

"That was my mom's office."

"Do you think she'd mind?"

"I'll go ask my dad."

They played for an hour. Linny joined them. With the door open, Caleb could hear people making excuses and saying their good-byes. The caterers made a final circuit, gathering up trash and empties.

Linny said, "It's weird, playing a game in my mom's office when she's dead."

Caleb understood her to mean she wanted absolution for going on with life without her mother. He gave it as best he could. "Your mother loved you?"

"Yeah, sure."

"Then she'd want you to get on with your lives."

"I guess."

"It's hard now. It'll get better—"

He was interrupted by Eileen Seely appearing suddenly in the doorway. "There you are, children—" She stopped with her mouth open, then she shut it. "I thought everyone had gone."

Josh said, "Jack's not everyone. He's our friend."

"Oh." Mrs. Seely clearly did not know what to say to that. "Where's your father?"

From the room behind her, Martin's voice said, "I'm here, Eileen." As she turned to face him, he came within Caleb's line of sight. He looked exhausted and depressed.

"I was just going to collect the children and take them home with me," she said, "so you can get some rest."

"That was thoughtful of you," Martin said. "But unnecessary. You're welcome to stay here with us if you like."

"No. I have to go. The children really should come with me. They need a mother."

Caleb looked at the children. Josh slid out of his chair and came over to cling to Caleb's arm. Linny's face hardened and she played with her Monopoly piece—a silver dog—without looking at her adult relatives. Caleb looked up at Martin, who was oblivious to him.

Martin's expression mimicked Linny's as he said, "Their mother is dead, Eileen. But they still have me."

She started as if she'd been slapped.

Martin said, "If you don't want to stay, let me walk you to your car."

As soon as they were out of the room, Josh said, "I have to go to the bathroom," and slipped away.

Linny turned to Caleb and said, "My father said it was an accident, but I know better. My mom was murdered."

There was no analgesic for the sort of pain she was feeling; he didn't try to offer one. "If someone caused your mother's death, he'll pay."

"How can you be sure? They never caught who killed Helen Brach."

"I know the detective in charge of the case."

218

"Detective Thinnes?" Caleb nodded. "He was at the wake. He made me feel like my dad does when I try to lie to him."

"You see? And he's relentless."

"Like Lieutenant Gerard?"

It took Caleb a moment to place the reference—the Fugitive's pursuer. He nodded. But as the girl turned away, Martin's words echoed in his memory: I'd die for my children.

Caleb wondered if he would also kill for them.

FIFTY-THREE

The green Ford van had no plates. Its paint was weathered, with little patches of rust and smudges of fingerprint powder everywhere. There were strips of rust around the lower edges of the doors, and shiny spots where fresh paint had been sprayed over gang graffiti. The rear bumper had a sticker: HANG UP AND DRIVE! and a Z Frank Chevrolet license plate holder. Each of the back windows had a bumper sticker, too: LET A UNION ELECTRICIAN CHECK YOUR SHORTS; and UNION ELECTRICIANS DO IT BETTER.

It was parked near the office of the central impound, where it had been towed from the alley it was blocking. Ferris was leaning against the hood of his department-issue Caprice, sucking pop from a Taco Bell cup through a straw. In deference to the unreal temperature—ninety-eight degrees—he and Thinnes had both ditched their suit jackets and ties.

"What's the story on this?" Thinnes asked.

"According to the DMV, it's titled to a Sean Fahey, though he hasn't had plates on it for two years. We asked. Said he sold it to his brother-in-law two years ago. Guess he didn't bother to change the registration."

"Let me guess. The brother-in-law's name is Terry Koslowski."

"Bingo! He reported it hijacked yesterday. Claims to be a private electrical contractor. The description he gave of the hi-

220

jacker sounded like a shithead I'm looking at on a previous beef. So I thought I'd come over and take a peek."

More like get out of the squad room before Evanger gave him something useful to do, Thinnes thought. What he said, was, "So why am *I* here?"

"Weren't you looking for Mr. Koslowski?"

"Yeah. You contact him yet?"

"No. I thought you might like to take it from here."

If Ferris would put half as much effort into his cases as he did into getting others to do his work for him, he'd be a crackerjack detective. Thinnes didn't say so, though. "What about the hijacker?"

"Doesn't look like he left any clues. All the prints are Koslowski's. The alleged offender took his tools—if you can believe he'd really leave anything valuable in his vehicle in that neighborhood—and battery and ditched the van. So, you want to take it from here?"

"I'm not going to get involved with processing any auto theft, but I'll notify Mr. Koslowski for you that we've recovered his wheels."

A District Nineteen beat car pulled up and let Oster out. He was also in shirt sleeves and tieless. He nodded at Thinnes and frowned at Ferris.

Ferris said, "Well, if it isn't our ten-o-clock scholar."

The frown became a scowl. "It figures you'd still be reciting nursery rhymes."

"Carl, you hear what O.J. said when the glove didn't fit?"

Oster looked at Thinnes. "If I shoot Ferris, can I plead temporary insanity?"

"I don't think so. The trial's been going on six months."

"Give up, Carl?" Ferris asked? *"Maybe I didn't do it."*

"See that, Thinnes?" Oster said. "A stopped clock's right twice a day, and Ferris finally got something right for once. He didn't do it."

221

Thinnes played along. "What?"

"Anything. He didn't do anything."

Ferris laughed.

"He *never* does anything!" Oster added.

"He's managed to get under your skin."

Thinnes didn't want to spook his prime suspect, so instead of going to pick Koslowski up, he left a message on his answering machine: to contact Detective Thinnes at Area Three about his van. While he waited for the fish to take the bait, he went on digging, by phone, into Helen Morgan's life and work.

Before she married Morgan, she'd been an RN, a good one according to former colleagues. Morgan had been a resident at the hospital where she worked. She'd made sure she caught his eye, to quote a former rival. She and the doctor had married a year later. The first child, Linet, had arrived close enough on the heels of the wedding to cause malicious speculation. Helen had quit her job two weeks before the baby was born and had gone from housewife/mother to society matron by the time the second child, Joshua, was two. She'd begun selling real estate when he entered kindergarten, three years after that. Most of the people Thinnes talked to were dazzled by her. Michael Wellman was unique in not being impressed, though based on his own run-in with her, Thinnes was inclined to favor the developer's assessment.

"Carl, did you check with that guy from the life insurance company on whether any other companies were accessing Morgan's records in the medical data base?"

"Nothing so far—"

The phone interrupted him. Thinnes picked it up and said, "Area Three detectives. Thinnes."

"Desk. Some guy named Koslowski here for you, Detective."

"Send him up."

While they waited, Thinnes said, "It seem like we're coming up with a lot of Ford owners who were somehow connected to Wiley Fahey?"

"Like who, besides this clown and Brother John?"

"John Mackie drove a Taurus."

"Yeah. I forgot about that. Very coincidental, don't you think?"

"It might be, if they all bought their Fords from the same dealership. Maybe you could run a title history on them while I talk to Mr. Koslowski."

Oster nodded. "Maybe I should call Waukegan and see if the Smith brothers left a Ford behind, too."

"Wiley Fahey never had a vehicle registered to him, but check on his sister, Koslowski's ex. If she doesn't have a car now, call and ask her if she used to."

Koslowski was five-ten and maybe two hundred pounds, but solid as a pro wrestler rather than fat. He had a square face, blue eyes under eyebrows that seemed too far apart, and crewcut brown hair. He was wearing a sweat-stained white T-shirt that proclaimed SHIT HAPPENS, dirty painters' pants, and tan leather boots. He smelled like an ashtray full of butts.

Thinnes took him in the conference room so he'd be less inclined to feel he was being interrogated. After having him go over the story of the hijacking and repeat his description of the offender, Thinnes dropped the big one: "Do you know a Brian Fahey?"

"Wiley Fahey?" Thinnes nodded. "Yeah. You think he's behind this?" The overdone incredulity was the giveaway. Koslowski knew about Fahey.

"When was the last time you saw him?"

Koslowski shrugged. "Before Christmas, maybe? What's this about?"

"I'm afraid Mr. Fahey is dead."

"No shit?"

Koslowski wasn't surprised, which didn't surprise Thinnes.
"What'd he die of?"

"Smoke inhalation."

"I always used to tell him he oughta cut back."

"You don't seem surprised he's dead."

"The guy always lived on the edge." He shrugged again.
"You push your luck and . . ."

Thinnes could tell that he was lying. And that he knew
Thinnes knew it.

"Listen, I thought you asked me down here to talk about
my van. I bet you didn't even find it yet."

"Actually, we did. It's down at Central Impound."

"So what's all this bullshit about Wiley?"

"He was a friend of yours. I thought you might be able to
tell us something about him."

"He wasn't a friend. He was my brother-in-law. And after
I got out of the joint, I never saw him. It would've violated my
parole."

"I thought you said you saw him before Christmas."

Koslowski stood up and leaned his bulk toward Thinnes.
"Look, just tell me how to get my van back and let me outta
here—unless you're planning to arrest me—then I want a
lawyer."

"The desk sergeant downstairs can tell you how to get
your van."

"Fuck you!"

FIFTY-FOUR

Rising smoke and steam were silhouetted against the street lights' orange glow, radiating from the city like the heat from banked coals. It was nearly 3:00 A.M. and still 88 degrees. Thinnes wondered how the fire fighters stayed conscious in their rubber suits. The frequent breaks for air and water wouldn't have done it for him. As he stood between Oster and Fuego, the heat and strobe flashes of emergency light were making Thinnes light-headed. He was thankful there was no crowd—heat usually brought out the killer in people. *This* heat, so far this summer, killed directly.

"The fire's struck," Fuego said, finally. He seemed unbothered. "We can't even *guess* at cause and origin 'til they're done with the overhaul." He meant the partial destruction of the building by firemen seeking hidden fire in walls and other enclosed places.

"Christ!" Oster said. "Time they get done, you're not gonna be able to tell there was a building."

Fuego shrugged. After a while, one of the firemen came over to announce that they'd just found a body. "Kind of expected it," he said. "Witness told us he saw someone go in just before the explosion."

"I didn't even think about not seeing the guy come out until the firemen asked if there was anyone in the building." The speaker, a male black in his late twenties, took a long pull from a sweating can of Coke. His outfit matched the customized eighteen-wheeler he'd parked fifty yards down the alley. Even with just parking lights, the truck looked like certain neighborhoods at Christmas. The driver was flashy, too, an urban cowboy with snakeskin boots, a diamond stud in one ear, and gold chains, and a Rolex. Thinnes wondered what kind of weapons he kept in the truck for protection.

"What were you doing down here?" Oster asked the driver. Oster was soaked with sweat and looked about all in.

"I got a delivery, but it's not 'til six in the mornin'. I was just fixin' to cop a few Zs when this went down."

"You don't worry about getting hijacked?"

The driver opened his eyes wide and said, "*Should* I be?"

"Yeah, smart guy."

Before the witness could get too worked up over the insult, Thinnes jumped in as the good guy. "We'd like to run you over to the station to look at some pictures while this whole thing's fresh in your mind. We'll have an officer keep an eye on your truck."

"Well . . ."

"Please. We think you might have seen the guy who set the fire. It's not often anyone gets a look at one of these creeps."

"Would I have to go to court?"

"Probably not."

"These bastards are usually happy to cop a plea if they're caught," Fuego added helpfully. "It'd just be nice to have something to prod 'em with."

"Yeah. Well, okay." He rolled his eyes toward his truck.

"We'll keep an eye on it for you," Thinnes reassured him.

They sent the cowboy off with a patrol officer and went to see the body. The smell of cooking meat made Thinnes glad he wouldn't have time for a barbecue any time soon. The body was burned beyond recognition. When you saw what was left, you could see why the Bible-thumpers threatened the damned with brimstone and hellfire.

One of the firemen, who'd been watching his fellows lift the remains into a body bag, came up with a portable phone. "Who's the primary detective on this one?"

Thinnes held out his hand. "Who'm I talking to?"

The fireman put the phone in it. "ME's office."

Thinnes put the phone to his ear and said, "Thinnes."

The man at the other end identified himself and asked a few cursory questions, then said, "Bag him and ship him."

Thinnes handed the phone back.

"Looks like he's got a wallet on him, Detective," one of the other firemen said. He held up an object that was hard to see in the poor light. Thinnes pulled gloves from his pocket and put them on before taking it. He walked over to the nearest fire truck to look the find over in the glare from the headlights. Oster and Fuego crowded around to kibitz. The license indicated that the victim was Terry Koslowski.

"This seem a little like déjà vu?" Thinnes asked.

"You mean just like Wiley?" Oster said.

Fuego made a face in the reflected light. "All over again."

FIFTY-FIVE

After Koslowski's autopsy, Thinnes just made it to the criminal court building at Twenty-sixth and California in time for the morning session. Oster was sitting in the hall outside the courtroom with his head in his hands, sweating heavily, and breathing like a horse that had run the Arlington Million.

Thinnes knew from what Oster never said that his partner was afraid to go to a doctor because of what he'd learn. Thinnes had brought the subject up once. Oster's response was, "What're you, my *wife*, now?" Short of going to Evanger with it, there wasn't anything more Thinnes could do. So he tried not to think about it. He *had* mentioned it to Rhonda, who'd said, "Karma."

"What's that supposed to mean?"

"What goes around comes around. Now you know how I used to feel when you'd tell me, don't worry about it."

"How's it going, Carl?" Thinnes asked.

"Been better, but I'll live."

They sat and watched two lawyers cutting a deal down the hall with a maximum of gesturing.

"Italian," Oster said.

"Southern Italian."

A private joke. One of the counselors was from Atlanta. It was funny, Thinnes thought, how you could carry on whole conversations with your partner and not say a dozen words.

"I'm still after that Ronzani woman," Oster said. "One of

228

the church ladies thought the name rang a bell, but she couldn't place it exactly. She's gonna check with her friends and get back to me."

It was nearly 7:30 P.M. when Thinnes finally walked in his front door. Toby was sitting at the foot of the stairs with his leash in his mouth. "Don't tell me nobody's walked you," Thinnes groaned. Toby thumped the floor with his tail.

Rhonda called from the kitchen. "Don't let him con you. He was out twenty minutes ago."

"Sorry, pal," Thinnes told the dog. He took the holstered .38 off his belt and put it on the top shelf of the closet, then went to find his wife.

She was emptying the dishwasher. She was wearing one of her going-out dresses, a cotton flowered thing that came below her knees but showed more of her cleavage than he liked to see displayed in public.

"Where's Rob?" he asked.

"Staying over night at Mike's."

Thinnes raised his eyebrows. "What's for dinner?"

"Reservations."

He suddenly felt tired. "What time?"

"As soon as you're cleaned up." She stopped long enough to give him a playful kiss on the mouth; he could feel himself waking up. She ran her fingers along his jawline. "If you're good, you might get lucky."

He must've been good. They went home early—for dessert.

Afterward, he had just drifted off when the phone rang. "Thinnes," the caller said, "you got a message here. Woman named Koslowski wanted you to call—urgent."

"Who *is* this?"

"Viernes. Thought you might want to know right away. It's about arson, according to this note."

"Yeah. Thanks."

As he wrote down the number, Rhonda murmured, "What is it, John?"

"Nothing. A screwup maybe. I've got to make a phone call. You go back to sleep."

Linda Koslowski didn't answer her phone, and it gave him a bad feeling. A weeknight. He knew she probably had to work the next day. He thought about calling District Seventeen and having a beat car stop by her place, but he'd feel pretty stupid if she'd just turned her phone down and turned in early. He headed back to bed, but the bad feeling got worse. When Rhonda stirred, he told her, "I got to check something."

He smelled smoke when he pulled on to Christiana. He had the AC off—it didn't work worth a damn—and the windows open. Linda Koslowski's house was dark, shaded from the orange glow of the street lights by listless parkway trees. There was room to park by a hydrant out front, but the nearest legal space was half a block away. He cursed himself for a fool as he parked in it. The neighborhood was quiet but not soundless. He heard laughter, a dog barking some blocks off, a car rumbling over uneven pavement, crickets—all muffled by the roar of air conditioners. Conditioned reflex—years as a beat cop made him grab the cell phone from beneath his seat and lock the car. As he neared the house, he had to step into the street to see the numbers on the keypad. He tapped out Koslowski's number. The phone rang; no one answered. The smell of smoke was stronger as he returned to the sidewalk. He looked at the house. Darkness seemed to be seeping out from around the windows. Seeping. Smoke! He debated with himself for a full second—charge in or call for backup? Training won again. He switched the phone off then on and called *999. "Fire," he said to the dispatcher and gave him the address. The screen door was locked but he yanked, and it gave. The inner door was old, solid wood reinforced for urban living. When he kicked it, it kicked back. There was no sign of light beyond the window next to the door. He remembered a warning from long ago: Don't stand in front of windows—they blow out. He spotted a small planter with hanging vines and flowers that looked black in the dim light. He jumped sideways, away from the window, as he heaved the planter through it. It touched the glass; the window blew out. Smoke pushing against it from within ignited. A cloud of orange heat and inky smoke flashed outward. He felt the explosion as he dived off the porch. He didn't hear it. Heat seared his skin. He smelled hair burning.

He landed face down on the parkway and covered his head with his arms. Embers and falling glass shards pricked his skin. He looked back cautiously. The front room of the house was an inferno. Smoke thick enough to shovel poured up from the top of the empty window frame. He got up and ran to the house next door. He kept ringing the bell while he pounded on the door.

An upstairs window opened. A man's head poked out. "What the hell? . . ." Then, "Fire!"

Having raised the neighbors, Thinnes ran down the walk between the houses and tried Koslowski's rear door. Locked. He was searching the smoky darkness for something to pry it open with when a silhouette materialized in the alley behind the house carrying a bar or short pole. Thinnes felt another hit of adrenaline. The arsonist?

A second shadow joined the first, pointing a gun in silhouette. A Maglight caught him. "Freeze!"

The familiar authority reassured him. Cops!

"Thinnes," he shouted. "Area Three!"

"Stand back!"

He stepped aside. The man with the bar attacked the door, and the wood around the handle splintered. The door flew open. A choking black cloud poured out and upward, searing his lungs, forcing him to retreat with the bar wielder. The coughing fit passed. He charged the doorway, but one of the cops grabbed his arm. Through the smoke, he could just make out an enclosed porch and an inner door. Orange flames licked the soot-smudged window in the inside door like a starving monster slobbering to get out.

"Too late, man," the cop said. " 'Cept for the firemen or a priest."

FIFTY-SIX

Fuego answered his page immediately, and when Thinnes had explained the situation, said, "Ten minutes." It took him fifteen. By then the firefighters had the flames knocked back and were beginning overhaul operations. Fuego came in his own car, a Fiero, which he pulled into a space vacated by a neighbor who didn't want his car damaged. Fuego's Fiero had both police and fire decals and a bumper sticker that said FIREMEN ALWAYS COME.

He set to work immediately—taking pictures of the spectators, interviewing Thinnes, the first cops on the scene, and the firemen during their frequent breaks to cool off. It was nearly 9:00 A.M. by the time they'd pronounced the fire completely out, removed Linda 's remains, and started to roll up the hoses.

Thinnes asked Fuego, "Now what?"

"Now we try to determine cause and origin."

"Can I watch?"

"If you put on a hard hat and boots and don't touch anything."

"This is how I figure it went down," Fuego said.

They were standing in the wreckage of the living room, staring at abstract patterns of uncharred wood on what had been the floor. He pointed to a circular, lightly burned spot on the most heavily charred part. Nearby were rectangular patches, nearly undamaged, with roughly rounded corners. "Looks like the fire started here, in the wastebasket, got going good, and spread to the sofa. . . ." He pointed to one of the rectangular patches.

"Then it started to run out of air—smoldered. I could probably calculate how long. . . ." He shrugged. "It just laid here, biding its time, gnawing on Koslowski and the furniture until you came along and broke that window." He shook himself. "The old fire devil's scarier than any monster Hollywood's cooked up."

"How can you tell it was a wastebasket?"

"Anything *on* the floor protects what's underneath because fire burns up. So unburned places show you where the furniture was. And that round spot on the floor matches the size and shape of a charred metal wastebasket I saw out front, where they dumped what they hauled out."

Thinnes looked around. Although much of what the fire had left had been removed, the remaining debris was black and soaking wet. "How the hell do you tell where it started?"

"Absent unusual conditions—which we don't seem to have here, fires burn upward and outward. So the most heavily damaged area, most burned, is usually the point of origin. And there's usually a V-shaped pattern of charring or smoke damage against walls or burned into combustible structures, or a big circle of heavier damage on the ceiling above the point of origin that points down to it. It's hard to tell here, because everything is so sooted up, but it's there." He pointed at the ceiling above the uncharred circle on the floor. "And you double-check that with the firemen who moved the stuff during suppression and overhaul and with people who knew where the furniture was before the fire."

Thinnes compared the unburned spots with his recollection of the room when he'd been in it last. Only the wastebasket mark was out of place. He didn't recall seeing a wastebasket and said so.

"That might not mean anything. People move things around."

"No!" Thinnes shook his head. "She wanted to talk to me—urgently. It's no coincidence she burned up. She knew something, maybe about her ex's death, and she was torched to keep her from telling us."

"It's going to be hard to prove unless the autopsy turns up something, because this all has the feel of an accidental fire."

"Wastebaskets just don't spontaneously combust."

"You mean spontaneously ignite. No. But people frequently drop lit cigarettes in them."

"She didn't smoke."

"She might have had a visitor who did. And she didn't have a battery in her smoke detector."

"The killer probably took it out."

"Try proving that."

"Maybe the ME'll find something. I'm sure as hell going to tell him to look at everything."

Oster put down the phone when Thinnes came into the squad room and asked, "You all right? You look like hell."

"Yeah." Thinnes had showered and changed clothes, but he could still smell the morgue—the odors of meat and bleach.

"Murder?" Oster asked. He was referring to Linda Koslowski, from whose autopsy Thinnes had just returned.

Thinnes nodded. "Unofficially, smoke inhalation, but the fire was suspicious origin. The ME's waiting on tox results before he goes out on a limb. You heard anything about funeral arrangements?"

"Guy from the funeral home said no wake, private burial."

"Whose turn is it?"

"Mine, I guess."

"You got a problem with that?"

"Nah. Better a funeral than an autopsy."

Linda Koslowski had been in the ground a week when they got the tox report back. She'd had alcohol in her system consistent with a single drink, and enough benzodiazepine to render her unconscious. Since she hadn't had a prescription or any history of mental problems and the fire didn't have a logical natural cause, and given the message she'd left Thinnes, the ME ruled it homicide.

"Just for kicks," Oster told Thinnes when they'd both read the report, "let's ask the ME to test Wiley and *Terry* Koslowski for benzodiazepines."

"Just for kicks, let's try to get permission to test Ronzani and Mrs. Morgan, too."

FIFTY-SEVEN

Dr. Martin Morgan looked like shit, Thinnes decided. Either he was really devastated by his wife's death or he'd killed her and was suffering remorse. Maybe both. When he showed up at the Area for the reinterview Thinnes requested, Oster showed him to a chair in the upstairs conference room and got him water. Then Oster took a chair against the wall and took notes while Thinnes asked the doctor questions.

"My attorney advised me not to talk to you," Morgan said when they were all settled, "but a mutual friend told me I don't have anything to worry about unless I killed Helen. I didn't kill her. What do you want to know?"

"What mutual friend?"

"Jack Caleb."

"How well do you know Dr. Caleb?"

"Well enough to know he's a friend in need."

Interesting answer, Thinnes thought. One he knew to be right from personal experience. "How well does he know you?"

"He's not my therapist, if that's what you're getting at."

"Your wife take tranquilizers?"

"Not to my knowledge. But it seems my knowledge of what she did is limited."

"You had her pretty heavily insured, didn't you?"

"We were both *adequately* insured." Thinnes waited. "I'll have to pay for child care and hire a full time housekeeper, possibly a part-time chauffeur. And we no longer have Helen's income, though my expenses haven't diminished."

"You haven't been very informative about her whereabouts the week she died, Doctor."

"My wife and I were living under the same roof, but we hadn't been living together for some time."

"Then why did you just recently file for divorce?"

"Inertia, I suppose. Or self-delusion. I'd only recently received proof that she'd been unfaithful."

"How's that?"

"When my daughter made a reference to 'Mommy's boyfriend,' I felt I had to face up to things. I hired a private investigator, one with a reputation for discretion, and asked him to get me proof one way or another. A week later he called back with results—he said he had pictures. I told him to forward them to my attorney, who filed for me."

"But she was still living with you."

"As I've already said."

"Why?"

"We both stayed for the same reason. Neither of us wanted to appear to be abandoning our children. We both wanted custody."

Enough to kill for? Thinnes wondered, but he wasn't ready to ask that yet. "Who was your wife getting it on with?"

"I don't know."

"C'mon, Doctor."

"It didn't matter. If it hadn't been him, it would've been someone else. She didn't care enough about him to ask *me* for a divorce. She liked the perks of being a doctor's wife. She didn't throw him in my face. I realized she wasn't trying to hurt me; she just didn't care. And the more I thought about it, the more I came to see I didn't care either. It was a relief to know we had an excuse to end it."

"But if she was having it both ways, why would she agree to end it?"

"She didn't. She wanted full custody of the children and most of my income. I'm telling you the truth because I believe it always comes out. In any case, you'd learn it when you talk to Helen's attorney."

Thinnes wondered if the doctor was brain dead, or was such a clever killer they'd never nail him. As if mind reading, Morgan said, "I know the police always suspect the husband, usually with good reason. But I didn't kill my wife and I don't want you to let her killer get away because you've made up your mind that I did it and stopped looking for anyone else." He looked at his watch. "I have to pick up my children at school. I'll ask my attorney to turn over the private investigator's file to you. I trust that you'll safeguard my wife's privacy unless you have to divulge something to prosecute her killer?"

Thinnes nodded. "Do you have any objections to our interviewing your daughter?"

He could see the wheels turning as Morgan thought about that. Finally the doctor said, "Not if Dr. Caleb is present during the interview."

"Why him?"

"*He* won't let you hurt her." Morgan stood up. "I have to go. You can call me if you have any other questions."

"There is one thing, Doctor," Thinnes said. "We think there might be something the ME missed on autopsy. We'd like permission to disinter your wife's body."

Morgan looked stunned. He stared at Thinnes for something like fifteen seconds, then blinked. "If you think it would help your investigation, go ahead." He nodded to Oster and walked out, closing the door quietly behind him.

Neither of them spoke for a few minutes, then Thinnes said, "That was too easy."

"We gonna interview the daughter?"

"Only as a last resort."

"There's something he's not telling us."

"There's always something they don't tell us, Carl. We'll just have to find out whether it's relevant to the wife's death."

FIFTY-EIGHT

They were sitting in the squad room later, when Oster said, "It's gonna be two weeks before we get any results back on those tox tests. What do we do in the meantime?"

"We could have another go at Sister Serena," Thinnes said.

"Let's call over and find out if she's coherent first."

"And if we can see her, let's take Dr. Caleb along to interpret in case she's still spouting gibberish."

On the way to the hospital, in the car, they pumped Caleb for information.

"One of the most ubiquitous symptoms," Caleb said, "is auditory hallucinations. Even though the individual may *know* they're not real, they sound real to him. Many of the disorder's other manifestations—the disordered thought, delusions, and paranoia—may be perfectly logical responses to phenomena the sufferer experiences but no one else even perceives."

"What causes it?" Oster asked.

"There probably isn't any one thing—head trauma, structural anomalies in the brain, and neurochemical dysfunction. Schizophrenia*s* might be a more accurate term for the syndrome. Some cases, but not all, respond to antipsychotic medications. Sometimes victims have spontaneous remissions. Bottom line is, it's terra incognita."

"Can it be cured?" Thinnes asked. *That* was the bottom line for him.

"The most recent data indicate that early intervention, particularly with the newer drugs, can limit the severity of episodes and improve prognosis."

"I take it that's a not really," Oster said.

"It can usually be managed. But there's something else to consider—not all the symptoms are due to the primary disorder. Many suffer from depression and anxiety because of the devastating way the disease interferes with their pursuit of a normal life."

"I never thought of it," Thinnes said, "but I guess it would be pretty depressing to hear voices or forget your own name."

"Don't confuse psychosis with retardation or memory loss," Caleb said. "Some schizophrenics have poor retention, but many have excellent recall."

There was a long silence while they digested it all, then Caleb added. "One of the most terrifying aspect of madness is that you're never quite sure of its boundaries. Once you're convinced that you're crazy, you never completely trust yourself again."

The doctor who'd agreed to talk to them about Serena's condition didn't look old enough to buy booze. She was hazel-eyed and naturally blond with perfect teeth and a Cover Girl complexion. She was wearing nurses shoes, and had a white lab coat over her street clothes. A little brass badge on her lapel announced that she was Lucinda Tambourine, M.D. She shook hands firmly with all three of them. "A few ground rules, gentlemen. You can have forty-five minutes with her—tops. She's not responsible for anything she did during a psychotic episode, so no third degree. If you need to ask her anything incriminating, you'll have to wait for her lawyer. And if she starts perseverating—repeating words or phrases, or running them together, it means she's getting tired or stressed—you'll have to stop."

Thinnes held his hands up like a patrol officer stopping traffic. "We're just here to get some details. She's already copped for the charge. She can't get in any deeper."

"I thought you said she's better," Oster remarked.

"Relatively speaking. She's still fairly detached, and probably still hearing voices—though she may not admit to it—and there's some loosening of associations. But she's not actively psychotic. Are you familiar with her background?"

"No," Thinnes said. "When she pled guilty, we didn't bother to follow up." He didn't explain why. Since mental patients don't get time off for good behavior, and fewer doctors were willing to risk a lawsuit by certifying someone safe to let out, mentally ill offenders actually spent more time locked up than those who were sane and guilty. Thinnes didn't care. Cecci was off the streets.

"It may be difficult to believe," Dr. Tambourine said, "but she was once a promising biblical scholar, and she has an IQ of a hundred eighty. She was very close to getting her master's when she had her first break—probably stress induced. Back then, unfortunately, the only antipsychotic they had was Thorazine. It's so sad. If she were to have her first episode today, she might be able to lead a normal life."

Maria Cecci was waiting for them in a cozy room without windows that reminded Thinnes of Caleb's office. It was like a living room without a coffee table—it had comfortable seating and lots of Kleenex boxes. Serena was sitting quietly on one of the couches.

If he hadn't seen it happen all the time for court appearances, Thinnes wouldn't have believed the change in her since he'd seen her last. She'd traded her army surplus clothes for an attractive dress, and she was clean and well groomed.

Thinnes walked over and said, "Maria, do you remember Detective Oster and me? It was hard not to think of her as Sister Serena, hard to call her by her real name.

She glanced at him, then stared at her lap and said, "No." She kept her hands still, not clasped, but one cupped in the other. "We've met?"

"We arrested you last March."

She seemed to drift away, then come back without moving. "I'm sorry. I don't remember. I was crazy last March."

Thinnes let it go. "This is Dr. Caleb. He's a psychiatrist." She nodded without looking up.

"Do you mind if we sit down?" Caleb asked.

She shrugged. She didn't say yes or no. They sat.

"Would you tell us about the Conflagration Church, Maria?" Thinnes said.

"It was like the voices I hear in my head—not real, but lifelike." They waited; she finally said, "But I was raised Catholic." There was another long pause, then: "I guess I needed something. . . . And Brother John had a way—he was so sure! He just dragged you along. . . . And he took me in and gave me a job."

She paused again. She seemed drugged or so depressed it was an effort to talk. Thinnes wondered if he thought of depression because she really seemed depressed or because Caleb had planted the idea in his mind.

Serena added, "Not many will hire the mentally handicapped. He had big plans. Brother John. He was gonna start a revolution. Huh! Malcom X was right. Revolution is like a forest fire, it burns everything in its path. John was gonna give the world a new savior." She shook her head. "Deep down all religions are the same. They promise you salvation if you'll just let them do your thinking for you. But *you* get to do the time. . . ."

Right on! Thinnes thought. He said, "Did John tell you the name of this savior?"

"No. I mean, I think he's just the Wizard of Oz."

Thinnes made a note to ask Caleb, later, what that was about. He said, "Ron Hughes told us how you and the others ambushed Officers Banks and Nolan."

"I must have, if you say so. But I don't remember. I'd been off my medication for a month by then."

"Why did they kill Banks?"

She looked away. "I don't know." Normal reaction this time. Guilt? Remorse?

Oster asked, "Did they set anything else on fire besides the police car?"

"Not that I know."

Thinnes asked, "What happened after the police car burned?"

She glanced at him, then looked away, shaking her head.

"Were they setting fires for profit?" Oster demanded.

She didn't seem to have heard.

"Maria," Thinnes said, "did Brian Fahey talk about retaliating against the police *before* the morning he killed Officer Banks?"

"He said he'd get even."

"When? And did he say how?"

She shook her head. "Nobody believed him that I recall. But I don't recall like I used to. I wasn't myself or I would have told him what Dear Abby said."

Caleb spoke for the first time since they'd sat down. "What did she say?"

" 'People who fight fire with fire end up with ashes.' "

FIFTY-NINE

Friday. The overnight low had been seventy degrees and most of the forecasts were promising ninety. Oster came into the squad room looking like he should be going out—to the nearest emergency room. Thinnes couldn't avoid asking, "You feeling okay, Carl?"

"Yeah."

"Oster," the sergeant called. "You got a request to call a Mrs. Sophie Renzi, ASAP." He gave Oster the number.

Oster said, "Thanks, Sarge." To Thinnes he said, "If you're goin' downstairs, bring me back something cold, will you?"

When Thinnes returned, he put a can of Diet Sprite in front of Oster.

"What the hell is this?"

"All that was left." It was getting hard to keep the machine stocked with anything cold. "I'll give it to Swann, if you don't want it."

Oster grabbed the can and popped the top. He took a long swallow, as Thinnes sat down, and wiped his mouth on the back of his hand. "Mrs. Renzi—she's my contact in the Catholic Ladies Bingo Society and Gossip Club—thinks she's run down Ronzani's sister." Thinnes waited. "Seems that a Maria Ronzani, just off the boat, fell into the arms—make that hands—of one Eduardo Limardi, thought by Mrs. Renzi to have been connected."

"That wouldn't be a relative of our car salesman?"

"His father. Anyway, the Ronzanis were married in a civil ceremony because—among other things—Ed senior was divorced from his first wife."

"Which would explain Mrs. Limardi's reluctance to introduce her new husband to her family."

"Exactly. Eventually Ed senior made his bones and the Limardis had two kids, a girl who died in a fire when she was ten or eleven and young Eddie. His old man came to the predictable bad end when the lad was eight or nine."

"You got all this while I was downstairs getting drinks?"

"You were gone half an hour, and Mrs. Renzi's a fast talker. But wait, it gets better. Mrs. Limardi remarried, this time in the church. And the guy she marries was Franco Ori."

"She's not the Mrs. Ori who owns our crime scene?"

"The very same."

"Making Maggot Man Limardi's cousin."

"How's that for a coincidence?"

"I don't believe in coincidences." Thinnes wiped the sweat from his forehead with his sleeve. "So, did Mrs. Ori have any other kids?"

"Nope. According to Mrs. Renzi, she used to say it was God's punishment for marrying Limardi. Mrs. Renzi's also pretty sure Limardi kicked her in the stomach shortly after young Eddie was born—hurt her so bad she couldn't have any more kids."

"And I s'pose he knocked Ed junior around while he was at it."

"Mrs. Renzi didn't say."

"You get confirmation on any of this yet?"

"No, but I got a few calls out."

"Well, keep on it. And while you're at it, see if you can find out who owns the house Mrs. Ori lives in."

"What're you gonna be doing?"

"I think I'll invite Fast Eddie to come by and talk about his family tree."

Thinnes asked Swann to bring Limardi in because he didn't want to pull Oster off what he was doing and Ferris would've let the cat out of the bag. Nobody else was free.

Swann put him in the interview room. When Thinnes went in, Limardi said, "I don't know any more about Helen Morgan's death than I did the last time I was here!

"Okay."

"I could've told you that over the phone." He wasn't mad enough to be an injured innocent, though it was amazing how many who *were* innocent put up with the inconvenience of coming down to the Area just because some cop implied they'd be thought guilty if they didn't. Almost as many as those who, like Limardi, thought they were smarter than the entire detective division. In spite of old Columbo episodes rerunning everywhere. They wanted to know what the police had on them and thought they could outcop the cops to find out. Wasn't there a fancy word for that kind of arrogance?

"Actually, we were looking into another matter," Thinnes said.

"Well?"

"Tell me about Dino Ori."

"He's a deadbeat."

"Your cousin?"

"My mother married his uncle. That doesn't make him my cousin."

"So you hated the guy?"

"It's more like I don't like him, and we've got nothing in common. He's a deadbeat."

"Was. He's dead."

Limardi shrugged.

"I'm surprised your mother didn't tell you."

"I don't see her much."

"When was the last time?"

"Easter."

"When was the last time you saw your cousin?"

"I told you, he's not my cousin. And if somebody shot the bastard, it's not my fault. I don't know anything about it or about him."

"Why would you think someone shot him?"

"To know him was to want to shoot him."

"Do you know a Brian Fahey?"

"Should I?" Thinnes waited. "No. Is he dead, too, or did he kill Dino?"

"Did I say Dino was killed?"

"Aren't you a homicide detective?"

"Violent crimes." Limardi shrugged. "Do you know Terry Koslowski?"

"No."

Thinnes thought he'd detected a slight hesitation. He said, "Linda Koslowski?"

"No."

This time there was a flicker of wariness, but was it because he was lying or because he was being asked about a woman? "Where were you the night of July seventeenth?"

"God, I thought nobody outside of B movies asked questions like that."

"Well?"

"I have no idea. Why?"

"Linda Koslowski was murdered July seventeenth."

"Not by me." Limardi seemed sure of himself. Either he *didn't* do it or he'd rehearsed his denial. "I'd like to go now. Or you can get me a lawyer."

249

Oster was still on the phone when Thinnes came out of the interview room. Swann was reading the *Sun-Times*, and the headline got Thinnes's attention: "Blood Placed on Simpson Sock: Expert." He walked over to check it out. Swann was his age or better, and when he put on reading glasses to study the paper, Thinnes was reminded—not for the first time—that they were both getting older.

Ferris came in and read the caption over Swann's shoulder. "How the hell could they tell that?" he demanded.

Swann dropped the paper on the table and pushed it toward Ferris. "I don't know. Read it yourself."

"Nah, it's bullshit." Ferris put his hands in his pockets and walked over to stand behind Oster. "You know what's the slogan of O.J.'s new limo service, Carl?"

"You're goin' straight to hell?"

"Close. We'll get you to the airport with time to kill."

SIXTY

Josh and Linny are spending the weekend with their grandmother," Martin said.

They were sitting in a quiet corner of the Palmer House bar. Morgan looked marginally better than he had the day of the funeral, but there were still worry lines, and dark circles beneath his eyes. There were also symptoms of attraction—dilated pupils, accelerated respiration, lingering eye contact. They'd been talking shop and weather, neither verbally acknowledging the electricity between them.

But there was something bothering Martin. Caleb was reluctant to ask what. Within his certainty that Martin couldn't have been behind his wife's murder there was a germ of doubt—given sufficient provocation anyone is capable. "Something's troubling you," he said. "What?"

Martin looked up from his drink and blushed. "Am I that easy to read?"

Moot question. Caleb waited.

"Linny said you told her Detective Thinnes is relentless."

"What brought that to mind?"

"The police hauled me in for questioning."

"Hauled?"

"Well, the very strong implication was that I'd fail to co-operate only if I were guilty. They asked me all sorts of personal questions: had I ever been unfaithful? why had I only recently filed for divorce? didn't I have Helen heavily insured? They asked questions I'd answered the last time I spoke with them. They acted as if it were just a matter of time until I get summoned before a grand jury."

"It's probably not personal. Until they figure it out, everyone's suspect."

"I'm sure they can sense guilt the way dogs pick up on fear. And I've been paralyzed by guilt lately. I wanted to be rid—I wanted to be free of Helen. Now, I feel as if I caused her death."

"Have a care for what you ask the gods. . . ."

"Precisely. But I didn't want her dead. And I didn't kill her. I know you've got no reason to believe me. My whole life to date has been a lie. No, not a lie! A mistake. But you must know people sometimes change, given sufficient motivation. God knows I have *that*!"

Of course he was right, Caleb thought. People change. Particularly when they reach a point when the pain is greater than the fear.

"I guess I'm asking you to trust me," Martin said.

Caleb wasn't one to trust a man he scarcely knew. In God we trust, he thought, all others pay cash. He really didn't *know* Martin.

Another maxim came to mind. Something he'd once seen on the notice board outside a church: Faith is not belief without proof but trust without reservation. He wished he could smother *his* reservations. He knew they were personal as well as interpersonal; faith in Martin was really faith in his own ability to judge character. He didn't believe Martin capable of premeditated murder but—he admitted—he'd been fooled in the past. And it was doubly hard to be objective when your soul cried out, this is the one. Self delusion? And was it his soul or his gonads?

SIXTY-ONE

There was a shrine in the darkened living room of Mrs. Ori's house. Oster hadn't mentioned it after his first visit, but he knew more about little old Catholic Italian ladies than Thinnes did, so maybe it was standard equipment. It was set up on a table in the corner of the room. A candle burned in a short red glass in front of a two-foot-tall statue of the Blessed Virgin Mary. Sharing the stage was the black-and-white picture of a grammar-school-age girl.

"My Bianca," Mrs. Ori said, when she noticed Thinnes looking. "An angel in heaven. With God." In case there was any doubt. "She died in that terrible school fire."

"Our Lady of Angels?" Oster asked.

Mrs. Ori nodded. She reminded Fuego of his grandmother, though she was about the age his mother would be if she were still alive. She had on a dress that came well below her knees. Her gray hair was piled and pinned up on her head. Her glasses were probably all the rage in the early seventies. "The same," she said. "God has His reasons, I'm sure. But it's hard."

Thinnes nodded, and waited. She invited them to sit; she took a chair facing the shrine. They sat on the sofa, and Thinnes got to the point. "We were wondering if you could tell us about your brother Aldo?"

"Aldo? I haven't seen him since I left Italy. I don't even

know if he's still alive. When I married Eduardo—my first husband—I was cut off from my family."

Thinnes glanced at Oster and got an I-told-you-so look.

"Eduardo—never mind. I won't speak against the dead. But Aldo. You've met him? You know him?"

"I'm sorry, Mrs. Ori. He passed away."

She nodded as if she'd been expecting it and waited for him to continue.

"He left you all his property in his will."

"I don't understand. What about his family?"

"I guess you're all the family he had."

She started crying softly. Thinnes looked at Oster, who shrugged. They waited. After a few moments, she said, "What about the arrangements?"

Oster said, "He's already been buried, Mrs. Ori. I'm sorry." He took a card from his pocket and handed it to her. "This is the name of your brother's lawyer. He can tell you about the arrangements and the terms of the will."

She took the card and held it in her lap. Tears made lines down her cheeks. "So many wasted years," she said. "Lonely, wasted years."

Thinnes looked around for a tissue box, located one, and offered it to her. She took a tissue; he put the box on an end table within reach.

"Is there someone we can call for you?"

"Father Raymond. Over at the church."

"I know him," Oster said. "I'll do it."

She pointed to a doorway on the far side of the room. "The phone's in the kitchen."

Oster left. Thinnes waited in silence with her. When Oster returned, he was carrying two glasses, both of which he offered to the woman. She took one and sniffed it. "My cooking wine?"

"Medicinal," Oster said. "Water," he added and put the

other glass next to the tissues. "Father Raymond will be here in twenty minutes." He sat down. "Mrs. Renzi's coming, too."

"That gossip?" She softened. "Well, she's in on *all* the marryings and buryings." She took a sip of wine and sighed.

Thinnes said, "I know this probably isn't a good time, Mrs. Ori, but we're still working on your nephew's death. Would you mind looking at some pictures for us? See if you recognize anyone?"

She nodded. Thinnes took a pack of Polaroids from his pocket and showed them to her one by one. The first three were District Nineteen tactical officers. She shook her head. The fourth was Limardi.

"That's my Eddie, my son!" She glared. "What's his picture doing with these criminals?"

"Those others were police officers." She seemed placated. "When was the last time you saw Eddie?"

"Eastertime." She must've realized how callous that made Eddie seem because she added, "He has his own life."

Thinnes nodded and showed her the next picture.

"Why, that's Brian Fahey."

"Where do you know him from, Mrs. Ori?"

"He went to school with Eddie. Long time ago."

"When was the last time you saw him, ma'am?" Oster asked.

"Three or four weeks ago." Thinnes and Oster looked at each other. "He was down on his luck. He said he lost his job and got evicted. I let him stay in Eddie's room. Eddie hasn't used it for years. He must've been in some very bad trouble, because he didn't say good-bye when he moved out."

They waited until they were sure she had nothing to add, then Thinnes showed her the sixth picture.

"Why that's another friend of Eddie's—Terry. He calls me Mom. He's renting Eddie's room from me—I would have let him stay for free, but he insisted."

"You seen him lately?" Oster asked.

"Now that you mention it, not for over a week. That's very strange. He used to come up all the time and ask was I okay in the heat? And did I want anything from the store?"

Thinnes looked at Oster; he shook his head. One bad news flash at a time. Thinnes showed her the rest of the pictures. She didn't recognize the two female patrol officers who'd stood in the lineup with Maria Cecci, but she recognized Cecci.

"That's a girl Eddie used to go with, years ago."

"Not recently?"

"Oh, no. She died. She went away to college, Eddie told me, and she died."

In a matter of speaking, Thinnes decided. Died for Limardi's purposes. He turned over the last picture, Helen Morgan, and was surprised when Mrs. Ori said, "I know her, too. I can't remember her name, but she used to have a crush on Eddie. She was always hanging around, mooning over him. He never cared much for her. I don't know why. She was nice enough but she wasn't so pretty when she was younger."

When was the last time you saw her?"

"Oh, a long time ago. Around the time Eddie graduated."

When they came back with Fuego and the warrant, the downstairs apartment, "Eddie's room," looked like the crazy uncles' place in *Unstrung Heroes*—wall-to-wall junk. Boxes had been piled up against the walls in the hallway to the point where you had to turn sideways to squeeze between them.

Thinnes walked to the "center" of the room and said, "Where the hell do you start?"

Fuego, who'd followed him, made a slow one-eighty degree turn, then pointed to a shelf of old notebooks. "Start with those. He must've had a reason to save them."

"Check this out." Oster held out a grimy photo album with age-yellow newspaper clippings glued to its pages. The glue made darker spots on the corners of the clippings. "We got any clue about this?"

Most of the articles were newspaper accounts of the Our Lady of Angels fire that had taken ninety-five lives in 1958, but there were a few pictures and accounts of other fires. There were also other albums filled with clippings about fires. The notebooks contained pages filled with neat lines of handwritten text, so small it could hardly be read without a magnifying glass. Thinnes tried to make out what it said; it reminded him of *Ulysses,* a book he'd had to read in school. One line—"I'd like to set the God-cursed city on fire"—seemed enough to justify seizing the notebooks as evidence, and the scrapbooks were a no-brainer.

"This is promising," Fuego said. "Let's get the lab to go over these for prints."

"Why?" Oster said. "Even if Limardi's prints are all over 'em, it's his room in his mother's house. He'll just say Fahey or Koslowski left it."

"Yeah, but he might have trouble explaining if *only* his prints are on things."

"And how do you know which is his stuff and what belongs to Fahey and Koslowski?"

"We'll sort it out. We got time. No statute of limitations on murder."

SIXTY-TWO

The Area Three squad room. Kate Ryan dropped her purse on the floor next to her chair; put down the rest of what she'd been carrying—large McDonald's soft drink, several files, a *Tribune,* and collapsed. Except for her red cheeks, she was a bright pink and beaded with sweat. She let out an exaggerated sigh.

Thinnes accepted the invitation. "Rough day?"

She laughed. "Day? Do you realize the average high for the *month* is ninety degrees?" She picked up her cup and rolled its sweaty surface over her cheeks and forehead, then took a long swallow.

The phone rang. Thinnes answered and told her, "For you."

"How'd they know I was here?"

"Good detective work."

She picked up and talked, then listened. When she hung up, she said, "That was the tac office. They've got my shooter in the Mackie case. He wants to deal."

Thinnes stood outside the interview room with officers Noir and Azul, the odd-couple tac team that had made the bust. Thinnes was admiring Ryan's technique, the other two critiquing her physique. The alleged offender was beginning to crumble.

"Jerry," she said. "We have an eyewitness. We have bullets recovered from the gun you were carrying. We have other witnesses who can put you in the neighborhood. What we need is why you did it. Maybe you had a good reason, a reason a jury would give you the benefit of the doubt over."

Jerry sat back and stretched his long legs out, and rested his scarred, gang-tattooed hands on his thighs. "I got the best reason there is." Ryan waited. "The man paid me to cap 'im."

"The man have a name?"

"Nope. He send me fifty shiny new twenties in a envelope with a note says I get the other half when this dude's history. Gave me the dude's car, an' plate, an' where to find 'im."

"Did you get the second installment?"

"Damn straight."

"From who?"

"Didn't give me no name. An' he was real careful that I didn't see his face. But he slipped up and I seen the car he was driving'." Ryan waited. "A big old white Mercedes."

SIXTY-THREE

Thinnes had discovered that the usual interview techniques didn't work on Dr. Caleb. The best way to get information out of him was to ask straight out. You didn't always get it, but you didn't get a load of shit either. Monday morning he left a message requesting that the doctor come in and talk.

By 2:00 P.M. the temperature was ninety-five degrees, and the *Sun-Times* headline pretty much described the situation: "City Goes on Heat Attack Cooling Sites, Hotlines Help Some Find Relief." Caleb came in looking like he'd just come from one of the cooling sites.

Thinnes noticed something different about him right off—hard to put a finger on what. If it had been one of the other detectives, he'd have asked if he'd just gotten lucky—but Caleb . . . He realized his unwillingness to ask Caleb was because the doctor was gay, and if he'd gotten lucky, Thinnes really didn't want to know.

The line from a song came to mind as he led Caleb to the conference room. "When a man loves a woman . . ."

What would a man do if he loved another man? Thinnes knew some of the things. He'd investigated enough domestic disputes turned ugly between gay lovers. Sometimes the only differences from straight lovers' quarrels was an increase in the violence because both combatants were strong and fueled by testosterone. He recalled the thought he'd had about Morgan at the funeral—maybe he was gay. He should have followed up on that.

When Oster'd joined them, and they were all sitting around the conference table, Thinnes said, "Tell us about benzodiazepines, Doctor."

Caleb looked surprised briefly, then said cautiously, "They're a class of drugs, including Librium and Valium, used to treat anxiety."

"You ever prescribe 'em?"

"Yes, occasionally."

"To Dr. Morgan?"

"He's not my patient. No."

"How 'bout Mrs. Morgan?"

"No."

"How well do you know Dr. Morgan?"

"We're friends."

"Close?"

"That depends on what you mean by close."

"Would you stick your neck out for him?"

"I might."

"Lie for him?"

"Possibly."

"To the police?"

"No."

"Would you sleep with him?" Thinnes heard Oster gasp. Caleb didn't seem fazed. "If he asked me."

"Did you sleep with him?"

"Did you ask him that?"

"You got a thing for Dr. Morgan?"

"Why do you ask?"

"It ever cross your mind that if you've got a thing for him, maybe he's got a thing for you?"

"It has. So?"

"Why'd he file for divorce?"

"Did you ask him?"

"Yeah. I want your version."

"He told me that his wife had been unfaithful, but that they'd been drifting apart for some time."

"That all?"

"Does there need to be more?"

"What about the kids? I didn't see that dragon-lady wife of his letting him have custody if she knew he's gay."

"Why do you assume he's gay?

"Hypothetically."

"Hypothetically, his wife's death wouldn't change anything. His mother-in-law is equally fierce and would also like to have custody."

"Maybe." Thinnes shook his head in frustration. "This isn't getting us anywhere. Talk to me, Jack. What do you know?"

"There's no hell as painful as uncertainty. Martin seems like a decent man, and I'm attracted to him. If I knew anything that would clear him or convict him, I'd tell you."

"Where do your loyalties lie?"

"With the truth."

"Which is?"

"I don't know," Caleb said. "But tell me this. Did you stop looking when you decided on Martin?"

"No, I didn't."

"What's this really about?"

"Money."

"No. It's more than that. People kill for money but they don't set fire to living beings for money."

"He had her insured for a lot of it."

"How much did she have *him* insured for?"

"You were a little hard on the doc, weren't you, Thinnes?" Oster asked. "I thought we'd established he's on our side."

"He's not telling us everything. It pisses me off."

Oster shrugged. "How long's he been gay?"

"Probably all his life."

"You know what I mean—you knew." There was a little resentment in his tone, implying, why didn't you tell your partner?

"Yeah," Thinnes said. "I guess we all got something we're not telling."

"Isn't that what I just said?"

SIXTY-FOUR

We got an impressive roster of victims here," Fuego said. He and Oster and Thinnes were sitting in the case management office, laying out the case for the sergeant, who was sitting on the edge of one of the desks; Evanger was sitting behind it. He had pen and paper handy.

"There's Mackie," Fuego continued. "And, probably, Ronzani, Fahey, Morgan, Koslowski, and Linda Koslowski."

"How 'bout the Smith brothers?" the sergeant said.

Thinnes said, "I think they were just criminally incompetent, and their luck ran out."

"Who're we looking at?" Evanger asked.

"Ed Limardi, Michael Wellman, and Dr. Morgan."

Evanger wrote down the names. "What have they got for motives?"

"I checked on Franco Ori's will," Oster said. "He set up a trust for the widow. She gets use of the house and income from the property during her lifetime. Then it's all split between Limardi and his cousins."

"Who are?"

"Were. Dino Ori. And an Angela Ori."

"Who's Angela Ori?"

"I'm workin' on that."

"So Limardi might've killed Aldo Ronzani," Evanger said,

"and Dino Ori—if we could prove he was murdered—to inherit. Why kill the others?"

"Maybe they knew too much," Thinnes said.

"What about Michael Wellman?"

"He stands to make a lot on the real estate he acquired. Ronzani wouldn't sell to him."

"Why would he kill the others?"

"Maybe they knew too much," Oster said.

"And Dr. Morgan?"

"He was divorcing his wife," Thinnes said. "And I think he may be gay. He'd lose a custody fight if that came out. Plus, he had a $500,000 life insurance policy on the wife—double indemnity. People have been killed for a lot less."

Evanger nodded. "And *he* might have killed the others because they knew too much. What have they all got for alibis?"

"Nobody's got much of an alibi for any of the deaths except Morgan's," Thinnes said.

"Wellman's is his chauffeur," Oster said. "He can't drive, so any place he goes, his chauffeur goes."

"And he's never heard of cabs or busses?"

Oster shrugged. "That's his story."

"Dr. Morgan claims he was home with his kids," Oster said, "every night but one the past year."

"Where was he the one?"

"Claims he had too much to drink and a friend checked him into a downtown hotel."

"Did the friend stay with him all night?"

"Not that he mentioned. The desk clerk remembered them. And that Morgan was too drunk to stand up."

"What about Limardi?" Evanger said.

"He has an alibi for Morgan's death and claims he never heard of the others. Wanted to know if I could tell him where *I* was on the other dates."

"Could you?"

Oster laughed.

Thinnes said, "But Limardi's mother told us he went to school with Fahey, Koslowski, Helen Morgan, and Maria Cecci, who was in on Banks's murder."

"What about Cox?" Fuego asked. "Cox is the real estate broker Helen Morgan worked for," he told Evanger.

"The killer drove a white Mercedes," Thinnes said. "That lets Cox off the hook. He drives a big black Cadillac with vanity plates—MR COX. Parks it out in front of his place in the bus stop."

"How do you know the killer drives a Mercedes?" Evanger asked.

"Mackie's killer told us."

"What else have we got?"

Fuego summarized: "One, we have a peculiar religious cult with enough money—from unknown sources—to buy and rehab a small church. It takes in excons, nutcases, and runaways. Two, Helen Morgan died in a fire of roughly the same MO Fahey tried to use to kill officer Nolan last spring. And three, we have the same MO in the deaths of Fahey, Ronzani, and the two Koslowskis—victim was drugged with a tranquilizer and died of smoke inhalation in a fire set up to look accidental or like a botched arson attempt. We gotta see all these cases as connected. Most of the players go way back together."

"So how do you figure it?" Evanger said.

"It looks like someone got the idea for Morgan's murder from Fahey's botched attempt on Nolan—maybe the same guy who killed Fahey."

"Who?"

Fuego said, "Probably Koslowski. He roomed with Fahey in Stateville—they must've talked about what they were in for—and he and Fahey both holed up in Limardi's mother's basement. My money's on Limardi being behind all of it."

"The three of them go way back," Thinnes added. "I think we can assume that what Fahey knew, Koslowski knew, and he told whoever he was working for."

"But why would Koslowski kill Fahey? And who killed Koslowski?"

"Whoever put him up to killing Morgan. With Fahey gone, Morgan's killer's our best bet. And, I'd be willing to put money on it, that it's either Limardi or Dr. Morgan."

"And one of them killed Linda Koslowski?"

"One of the three," Fuego said. "Limardi, Morgan, or Wellman."

"I'm going to talk to Nolan tomorrow," Thinnes said. "Maybe he'll remember something helpful. Meanwhile, we'll just keep turning the pieces around until we fit them—"

Evanger interrupted him. "What can we do for you, Doctor?"

Thinnes turned around; Caleb was standing in the open doorway. He wondered how much of the conversation the doctor had overheard.

"I want to help," Caleb said.

"Forget it, Doc," Thinnes said. "Go home. Let us deal with it."

SIXTY-FIVE

It was Patrolman Nolan's day off. Thinnes located him at home, and when he opened his door, he was covered with paint. "Mind coming in the kitchen?" he said, after inviting Thinnes in. "I promised my wife I'd have it done when she gets home from work. She's having some friends over."

Thinnes sat on a chair and watched him roll pale-green semigloss on the wall over the sink without wasting time or paint. He probably didn't spend as much thought on Thinnes's questions as he should have, but he repeated the story he'd told at the hospital without any changes or omissions.

"I looked over the rap sheets and arrest records of the ass-holes you nailed—hope they fry in hell," he said. "None of 'em anyone I know or ever arrested." He got down from the chair he was standing on and filled his roller with paint, then climbed back up to apply it to the wall. "What's this about?"

"We had an agg-arson recently, car fire. Same MO as yours."

Nolan got down and put down his roller. "That the Mercedes that was torched?"

"Yeah."

"My wife knew the victim. Went to school with her."

"No shit! Did *you* know her?"

"Nah. It was in high school—before my time. And she

didn't know her well enough to go to the wake or anything; she just recalled the face when she saw it in the paper."

"What time does your wife get home?"

"Five-ish."

"I'll be back. Meantime, watch your back. If I'm right, whoever was behind Banks's murder may have really been after you."

"What in hell for?"

"If we knew that, we'd know who we're looking for."

"I thought you finally got all the assholes that killed Banks."

"I wouldn't bet my life on it."

Angela Ori Nolan—Angie—lit a cigarette and took a long drag before she answered the question, "What was Dino Ori to you?"

"My cousin. But we weren't close."

"Your father and his father were brothers?"

"Yeah. They're both dead now. So's my aunt. Dino was her and my uncle's only kid."

"He was a waste of sperm," Nolan volunteered.

"Don't, Paul," she said. "It's bad luck to speak ill of the dead." Nolan made a face and shook his head. Angie continued. "I didn't even go to his funeral—not that I missed anything. My aunt went—another aunt, not Dino's ma. My aunt told me she and the priest and Mrs. Renzi were the only ones who showed up, which shows how much of a deadbeat Dino was. He didn't even have a friend who'd come to his funeral."

Thinnes said, "I understand you knew Helen Morgan?"

"Yeah."

"Well?"

"Nah. And she wasn't Helen Morgan then, she was Helen Kerrigan. Morgan must be her married name. In high school, she had the hots for another cousin of mine and was always hanging around his house. I don't know why. He was dating someone else."

"Who?"

"A girl named Maria Cecci."

Serena.

". . . And after Maria died, he asked me out a couple of times." Angie took another pull on the cigarette and gave her husband an affectionate look. "That was before I met Paul."

Thinnes said, "What did Maria die of?"

"Eddie told me a drug overdose. It was years ago. She was in college. He didn't go into detail. I thought he just didn't want to talk about her because it kinda ticked him off that she went away to school instead of marrying him."

"Would it surprise you to learn that she's still alive?"

"No!"

"Yes."

Angie said, "Why would that lying? . . . Eddie. I'll bet he couldn't admit a girl would throw him over."

"Where is she?" Nolan asked.

"In a hospital for the criminally insane. She was the woman who flagged you down in the alley that night."

"No shit!"

"I'm amazed you didn't know."

"I was pretty out of it for a while. And by the time I got back to work, they told me I wouldn't have to testify 'cause the douche bags that killed Arlette had copped pleas."

Thinnes said, "Angie, tell me about your cousin Eddie."

"Eddie Limardi. We used to call him mostly Malarky 'cause he was full of it, but he could talk people into things. Most of the time, I think *he* even believed his BS."

"What's he doing now?"

"I haven't kept in touch, but his ma—she's the aunt that

went to Dino's funeral—tells me he's selling Mercedes-Benzes. Like that makes him not a car salesman."

"You ever meet Martin Morgan?"

"Helen's husband?" Thinnes nodded. "No."

"How about Michael Wellman?"

"The name sounds familiar but . . ."

"The developer?" Nolan interrupted.

"That's him."

They both shook their heads.

"Did Eddie have any close male friends?"

"Oh, sure, in school. Back then, we didn't have these vicious gangs—Kings or GDs or Vice Lords. Most of the guys hung out with other guys from their neighborhood. And they were mostly divided up by nationality—you know, Irish or Poles or Italians." She looked at her husband. "We got a lot of flak 'cause we didn't marry 'our own kind.' " She took a drag on the cigarette and tapped the ash off into an ashtray. "Eddie and his friends go way back—went to Catholic grammar school together, then public high school. 'Til Brian—I can't remember his last name—dropped out. We used to call 'em the unholy trinity cause it wasn't natural—them being all different. Eddie was Italian, of course, but the other two were Irish and Polish. The Polack was Terry something—I forget. But I think I got an old yearbook somewhere if it would help."

It would.

SIXTY-SIX

Thinnes," Oster said, "Angela Ori is—"

"Nolan's wife."

Thinnes was instantly sorry he'd said it.

"So what did I spend half a day burning up the phone lines to find that out for?" Oster looked like he'd spent half a day digging ditches.

"Corroboration? Why don't you take the other half the day off?" This in spite of the fact that it was almost 7:00 P.M.

"What, are you my boss now?"

Thinnes let it go.

"You got a request to call Dr. Tambourine at her hospital or stop by and see her. She gets off at nine." Before Thinnes could comment, Oster went back to what he'd been doing.

Thinnes looked up the number in his case notes and called. He had to wait a long time for the woman who answered the phone to tell him the doctor wouldn't be free for half an hour.

Half an hour later, an aide led him to the room in the hospital that they'd used to interview Serena. Dr. Tambourine was sitting cross-legged on an end of one of the couches with a tissue box next to her. She gestured toward the couch's other end. She looked older than Thinnes, even older than he felt. She said, "Please sit down, Detective Thinnes." He sat. "I thought you'd want to know. Maria Cecci killed herself last night."

"Are you sure she wasn't—"

"She locked herself in the shower room, plugged up the toilet, and drowned in it. The door was locked from inside—we had to break in."

"How the hell did she *do* it?"

"She put her head in the bowl and wrapped her arms around the joint between the base and the tank. And she tied her hands together with a strip of towel so she wouldn't save herself by falling off when she passed out."

"Christ!"

Dr. Tambourine shook her head and blinked back tears.

Thinnes softened his voice.

"Did she have any visitors or phone calls recently?"

"A phone call. A man who said he went to school with her. He said his name was Brian Fahey."

Not! as Rob would say. Chalk up another victim. Thinnes wondered what Limardi had said to her to make her do it. He was sure it was Limardi.

"Ordinarily, we wouldn't have let her take the call, but the regular aide was off. . . . Two hours later, she'd drowned."

She handed Thinnes a small, leather-bound book. "Someone sent her this, day before yesterday."

It was a Catholic version of the Bible. As Thinnes paged through it, a small piece of paper fell out. He retrieved it and read it. "One dies in fire. One dies in water. So do we all belong to death and go to our place." He held it up. "What *is* this?"

"Something she told me she found in *Gale's Quotations,* a proverb from Togo."

"It sounds to me like a suicide note." He read it again and added, "or an epitaph."

One dies in water.

"You're a popular man tonight, Thinnes," the sergeant said, when Thinnes walked into the squad room. "Packages . . ." He handed Thinnes a messenger service envelope. "Visitors . . ." He hitched his thumb toward the desk nearest the coffee setup, where Dr. Morgan was sitting, drumming on the desktop with his fingers. Good timing.

Morgan spotted Thinnes. He got up and hurried over with a grim expression. He was carrying a letter-size manila envelope.

"Come with me, Doctor," Thinnes said. He led the way to the conference room. "You want some coffee?"

Morgan shook his head.

When they were seated at the conference table, Thinnes opened the envelope and took out a letter. Printed. Probably on a laser printer, which made it essentially untraceable. Unsigned. It said, "You've gone to a lot of trouble to remove certain obstacles to your success. For a modest additional investment, you can insure your efforts won't have been for nothing. Page me." There was a phone number. Also inside the manila envelope was a plain white business envelope with "Dr. Martin Morgan" printed on it above Morgan's home address. The stamp was an American flag. The postmark was local. Thinnes looked up to find Morgan watching him.

"Someone thinks I'm guilty of something," he said. "And that I can be blackmailed. I want him caught."

Thinnes studied the letter. The number was familiar but it took a minute to place it.

"I'm sorry," Morgan said. "I handled it before I thought of fingerprints."

"That's all right." He opened the messenger envelope that the sergeant had given him. It was from Michael Wellman. It contained a copy of the same "blackmail" letter Morgan had just given him, along with a note to Thinnes stating that this was the sort of "offer" Wellman thought was made by the "wrong element." Thinnes put it back in the envelope.

"Who's watching your kids?" he asked Morgan.

"They're spending a few days with their grandmother. She's—"

A tap on the window between the conference and squad rooms interrupted him. Evanger was outside, crooking his finger at Thinnes.

"Excuse me a minute, Doctor," Thinnes said. He brought the letters out to the squad room with him.

As he closed the door, Evanger was telling Oster, "Go home, Carl." He turned to Thinnes. "What's this about?" He handed Thinnes a photocopy.

Evanger hadn't worked nights since the department went to permanent assignments, so Thinnes ignored his question and asked the obvious: "What's up?"

"Rossi called in sick. "You know anything about this?" He tapped the photocopy he'd handed Thinnes.

Thinnes read it—the photocopy of a letter sent by James A. Caleb, M.D., informing the department that he was resigning as a consultant due to a conflict of interest. Copies to Commander, Area Three Detectives. It had the same font style and size as the two "blackmail" notes.

Thinnes put it together immediately. "Dr. Caleb's a loose cannon," he said. "He can't take no for an answer, and it looks like he's gone on a little bear hunt with himself for bait." He handed Evanger the letter Morgan had given him.

Evanger read it and said, "Where'd you get this?"

Thinnes pointed to the conference room window, through which they could see Dr. Morgan.

"Has it been dusted for prints?"

"No need. If it has any, they're Caleb's. That's his pager number. He sent the same letter to Michael Wellman. And I'll bet he sent it to Limardi, too."

"Why, for God's sake?"

"Not God's sake. For Dr. Morgan's sake. Apparently

275

they're good friends, and Caleb can't stand the suspense of not knowing whether his friend is a murderer."

"Presumably, when he gets this, the killer will try to pay Dr. Caleb off, or kill him?"

"Yeah. And I'm pretty sure that'll be Limardi."

"Well, throw a net over Dr. Caleb and talk to the state's attorney about getting a warrant for Limardi before he kills someone else."

Thinnes tried Caleb's pager first—the number on the "blackmail" notes. He didn't really expect an answer, but he left his cell-phone number anyway. He called Caleb's condo and left a message on the answering machine, then called his office. He got the answering service number from the answering machine's recorded message and called the service. If this was an emergency, they could page Dr. Caleb or Dr. Fenwick. "I paged Dr. Caleb already," Thinnes told the woman. "Give me Dr. Fenwick's number."

"I'm sorry. I can't—"

"I'm a police officer and Dr. Caleb may be in danger," Thinnes told her. He gave her his star number and told her to call him back at Area Three detective headquarters. After a few minutes, she did. Her standard procedure was to page the doctor, which she'd done as soon as Thinnes called. Dr. Fenwick had not returned the page, so under the circumstances, she agreed to give Thinnes his number.

Thinnes called. Dr. Fenwick didn't know where Caleb was either, but he did know his partner's plans for dinner. Thinnes had to threaten to send a squad of uniformed cops to interview everyone in the restaurant in order to confirm that Caleb had been there and to get Caleb's waiter on the line, but it was worth it. The waiter was able to say that Caleb had been paged during dessert and had ordered a cab. He even saved Thinnes the hassle of trying to track down the cabby—he'd heard Caleb tell the driver where he was going.

Oster was still there—sitting at his desk in a haze. When Thinnes hung up, Oster came out of it and said, "What's up?"

"Dr. Caleb may have just caught our tiger by the tail."

Oster wiped his face with his hand and yawned. "Where're we going?"

"Sears Tower. It has to be Wellman's office."

"What about him?" Oster hitched his thumb toward the conference room.

Through the window Thinnes could see that Morgan had put his head on the table and apparently gone to sleep. Thinnes hurried in to wake him. "Doctor, go home."

Morgan stared at him and stifled a yawn. "Did you find him?"

"Who?"

"The blackmailer?"

"Not yet. You go home. We'll be in touch."

Out in the squad room, Oster was bringing Evanger up to speed. ". . . Caleb went to the Sears Tower. He may be in trouble. . . ."

Morgan obviously heard. He stopped.

Thinnes said, "Good-bye, Doctor."

Morgan walked out without arguing. But when Thinnes pulled the Caprice out onto Clybourn Avenue, a white Volvo wagon fell in behind.

SIXTY-SEVEN

Caleb arrived at the Sears Tower and bypassed the desk. The security guard on duty apparently didn't think a well-dressed man a threat, because he didn't challenge him. The elevator let him off on a deserted floor and he followed the numbers to Wellman's offices. He knew the developer slightly, having met him at various social functions. He would not have guessed Wellman was a killer.

Fridays most people left early, and this late on any evening one would expect the office floor to be deserted. The door to Wellman's suite was closed but not locked, the reception area empty. Caleb called out; he got no answer. He played the cat, silently prowling the carpeted hall. The door at the end of the hall was open, and he stepped into Wellman's private preserve. It had a spectacular view of Grant Park, the lake, and Lake Shore Drive. Wellman, himself, was sitting propped in his chair behind the huge table that functioned as his desk. His pupils were dilated, his breathing dangerously slow. Caleb felt for a carotid pulse and found it weak and irregular. As he reached for the phone, he caught a movement off to his side.

"Don't touch that!"

Caleb turned to see the speaker, a blond man with pale blue eyes and a deep tan. The impression made by the expensive suit and haircut was unmade by the pistol he was pointing.

"Mr. Limardi, I presume," Caleb said. He turned so that his right side was toward Limardi and he could keep an eye on Wellman, to his left.

"Who the hell are you?"

"A friend of Dr. Morgan's."

"Where is he?"

"At home with his family."

"How did you find out about me?"

"It didn't take too much effort." Caleb kept his right hand at his side, where Limardi could see it, and reached into his suit-coat pocket, with his left, for his cell phone. He slid the cover up and pushed the on button, then pressed *999. He'd practiced this for the odd emergency until he could do it with either hand. "Mrs. Morgan was in real estate," he said, by way of a distraction. "Someone profited from her death or her silence, and it wasn't her husband."

"No, it was Wellman here."

"I think not. I think she knew something about *you* that made her a liability."

Limardi seemed shaken. "Do the police know this?"

"I have to believe they do. Collectively, they're at least as able to make an inference as I."

"Too bad for you. What have you got in your pocket?"

Caleb let go of the phone—carefully, so as not to inadvertently turn it off—and took hold of the other item he was carrying. He switched on the tiny pocket tape recorder as he pulled it out and held it where Limardi could see it.

"So this wasn't about blackmail after all," Limardi said. "You thought you'd trap me." Caleb said nothing. Keeping the gun on him, Limardi glided forward and snatched the recorder. He shut it off and put it in his pocket. "He who rides the tiger . . . You have as long to live as Wellman here—until he stops breathing. That should be very soon."

"What did you do to him?"

279

Limardi smiled. "He's taken an overdose of Valium. Washed it down with too much Chivas. Too bad."

"The police will trace the pills."

"Oh, it was his own prescription. Bought so long ago the pharmacist's delivery boy won't remember him. He's used it to kill a number of people."

"Who?"

"Let's see. There was Brian Fahey and his buddy Terry, and his fucking sister, and old man Ronzani. Ronzani had some property Wellman wanted. And he got it."

"What did Mr. Wellman do to you?"

"Not what he did. What he didn't—acknowledge my existence. He was too good to even pick up the car he bought from me—he sent a flunky. He could've been my partner. . . ." He waved the gun impatiently. "How did you find out about me?"

"Helen Morgan." It was from the newspaper account of her death, actually, and what he'd overheard at Area Three but . . .

"Why would she tell you?" Limardi demanded.

"You think you were the only one she was fooling around with?"

That got to him. His jaw clenched briefly.

"Why did you kill her?"

"The faithless slut thought I was going to marry her. After cheating on a man she'd been married to for fifteen years, she honestly thought I would trust her to be faithful to me!"

Both of them looked at Wellman. He took a deep, hiccupy breath and expelled it.

"Why did you kill Brian Fahey and . . . Terry, was it?"

"Brian was an incompetent fool! I sent him to eliminate Nolan and he killed some woman, instead. Terry fucked up, too. The greedy bastard hijacked a truck. And he expected *me* to help him hide it!"

"I see."

"You have no idea what this is about!"

280

"It's about power, isn't it?"

"Is it?"

Caleb waited, let the suspense of his silence drag the answer from the man.

"I could cheerfully burn down this whole fucking city."

"Why?" He said it softly.

"Complete combustion yields heat and light and clean elements."

Or what seems like elements, Caleb thought. Fire as Kali, goddess of destruction. Very Jungian. And the aftermath of fire is a new start, rebuilding, redevelopment.

"My sister died in a fire," Limardi said. "The Our Lady of Angels fire—December first, 1958. I was five. She was in eighth grade. And just ten years later, the '68 riots, I watched Watts and the west side burn."

From the safety of his parents living room, no doubt.

"Look at the west side now!" Limardi grinned. "Rebirth!"

Caleb ventured a glance at Wellman—pale, but still breathing—barely.

Fire was the rapid oxidation of a combustible material, releasing energy that could be used for good or evil. There was terror as well as attraction in the idea of controlling something so powerful. It paralleled the child's love/hate relationship with his omnipotent parent, or in this case, a God that failed. "What happened to your sister?" Caleb asked.

"The *blessed* nuns. Not a competent adult among them. *They* let her burn. They prayed the rosary when they should have been *doing something*. They put their faith in God—there *is* no God! No! *I'm* God. I have the power of life and death. *I control fire.*"

We all try to master our fates. "Your sister was very important to you."

"She was more a mother to me than my mother ever was." Limardi smiled. "Fire's more powerful than God! I control fire. That makes me more powerful than God!"

SIXTY-EIGHT

When they pulled up outside the Franklin Street entrance to the Sears Tower, Thinnes was afraid they were too late. The backup he'd called for was parked in front with Mars lights blazing. Thinnes pulled behind them, and they ran inside. The lobby seemed to be filled with cops and security guards— people with radios milling around near the elevators. With Oster in tow, Thinnes pushed his way to the center and flashed his star. "Thinnes, Area Three. Where are we?"

A patrol sergeant answered. "We had a *999 call in from here before you called, and we'd already started looking for the caller. Can we assume it's your guy?"

"Phone registered to James Caleb?" The sergeant nodded. "It's him."

The security supervisor, ID clipped to his lapel, said, "Mr. Wellman's up there. I sent someone up when we got your call. When he saw a man up there with a gun, he called down for backup. He's been keeping an eye on the suite entrance."

"Let's get up there," the patrol sergeant said.

"Let's get organized first," Thinnes said. "We haven't got a clue what we're going to find, and we don't need any bystanders getting hurt." He tried to recall the layout. "Is there a back way up?"

One of the security men reversed a form on his clipboard

and sketched the floor plan of Wellman's suite. The inner office was L-shaped, and if you stood against the outside wall, you could see the whole room. Not much chance of a surprise attack. Trying to come up with something, Thinnes looked around. He spotted Martin Morgan coming through the door. The doctor stopped just inside. Thinnes pointed him out to one of the uniforms. "Get that civilian out of here."

The copper walked over and started to push Morgan out. Morgan resisted. "I want to help, Detective," he shouted. "My friend's up there."

The cop looked at Thinnes. Thinnes got an idea. "Let him come," he told the cop.

"You fuckin' nuts?" Oster demanded.

"We need a diversion. Dr. Morgan can call Wellman and raise hell over the phone while we get in position. If he can get Caleb on the line, maybe *he* can let us know what's going on."

"I'll get more backup," the patrol sergeant said, "and clear the street in case somebody decides to start shooting."

The phone had been ringing for five minutes when Caleb said, "They know someone's here. If we don't answer, they'll just come up."

Wellman was still breathing—barely.

"Answer it," Limardi said. His grip tightened on the pistol. His hand shook. "Be careful what you say."

Caleb picked up and said, "Hello."

"Jack, is that you?" Martin's voice.

Caleb said, "Yes," cautiously.

"Thank God you're alive."

"Who is it?" Limardi demanded.

"Martin Morgan."

"Is there someone up there with you?" Martin asked.

"Michael Wellman."

"What's he saying?" Limardi growled. He cocked the gun.

Caleb put a hand over the mouthpiece. "He wanted to know if anyone else is here."

"Tell him no. Ask him what he wants."

"Tell him," Thinnes said, "That you figured out who killed your wife and you want to talk to him about it. Tell him you're on your way up."

The security guard on lookout greeted the reinforcements like the Bulls welcoming M.J. back. Thinnes sent him down to the lobby. He left Dr. Morgan by the elevators with orders to stay out of sight. "Give us two minutes, then call and say the outside door is locked."

Thinnes, Oster, and the two uniform coppers slipped into the suite and took cover in the reception area. After what seemed like forever, the phone rang in Wellman's inner office.

It stopped ringing. Nothing happened for a full minute.

When the door at the end of the hallway opened, a man was silhouetted in the doorway, backlit. Jack Caleb! Behind him, parts of the room were visible in reflection from the wall of windows. Eddie Limardi was out of Thinnes's direct line of fire, but Thinnes could see his blurred image in the distorted mirror of the windows. Thinnes aimed beyond the silhouette of Caleb and said, "Hit the floor, Doctor."

Caleb dropped into the hall.

In the reflection, Limardi darted for the door and slammed it shut.

Caleb said, "Wellman's in there." He started crawling toward the cops.

"Come on out, Limardi," Thinnes shouted.

"Go away or Wellman's a dead man!"

Standoff.

"Now what?" Oster said.

"Now we wait," Thinnes said. "Call in the SWAT team and hostage negotiators."

"Wellman will die," Caleb said, "if he doesn't get treatment immediately."

"I'm open to suggestions. Doctor?"

"We're not dealing with a rational individual."

"What gave you your first clue?" Oster said.

Thinnes's radio crackled as the SWAT team commander announced they were coming up. "Don't shoot the civilian in the hallway," Thinnes told him.

"He's being awfully quiet in there," Oster said. "Doc, can you talk to him?"

Caleb nodded.

"Stay out of the line of fire," Thinnes said.

Caleb moved to the corner at the end of the hall and called out, "Edward. Edward, you need to come out now."

There was no answer. The absence of gunfire was the only hopeful sign. The SWAT team slithered into the room and deployed themselves. The leader came up behind Caleb with a bullhorn and said, "Edward Limardi, put down the gun and come out." Moments passed. Caleb retreated to the reception area. Thinnes looked over and saw Oster ease himself into a sitting position on the floor and begin to rub his chest. The SWAT team conferred among themselves in whispers.

Then all hell broke loose. They smelled smoke at the moment an alarm began to sound. Smoke began pouring out above Wellman's office door. Caleb suddenly charged past the SWAT members in the hall and started kicking in the door. "Cover him!" Thinnes shouted.

The door gave. Caleb fell into the office as choking smoke poured out. He crawled into the smoke-filled room and disappeared.

Thinnes charged after him, past the SWAT team. Smoke filled all but the lower two feet of the room. There was no light, not even from the fire. He dived under the smoke. The alarm vibrated through the choking atmosphere, filling the room with panic. Automatic sprinklers added water to the chaos.

As Thinnes dropped his face to the floor to breathe, his face met with Caleb's foot. Thinnes was forced to back up as the foot came toward him. He grabbed it and hauled as he scrambled back into the hall. Caleb was pulling someone out by the shirt collar. Both were gasping and wheezing. In spite of the confusion, Thinnes was aware of the SWAT team moving closer to cover them. He hacked and lurched forward to help Caleb. As they dragged the body toward the fresh air, Thinnes realized that it was Wellman. "Offender's still in there," he managed to gasp. He and Caleb kept backing up. The SWAT team stepped over them, into the smoke.

Dr. Morgan was waiting in the reception area, hovering over Oster. When they dragged Wellman in, Morgan transferred his attention to the developer. He and Caleb moved Wellman out near the elevators and began doing CPR without missing a beat.

As Thinnes located his radio to call for paramedics, the SWAT team came gasping back down the hall. "He's gotta be done for," one of them said. "Nobody can breathe in there."

It took sixty seconds for them to strike the fire, once they got the hoses in place, and another fifteen minutes to evacuate the smoke. They found no trace of Limardi. "He was in there," Thinnes insisted. But after they'd gone over the entire office suite he began to wonder.

"Detective," one of the firemen said. "Here's where it started." He pointed to the charred remains of a matchbook under Wellman's pool table. "The old cigarette in the matchbook device." The fireman shook his head. "Simple but effective. Gotta give this guy credit. He started it where the sprinklers wouldn't put it out right away."

Thinnes shook his head. "All I want to know is how he got out of here."

"Probably through there." The fireman pointed to the dropped acoustical tile ceiling from which several squares were missing. "If he was in good shape, he just hoists hisself up and waits 'til the fire gets going good, then drops down on the other side of the wall and walks away in the confusion." He led the way back out of Wellman's office and down the hall to a point in the reception area opposite the missing ceiling panels—the door to the washroom.

Thinnes took out his gun and aimed at the door, then jerked it open. The room was empty. But there were ceiling panels missing in there, too. "Damn it!" He backed back into the reception area and looked out into the outside hall.

Caleb and Morgan had relinquished care of Wellman to the paramedics, who were strapping him onto a stretcher. Oster was sitting on the floor against the wall, looking gray, breathing as if it hurt. Firemen and cops were coming and going; two security guards were standing by, gawking. Any number of people could have passed through since the fire was struck. "Somebody got a working phone?" he asked. Caleb did. Thinnes called Evanger and got Limardi's description out.

As he handed the phone back, he saw Morgan go over and kneel next to Oster. Morgan took hold of Oster's wrist. Oster made a half-assed attempt to pull away, but the MD persisted. "You're having a heart attack, Detective." he said. "You need to go to a hospital immediately."

"You don't get it," Oster said. "I check into a hospital with a bad pump, I'm finished as a cop."

"There is life after the department, Carl," Thinnes said.

"Yeah. Move to Wisconsin and open a bait shop."

"Or become a consultant," Thinnes said. "And make three times as much for what you're doing now. You gonna check out and leave Norma to deal with the mess?"

Oster glared at him. "Damn you, Thinnes." His expression softened. "At least we ID'd the SOB"

"And we'll get him."

Oster looked from Thinnes to Caleb. "Fuckin' three musketeers."

"Look at the bright side, Carl." Thinnes said.

"There's a bright side?"

"This'll get you out of the paperwork."

SIXTY-NINE

While they were loading Oster in the ambulance, Thinnes noticed Caleb give Morgan a hug. For the briefest moment, he envied them—straight men made do with handshakes; hugs were only tolerated at wakes and funerals—barely. Caleb met his gaze, then looked away. The moment passed leaving Thinnes feeling—as he had before—that the doctor was a step ahead of him.

Morgan went with Oster to the hospital. Thinnes kept Caleb with him. "We have a little paperwork to do, Doctor," was the closest he came to giving Caleb a piece of his mind.

Thinnes was sure Limardi was long gone, so they didn't wait around for a complete search of the building. They left it to the uniforms and building security. Thinnes called the Area to report to Evanger and sent patrol units to Limardi's apartment and Mrs. Ori's house. They were halfway back to headquarters when Caleb's cell phone rang—Dr. Morgan calling from the hospital.

"Detective Oster insisted that I call with information he'd forgotten in the excitement. He asked me to tell you that Limardi owns the storage building south of the factory where you found Dino Ori. He said it's a long shot, but you need to know anyway."

"Thanks, Martin." Caleb hung up.

Thinnes borrowed the phone to call Fuego at home. "We'll meet you there."

Fuego was waiting for them outside the warehouse. Thinnes hadn't paid much attention to it before. Now he got out of the car and studied it carefully—old, solid brick and masonry, two stories, the top floor disappearing into the darkness above the reach of the streetlights. It was closed up tight, with iron grills covering high, grime-coated windows on both upper and lower stories. It had two overhead garage doors and a standard door facing the street. In back, a metal door opened outward into the alley, where an unmarked car was parked in the shadows. The two tactical cops in the car made Thinnes for a detective as soon as they spotted him. "What's happenin', man?"

"We've got a search warrant coming. When it gets here, how 'bout you back your car up against this door so it won't open?"

"Yeah. Meanwhile, we'll just prowl around, keep an eye on things."

Thinnes strolled casually to the end of the block as if walking an invisible dog. The only sign that Oster's hunch was on target was a Mercedes convertible with dealer plates parked around the corner in a residential block. Even surrounded by other cars, it jumped out at him.

He went back to his car and alerted patrol, asking for a car to come out and watch it. Then he called Evanger to expedite the paperwork on the search warrant.

"Now what?" Fuego asked. He was sitting in the front, next to Thinnes. Caleb sat in back.

"Now we sit on the hole and wait for the rat to show his nose."

To pass the time, they compared notes. "What happened up there, Jack?" Thinnes said, "What did he tell you?"

"More than he would have if he thought I'd get away. He let his mask of sanity slip, going on about controlling fire and being more powerful than God. I gather killing Arlette Banks was a mistake. He sent Brian Fahey and Maria Cecci to kill Officer Nolan, but I'm sure he never revealed his real agenda. When I intervened, they murdered the cop they had at hand because Fahey thought they were just avenging Brother John."

"Maria Cecci's dead, by the way," Thinnes told him. "Suicide, with a little push over the edge."

"Why Nolan?" Fuego asked.

Thinnes answered. "So Nolan's widow would be free to remarry. Limardi. He signed her yearbook, 'Your kissing cousin.' "

Fuego thought about that. "I can see why he had to get rid of Fahey, but what about the others?"

"Ronzani was his maternal uncle," Thinnes said. "Limardi must've found out how the property was left—maybe from Helen Morgan. Once his mother inherited, it was just a matter of time before the property came to him."

"But why kill Ronzani? He was an old man. Why not wait and let nature take its course?"

"Control," Caleb said. "He can't leave anything to chance."

"And he may have worried that Ronzani would change his mind and sell to Wellman, or change his will. The old man didn't know his sister was still alive. He could've left his money to the church—he was a practicing Catholic—or to some charity. Limardi couldn't risk it.

"He killed the Koslowskis to keep them quiet," Thinnes continued. "My guess is he got Terry Koslowski to kill Morgan, then killed him and his sister to keep them from talking. Linda must've put it together. That's why she tried to contact me. And Limardi paid a gangbanger to off Mackie for the same reason. I'm sure it was no oversight that the chump got a look at a white Mercedes—made it more likely we'd look at Morgan for the killer if the trigger man ever tried to cut a deal."

Fuego nodded. "Which is just what happened."

"Speaking of Helen Morgan," Caleb said, "where does she fit in?"

"She was one of the gang from the old neighborhood," Thinnes said. "Nolan's wife loaned me her high school yearbook and I looked her up—Helen Kerrigan back then. She wasn't much to look at, and if you can believe Angie Nolan, Helen, being Irish, might as well have been black as far as Limardi was concerned. But over the years, she fixed up her looks and came into money. I think Limardi may have been telling the truth when he said he met her when she came in to buy a car. It probably *did* look like a chance for 'safe sex' and, of course, there was the real estate angle. I'll bet we weren't out of the building before she was on the phone to tell him we were asking about his old buddies."

"Limardi told me she expected him to marry her," Caleb said.

"Her mother told us he bought her a ring. We checked. At dinner the night she died she had on a rock the size of a pigeon's egg. There wasn't a trace of it on the remains."

"Where does this nutty church come in?" Fuego asked.

Thinnes shrugged and looked back at Caleb.

"Another way to manipulate people," Caleb said. "His original plan may have been to set up Brother John as some new messiah—he had the charisma—and in a few years, he'd have been the man behind the curtain. The Wizard of Oz."

"I don't like all the coincidences," Fuego said.

Caleb shook his head. "The only real coincidence is my meeting Martin and befriending him. The others were all connected since childhood."

Thinnes said, "Everything that gets done in this city depends on who you know or how much clout you have. What makes this whole thing seem complicated is that it's hard to see the connections if you're not part of the game. Limardi killing his uncle and cousin for money, or trying to bump off a rival for the woman he's after isn't any more unlikely than the sordid domestic murders we handle every day. It's just more sensational when the offender wears a Rolex and drives a Mercedes."

"How the hell did he expect to get away with it?" Fuego demanded.

"People tend to repeat behaviors they see as successful," Caleb said. "Limardi killed at least four times without being suspected."

"But what about his method?" Thinnes asked. "Pyromania's way off the deep end."

"Some obsessions are an attempt to get control of what's feared."

"Which is?" Thinnes said.

"Maybe fire. His sister died by fire. Maybe rage. Anger's one of the most common and normal emotions accompanying the death of a loved one—the least acknowledged. It's almost always proportional to the loss, and if it's not addressed, it can go underground and smolder like a fire deprived of air."

" 'Til something gives, and you get a backdraft," Thinnes said.

Fuego turned to Thinnes. "How long before it starts getting light?"

Thinnes looked at his watch. "About an hour."

"Hey! Something's up!"

They all looked at the building. One of the overhead doors was going up. Beyond it they could see a delivery dock with a large truck backed up to it. Thinnes started the engine. "Fasten your seat belts." As he maneuvered the Caprice to block the truck, the door started back down. A shadow dodged under it—one of the tac cops.

Fuego was out of the car before Thinnes could figure out what he was doing. Caleb was right behind. The doctor made it under the door by ducking; Fuego dived under in a forward roll.

"Shit!" Thinnes pounded the steering wheel in frustration, then reached for the radio to bring their backup up to speed. He turned off the car and got out. A beat car pulled up with all its lights flashing.

Caleb didn't slow to think what he was doing until the overhead door cut them off from Thinnes. It cut off all the light, too. He didn't want to consider why he'd done it.

He heard Fuego yell, "What the hell are you doing?" Then there was an explosion of gunfire, shockingly loud in the enclosed space. For a moment the muzzle flashes were the only light—Limardi firing from the dock, Fuego and the tac cop firing back. Caleb tried to count the shots. Limardi was firing wildly, the cops returning one shot for three. He heard a gasp, and an unfamiliar voice cried, "I'm hit." He heard the body fall. Then there was the odor of fuel oil and the deafening scratch of a flare igniting. A neon-red glow blossomed, throwing Limardi's face into infernal relief. Then the flare arced overhead, reflected from a growing pool of diesel. . . .

"Shots fired! Officer needs assistance!"

"Holy shit! Somebody started a fire!"

No time to think. Thinnes started the Caprice and aimed for the door next to the one with the truck behind it. What's behind door number two?

Firelight burst into being the instant the flare hit the fuel oil. Almost simultaneously, the truck lights came on. Someone dropped out of the driver's side. It was too fast, and the flames too frightening for more than an impression: the loading dock with fifty-five-gallon drums; the trickle and splash of leaking fuel oil; liquid fire racing across the floor, under the truck, reflecting in the liquid before igniting it; a man lying just beyond the flaming pool; a HAZMAT placard with the word

EXPLOSIVES; Fuego dragging the injured man in the flickering light; and Limardi, gun at his side, standing transfixed by the fire, eyes reflecting it.

Fuego's movement caught him, and he raised the gun. Caleb shouted. The gun pointed his way. He dived behind the truck, heard the explosion of the shot, the thunk when it hit. A fire alarm sounded. Smoke seemed to be settling down like black fog, meeting the dancing orange flames and inky rising soot. Caleb peered around the truck and saw Limardi fire again, heard the metallic snap of a misfire.

Limardi threw the gun at Fuego and turned to the door behind him on the dock. He went through it, slammed it shut.

Smoke settled beneath the ceiling to waist height. Caleb dropped to his knees. The very air was burning. There was a beast of fire hunting beneath the truck, sniffing the explosives. Fuego screamed, "Doctor!" The only way out was blocked by fire.

The way out.

Caleb squatted down and took a breath. And ran.

Déjà vu. Pain. Heat. A dark form striking him to the ground, rolling him.

Thinnes had to hit the door twice to break it.

Then salvation! The wall—no it was an overhead door—split as the front of a car broke through. Smoke and fire rushed out. Men came rushing in.

Beat coppers climbed into the breach before he could even back the car away. Fuego came staggering out, bent over, heaving for breath. Someone shoved a body through the breach and shouted. Thinnes jammed the car into park and ran to pull the tac cop free. A beat copper dodged out after him, singed and soot-black. Then Caleb came tumbling after, then the beat copper's partner.

Thinnes shook the tac cop, who was bleeding. "Where's your partner."

The partner came tearing up like an answer to prayer, yelling, "Jesus Christ!"

Caleb got to his knees and yelled "Explosives! Everybody run!"

They all ran.

From the safety of the other end of the block, from behind a fire truck they watched the doors blow away and waves of orange and yellow flame billow out as, one by one, the drums exploded. The show lasted fifteen minutes. Rockets and starbursts and screamers—Thinnes didn't know their official names— came pouring out the doors and blown-out windows. It was the grand finale on the fourth of July—only up close, it wasn't awe-inspiring, it was fucking terrifying.

Limardi came out last. They heard him scream from an upper-floor window. The bars held him in. There was nothing they could do but watch. Or not watch. They couldn't not hear. It was over mercifully fast—the screams, the flames, and then the water hit. Limardi was lost in smoke and steam.

One dies in fire.

Thinnes turned to find Caleb standing behind him. The doctor was blackened and scraped but not badly burned. He couldn't speak. He looked like he'd just been through Armageddon. And as Thinnes led him to the waiting ambulance, he felt as if they'd just seen the Judgement.